VIRUS

IRON MAN

VIRUS

ALEX IRVINE

BALLANTINE BOOKS • NEW YORK

A Del Rey Mass Market Original

Copyright © 2010 Marvel Entertainment, Inc., and its subsidiaries. Marvel, IRON MAN, and all related characters and the distinctive likenesses thereof: TM and © 2010 Marvel Entertainment, Inc., and its subsidiaries. Licensed by Marvel Characters B.V. www.marvel.com. All rights reserved. SuperHero(es) is a co-owned registered trademark.

Published in the United States by Del Rey, an imprint of The Random House Publishing Group, a division of Random House, Inc., New York.

DEL REY is a registered trademark and the Del Rey colophon is a trademark of Random House, Inc.

ISBN 978-0-345-50684-9

Printed in the United States of America

www.delreybooks.com

9 8 7 6 5 4 3 2 1

prologue

Through the tinted windows of a limousine that looked like any one of the other ten thousand limousines clogging the freeways of Long Island, Madame Hydra regarded the passing landscape and considered the new day that was soon to dawn for HYDRA. Facing her, Arnim Zola was lost in his thoughts . . . or, for all she knew, her own.

She had taken him in with the mixture of ambition and trepidation one felt when one handled a dangerous weapon. He had much to offer HYDRA, particularly when they had lost so many during their last unfortunate episode with Tony Stark and SHIELD; yet she was loath to admit that HYDRA—that she—had need of this body-hopping monstrosity, who emerged from scheming anonymity only when he felt he had something to gain. Madame Hydra did not desire to be someone from whom things were gained.

"These are new days for HYDRA," Zola said. Madame Hydra looked over at him and had to readjust her glance downward. She had known him for years, but she still re-flexively looked at where his face would be every time he spoke. To have her gaze met by the ESP Box was deeply unsettling. What had this body looked like when it still belonged to a man? She could see that it had been strong, well built. The shoulders were broad and the torso heavy and well developed enough that the television screen built into the front of Zola's chest did not deform the overall outlines of the body. Which were pleasing, until one reached the head. Or, more accurately, where the head was supposed to be. Instead, one saw a rectangular apparatus of gleaming metal, anchored to the shoulders by a steel column that connected—she assumed—into the body's spine. Antennae sprouted from the top of the box. The ESP Box received and deciphered any electromagnetic signal, from brain waves to microwave-burst transmissions, and with it Zola could issue signals of his own. Madame Hydra had met many men who professed mind-control ability. Never had she seen it in practice the way Zola could practice it.

She did not know, in fact, whether he was choosing to manipulate her thoughts at that exact moment.

On the torso screen, Zola's face was smiling. "New days," he said again. "We are going to do great things together."

"HYDRA has done great things before," Madame Hydra said icily.

Zola's head inclined. "Deepest apologies if I have given offense. That was not my intent. I am a creature of ambition, as you know. I look forward. It is sometimes difficult for me to remember that in looking forward I must not belittle past achievements."

The limousine passed through the gate onto the saccharinely named Arrival Avenue, which looped past the airport's terminals. "I trust that you will return from your visit to Washington in time to see the newest creations," Zola said.

"And I trust that you will wait for my return before putting our newest initiatives into action." The limousine stopped.

Madame Hydra waited for the driver to open the door. She stepped out onto the sidewalk, aware that heads were turning. In black and emerald green, she cut the kind of figure people assumed must belong to an actress whose name they couldn't quite bring to mind. It was a useful and harmless deception, of advantage to both deceiver and deceived.

From within the car, Zola said, "All of us, at times, must hide our true natures from the world."

Madame Hydra sighed. "I am well aware of your abilities, Monsieur Zola, and I find your constant need to display them tiresome."

"Beg pardon," she heard from within the limousine. Then the driver shut the door and Madame Hydra walked into the terminal accompanied by a skycap who carried her single bag. She tipped him one hundred dollars and waved her Latverian diplomatic credentials at the security personnel. Once seated on the commuter flight to Washington, DC, she considered Zola's words. What might he be hiding from her? It was he who had suggested that she use a regular flight. SHIELD was monitoring private charters intensively. Perhaps there was good sense in this. The people she was going to see preferred as little attention drawn to them as possible. They were HYDRA, as she was HYDRA. Many heads, some hidden and other simply disguised.

Zola, she supposed, was also HYDRA. His was a head she did not welcome, but its presence was necessary. Once he had served his purpose, she intended to cut that head off and see what else might grow in its place.

Until then, yes. True natures must be hidden from the world.

i.

PROVISIONAL APPLICATION FOR PATENT

TITLE
  Pulse bolt armament system, suit-borne

DESCRIPTION
  A generation and delivery system for the production of concentrated bursts of kinetic energy that increase in force as they travel by drawing power from the displacement of air. Designed for use in conjunction with personal armor such as Stark Industries patents [redacted], [redacted], and [redacted]. Improved pulse-bolt projection capability is a dramatic force multiplier in battlefield situations, and the technology has industrial applications as well, among them mining, propulsion systems, and construction/demolition.

CLAIM
  Develops and extends technological innovations in previous Stark Industries patents [redacted], [redacted], [redacted], and [redacted]. Specific improvements include: higher kinetic energy per unit of generating power, refinements in delivery and lensing to reduce need for cooling systems at point of generation. These improvements increase utility of pulse-bolt technology in applications demanding portability and ease of use, including the fields of civilian crowd control and light infantry engagements.

SECURITY STATUS
  Project undertaken under the auspices of Stark Industries agreements with the Department of Defense, SHIELD, and other governmental agencies outlined in Senate Amdt. [redacted] to

Senate Amdt. [redacted] to H.R. [redacted] (110th). Technology is proprietary to Stark Industries but will be shared fully with all eligible entities. Technology is classified and will not be licensed until such time as classification order is rescinded.

On his way out the Long Island Expressway to the new lab, Tony Stark got a call from Nick Fury. "Answer," he said to the phone, and then greeted Nick. "Sarge," he said. "How's the war?"

"Funny," Fury said. "Where are you going? I'm getting memos from senators who are worried that you're not going to deliver on certain items of interest to the United States Government."

"Spare me the bellyaching of senators." Tony watched through smoked and bulletproof windows as his driver swung down the off-ramp onto an access road that led to the lab. He was more excited to get to work than he had been in months.

"Maybe I'll spare you the next round of contracts, too," Fury growled.

Tony laughed. "Nick, come on. I think Stark Industries will survive without government handouts."

"Not if DOD classifies everything you've ever done with government handouts, you won't," Fury said. "And just to clarify, that's not a direct threat, but it is something I heard discussed in a committee meeting yesterday afternoon."

"The only thing that'll do is make my lawyers rich," Tony said.

"Most senators are lawyers," Fury said. "Remember that."

Tony sighed. How many times had he done this dance with Fury, with SHIELD, with staffers from senatorial and Defense Department offices? "Tell you what," he said. "Come on up to the new lab. I'll show you what I'm working on, and you can go back to the Hill and tell the crybabies that their supply of Stark Industries goodies is going to continue uninterrupted. They just might not get what they thought they were going to get."

The car pulled up to the security gate. The gate systems recognized the car, but the booth guard did a visual check per Tony's mandated admissions protocol. Tony winked at him and the gate slid open.

"I was hoping you'd say that," Nick said in Tony's ear. "Leave the gate open for a sec; we're right behind you."

So Tony was ever so slightly fuming as he led Nick and Rhodey on a tour of Stark Industries' Real-Time Interface Lab. Wiseass, he thought. Fury's always got to play these games to show me who's boss. He was upset with himself as well. It was a dumb move on someone's part not to have noticed Fury and Rhodey trailing him right up to the laboratory complex gate, and Tony was inclined to blame himself. He visualized schematics for a satellite-linked camera system that would identify every car in his proximity. It would be easy enough to find out who every car belonged to, and where it had been. The idea fit neatly into the Instant Control Project, which was his reason for building this new lab in the first place.

Instant control.

He loved the sound of the words in his head. Also he loved the idea that from anywhere, he could immediately interface with and control any asset linked to Stark Industries—through the nerve center of the Iron Man suit. The last brush with HYDRA had brought home to Tony just how important command-and-control systems were. He'd always known this in a theoretical sense, but Iron Man had always been able to suit up and ass-kick his way out of trouble. What if he could add real-time, multiple-interface battlefield control systems that deployed more assets than just the suit?

First things first, Tony told himself. There are plenty of technical obstacles to overcome in the new neurointerfaces.

He spun on his heel, deliberately snapping out of his annoyed funk to clap Rhodey and Fury on the shoulders and then lift his arms impresario-style, taking in the gleaming new facility. "Not a penny in tax breaks did I accept for this," he said to them. "Since the topic of public-private partnerships has been broached. Now let me tell you what it's all about."

The main lab building was L-shaped, with an outside testing area built into the inside corner of the L. The shorter leg was occupied by smaller clean labs for development of individual components of the neurointerface system. The longer leg was a single manufacturing and testing floor, extending maybe five hundred feet along the banks of a creek that determined the northern boundary of the lab property. "I spent a hundred million dollars on this lab," Tony said with some pride, "and it went from groundbreaking to fully on line in ten weeks. Take that, government."

"Funny," Rhodey said. "You got any other zingers stored up, or should we get on to what you're actually doing here?"

"Zingers aplenty, Rhodey my friend," Tony said. He let a panel set into a sliding steel door examine his retina. As it slid open, he added, "But I'll keep them in storage for right now."

They walked out onto the testing floor. Under a forty-foot ceiling, the facility was divided lengthwise into two areas. On the left, a row of workshop benches and small-scale manufacturing assemblies. On the right—the side next to the exterior testing area—a long, open runway, bracketed at intervals with sensor arrays and instruments designed to measure everything from laminar flow to the chemical consistency of the suit occupant's sweat. "I've got the full assembly works downstairs in another clean space," Tony said, pointing to a set of freight elevators halfway down the left wall. "Components up here, assembly downstairs, testing up here and outside. You wouldn't believe the results I'm already getting."

"We might if you told us," Rhodey said. Nick Fury was taking in the facility with his typical reserved calculation. Sooner or later, Tony thought, he's going to tell me what he thinks. I have a feeling that even if he's trying to be nice— however unlikely that is—I'm not going to like what he has to say.

"I'm thinking of it in historical terms," Tony said, and forged ahead over Fury's muttered Kee-rist. "When war was two guys with swords, it didn't matter what happened around them. All they needed to know was what the other guy was doing. Then, the more technological advances get involved in warfare, the more you need to know, and the more you need to know all at once, over a broad area, to get the job done. In World War Two, you had to synchronize radar, radio, visual communications—if you didn't, and the artillery barrage comes at the wrong time or the bombers let go over the wrong spot on the map, you get Market Garden instead of D-Day. Timing. You've got to decrease the time it takes to make command decisions using a large number of inputs spread over a wide area." He guided them over to a seven-foot flat-screen set over a workstation near the doorway. It displayed a tangle of equations and histograms.

"So," Tony went on. "What if you could build an independent battlefield system that knew everything about every factor that influenced combat circumstances? And what if you could not only know everything about those factors, but exercise instant control over every asset on your side? That's the goal. It's a ways off yet, but I'm making some interesting progress."

"I don't have to quote that old saw about plans surviving contact with the enemy, do I?" Rhodey asked.

"Nope. It's true. But what if plans could be remade instantly—I mean instantly—as contact with the enemy evolved?"

"You got the general's God complex, Tony," Fury observed. "Nobody can stop time, and no system can handle that many different inputs at once in real time."

"Not yet," Tony said. "But if you'll take a look at this—"

Fury cut him off. "Tony. You tried this, remember? Doing your cyborg thing with the suit? How long did it take to put your nervous system back together?"

"Nick, I will freely admit that that was kind of a bad idea given how little I knew about what I was doing at the time," Tony said. "But now, with the tech I'm developing in this lab, I'm figuring out how I can decrease the lag between my nerve response and the corresponding suit action as close to zero as the speed of light will allow. That's the first step in instant control. All external for now."

"For now?" Rhodey said. The qualification appeared to have caught Fury's attention as well.

"Never say never, gentlemen," Tony said. "Just because I had a bad experience with neuromuscular interfaces before doesn't mean they're a bad idea on principle. But I'm not going to turn myself into a cyborg. Don't you worry."

"Turn yourself into whatever you want, Tony, long as you keep delivering what you signed contracts to deliver," Fury said.

"Fear not, Nick Fury of SHIELD," Tony grinned. "Never shall the bond between Stark Industries and its best clients be broken."

But behind the grin, he wanted them out. He wanted to dive back into the lab, surround himself with measurements of tensile strength, experimental polymers, high-volume nanoscale communication channels.

Instant control.

With true instant control, it wouldn't matter where he was in the world; he'd be able to work the suit like he was in it, and run an array of drones or mechanical infantry or satellites like they were a school of fish all darting in the same direction at once with no visible cue or order. He would be everywhere at once, no matter where he was. And when he turned it off, he'd be back in the quiet of his study. Nobody else around. The more he learned about the potential inherent in the idea, the more he liked that part of it. Action at a distance, and nobody there to bother him when it was over. That was the next step in instant control. The final step.

"So, gentlemen," he said. "If there's nothing else . . ." He started walking back toward the door. "I can't get anything done with you two hanging around," he said when they were outside, meaning it as a joke but hearing a harder edge in his voice.

"If this is what you're doing when we're not around," Rhodey said, "we're going to stop by more often."

Fury took a harder line. "You have obligations, Tony. When you don't live up to them, people are in danger." He started to walk away, and Rhodey followed him. "Time to think about someone other than yourself, Mr. Stark," Fury added without looking back.

A flash in the sky caught their attention. Tony took it all in at once: the blackening fireball, the trails of smoke curving away from it toward the earth, the gleam and flash of sunlight on falling metal. A jet collision, over near Islip. The rumble of the explosion reached them as they stood watching in the parking lot. Rhodey was on his phone by the time the echoes had died out of the sky. Tony watched the smoke slowly stretch away to the south over the airport. He wondered if they were close enough to hear sirens, and thought about how many people must have been on those two planes. Rhodey's voice, quiet and commanding, was the only sound in the parking lot until Tony turned to Nick Fury and said, "instant control, Sarge. If those planes had instant control, or the control tower had it, we never would have seen that again. Now you tell me who's thinking of themselves."

ii.

I bring to you news worth celebrating: Madame Hydra is dead! Madame Hydra is dead! Madame Hydra is dead! No longer does HYDRA labor under her tyrannical blindness; no longer do you, the soldiers of HYDRA, march off to your deaths for the satisfaction of her whims. Madame Hydra is dead! But HYDRA lives. HYDRA grows. Its head is cut off, but another grows in its place, stronger and better than the last. I am that head. I am your guide. I will re-create you in my image, in the image toward which HYDRA has always aspired. Together we will be the hydra-headed colossus that will at last achieve the goals that weaker leaders envisioned. They could not bring their visions to pass; we can. HYDRA can. A new day comes, born from the fire and ashes of the demise of the old. A new HYDRA rises, resolute and indomitable, from the pruning of the weak heads that for so long have misled you. Now we rise to claim what is ours, to claim through strength what has for so long been grasped at but failed by weakness. You are HYDRA! I am HYDRA! We are HYDRA!

From the tar-papered, garbage-strewn roof of an abandoned chocolate factory, Arnim Zola watched the distant bloom of smoke in an otherwise clear blue sky. "Excellent," he said to his clone, which in a fit of literary whimsy he had named Maheu. "Thus ends the nettlesome life of Madame Hydra."

"Unless she was late to the airport," Maheu said.

On the television screen that dominated the front of Zola's torso, his face frowned. "She was not. I have reports."

"Do your reports confirm that she got on the plane?" the

clone asked. "Have you heard definitively that everyone on board both planes has died?"

"Human beings do not survive midair collisions between jet aircraft traveling hundreds of miles per hour," Zola said.

"Not often," Maheu agreed. "But still."

Zola briefly reconsidered the wisdom of cloning himself. The idea had been that a clone would be an optimal advisor, his equal in intellect but socialized to believe itself subordinate to him. What seemed to have happened, unfortunately, was that the clone interpreted its role differently than Zola had intended. It was meticulously fault-finding, contrary, and often disrespectful. He had a private theory that something had gone wrong with the clone in its accelerated childhood, and that it resented the modifications to its original human form. Its ESP Box was much less powerful than his. Perhaps, Zola thought—and not for the first time—it would prefer to be a normal human.

But this was not possible. Even a second-iteration Arnim Zola could not be normal. Far from it. Zola had made thousands of normal clones—and many thousands more subnormal accidents. Those were different than his more focused attempts to re-create a version of himself that would be useful to him. Maheu was the best, so far, of those.

Despite his irritating pessimism.

"It's too good to be true, really," Maheu said. "To infiltrate and usurp an organization as nebulous as HYDRA in a matter of months? Surely there is something we have missed."

"Surely?" Zola echoed. "If you're that certain, perhaps you can tell me what."

"Do we know that we have completely suborned all remaining HYDRA personnel?"

"The remaining HYDRA personnel do not include anyone capable of initiative," Zola said. "Much less the kind of initiative and cunning it would require to push back against our takeover. Tell me I'm wrong."

"I can't tell you you're wrong," Maheu said. "But neither can I confirm your belief that you're right. This is exactly my point."

Zola reflected that if there was one thing he missed about working for the Führer, it was directness. There had been none of this philosophical logic-chopping during the Reich. One had seen what was necessary, and one had done what was necessary. It was unfortunate that the Führer's irrational opinions on the topics of the Russian front and the Jews had ultimately undone what otherwise might have been a most suitable environment for the pursuit of the science of dominion.

Events had unfolded otherwise, however, and Zola had learned to work with what materials were available. When the HYDRA opportunity had presented itself, he had assessed its potential and then made decisions based on that assessment . . . with, it must be admitted, the valuable but gloomy counsel of Maheu.

How Maheu had emerged from the cloning process with a personality so different to Zola's own was a scientific problem of delicious complexity. Had he been in a position to do so, Zola might have published the results to justified acclaim. Briefly he had considered cloning himself again for the purposes of installing the product in a university where it could make known the more invigorating results of Zola's research. Time and circumstance had thus far not permitted this luxury, which further whetted Zola's appetite for the conclusion of his plans for HYDRA. Once he had achieved the pinnacle of his power, no learned institution or scientific establishment would be able to afford to ignore him—no matter what he said.

This was a goal worth striving for. It was one thing to recognize and be comfortable with one's megalomania, and Zola certainly was that; but to channel one's megalomania into an enterprise that would benefit humankind . . . Marvelous! And what was the highest expression of humankind, if it was not the advancement of science? And what was the highest advancement of science, if it was not the creation of a better race of human beings, who would then in turn create one still better?

But like all plans, this one depended on a carefully constructed progression of steps. Zola had the scientific know-how. He'd created his first clone in 1940, and refined the process continuously since then. The second stage, to seize power where it would not be given—this had eluded him. In retrospect, he could laugh at some of his earlier missteps, as painful and embarrassing as they had been. He had learned valuable lessons, and now was poised to put them to use. Once HYDRA was under his complete control, he would move on to the next stage of the plan: the elimination of known opponents, and the prevention of new opponents from emerging.

A soft ping, emanating from the inside of the ESP Box and inaudible to anyone but Zola himself, signaled an incoming communication. "Verified that target boarded the plane, Master," said the operative Zola had installed in the Islip airport's control tower staff. The operative disconnected without waiting for Zola to respond, exactly as he had been instructed.

"There's your confirmation, Maheu," Zola said. "She was on the plane. Do you suppose we must wait for her body to be pieced back together before we can celebrate?"

Inside the abandoned factory, on a catwalk outside the command center whose construction he had personally overseen, Zola watched his labor clones at work. Where once a confectioner had mixed truffles and bonbons, Zola now guided the creation of his next great project, and the enterprise that would once and for all cement HYDRA's dominance over its worthy but doomed opposition. He had watched and learned as HYDRA fought SHIELD and Iron Man just a year ago. When the dust had barely begun to settle from that confrontation, he had moved the way a predatory CEO moves when he sees a distressed but potentially valuable asset: quickly and without mercy. HYDRA's remaining command structure was swiftly wiped away, its depleted ranks replenished with operatives of his own creation. Now that Madame Hydra's death was confirmed to his satisfaction, Zola's control over HYDRA was complete.

The ESP Box whispered and breathed with the communications and passing fancies of his underlings. In different tones, he heard the voices of police officers, disc jockeys, pilots, taxicab drivers . . . the airwaves were a symphony, and he alone was attuned to it in its glorious entirety.

"You," he said to one of the clones who stood near him awaiting instruction.

"Master," the clone said.

The identity of our operative at the airport is known to you now, Zola said, slipping into the voiceless communication of the ESP Box.

Yes, Master.

There is a 1990 Plymouth Sundance, color blue, parked on the street directly opposite from the loading docks of this building.

Yes, Master.

In its glove compartment you will find a firearm and instructions.

Yes, Master.

There is one further instruction: When your operation at the airport is complete, you will use that firearm to eliminate yourself.

Yes, Master.

Go now.

The clone left, walking briskly down the length of the catwalk and into a stairwell at the corner of the building. It was of a model that had served Zola well, and he had no doubt that it would complete its mission.

"You take an enormous risk," Maheu said.

"I think not."

"Obviously, or you would have made a different set of choices," Maheu said.

Zola ignored his clone. He had assessed the risk, and found it acceptable. Far more risky to have the operative's identity uncovered during the bureaucratic witch hunt that would surely follow in the aftermath of the airborne collision. A murder-suicide on Long Island? Hardly news.

"It is always a critical mistake to underestimate one's adversary," Maheu said.

"There's no arguing that," Zola agreed. "It is our great fortune that I am not."

"It is perhaps your great misfortune that you believe you are not."

Zola sighed. "Maheu," he said. "If I had known you were going to fritter away the intelligence I gave you on wordplay, I might have made a different set of choices in that regard. Madame Hydra is dead. Our links to the airport will soon be severed. Our plan proceeds apace."

"As do all plans, until they collapse."

"You seem to have confused the role of advisor with the antics of a Shakespearean fool," Zola said. "If I wanted a memento mori, I need only consider all of the bodies I inhabited previous to this one."

"And whose deaths seem to have failed to teach you their lessons. You move too fast," Maheu said.

"How slowly would you have me move?" Zola said. "Now is the time. Hesitation in the face of opportunity is as disastrous as reckless action. You have advised. I have heard your advice. Kindly refrain from offering it until I ask for it again."

Maheu withdrew, and Zola soaked in the afterglow of success. Certainly it was wise to be cautious where caution was called for. But it was foolish to retreat from a battlefield already won. *My followers, my warriors, my army,* he said through the ESP Box, *HYDRA is ours.*

All activity on the factory floor stopped, and as one the workers turned and saluted him. "HYDRA is ours!" they boomed. Zola felt the heat of their unified commitment in his mind as his ears rang with the echoes of their words.

And now we must redouble our efforts to drive our plan forward. HYDRA is only part of it. To work, my followers, and bring our project to its glorious fruition!

Again in perfect unison, the workers and technicians below him returned to their tasks. There were materials to synthesize, temperatures and pressures to monitor, training and cognitive-acceleration processes to administer. The factory floor ticked into action and within seconds was just as it had been before Zola had paused it to deliver his brief address. Maheu appeared on the floor, weaving through machinery and moving bodies on his way down to the subterranean training facilities whose operational efficiency remained unacceptably low.

The next phase of his project unfolded. Even the predatory CEO knows when to act and when to await the proper time for action, Zola thought. It's all just business.

But when was business anything but a metaphor for war?

PROVISIONAL APPLICATION FOR PATENT

TITLE
Uni-beam projector and calibration assembly, suit-borne

DESCRIPTION
Derived from the same technology as the repulsor ray integrated into previous versions of Stark Industries personal body armor (see list of existing patents, attached), the uni-beam combines electromagnetic and heat energy with a highly variable light frequency that can be automatically adjusted to enhance its power. Available frequencies extend from the infrared through ultraviolet, creating a single weapon that presents multiple challenges to any given enemy defense.

CLAIM
By integrating the functions of several individual previous weapon systems, the uni-beam creates a new category of offensive capability. No existing weapons system with the exception of tactical and strategic nuclear weaponry attacks a target with simultaneous heat, kinetic, and electromagnetic deliveries. This design has the further virtue of seamless integration into existing Stark Industries personal body armor systems, enhancing their capabilities and creating potentially transformative new possibilities for battlefield infantry and light armor units.

SECURITY STATUS
Project undertaken under the auspices of Stark Industries agreements with the Department of Defense, SHIELD, and other governmental agencies outlined in Senate Amdt. [redacted] to Senate

Amdt. [redacted] to H.R. [redacted] (110th). Technology is proprietary to Stark Industries but will be shared fully with all eligible entities. Technology is classified and will not be licensed until such time as classification order is rescinded.

After a long week spent trying to placate Fury and whoever was holding Fury's leash back in Washington, Tony figured out that he was in the kind of rut that could only be gotten out of by a night on the town. He needed music, he needed a girl on his arm, he needed some time for the finer things. Pepper Potts, assistant extraordinaire and the finest woman Tony had ever known, walked into his office while he was flipping his finger back and forth across a touch screen, deciding who to call. "That tough a call?" she asked wryly.

"The tyranny of choice," Tony said.

"Make it someone you won't necessarily want to see again," Pepper advised. "That usually works best when you're only going out because you're sick of looking at the walls in the lab."

Tony stopped his touch screen eenie-meenie-meinie-moe. "What are you talking about?"

"I swear, Tony. Sometimes it's like you rely on me to know your personality just like everything else. When you get in this weird zone you've been in at work, every time you try to snap out of it by going on a date, you end up being a prize ass." Tony looked blankly at her, and he watched Pepper mimic the expression and turn it up a notch. "You seriously don't remember the conversations we've had about this before?" she asked him.

"I seriously don't," Tony said. "But I'll take your word for it, since you know me. Hm," he went on, returning his attention to the screen, "someone I won't want to see again. How about . . . Serena Borland? Pep, who's Serena Borland?"

"Sometimes I could kill you," she said, and walked out of the office without ever telling him what she'd come in for.

He picked up Serena Borland at ten, after running himself through an Internet-assisted refresher course on who she was. They'd met at an art opening two years before at the Whitney, and Tony had called her a few times since, but this was the first time their schedules had come together. She was the right kind of girl to be seen on the arm of Tony Stark: a knockout with the right kind of profile (politically active family whose work consisted of taking care of its previous generations' piles of money) and interests (art, children's welfare, high-minded causes of every kind) who didn't take herself too seriously. That last quality was the only one he genuinely remembered from their initial meeting, and the only reason he remembered that was because she was able to make fun of an Alexander Calder piece while the TV cameras were on. Not because she was stupid and didn't understand art, but because she did understand art and didn't like Calder and didn't care who knew it.

Good choice, Tony told himself as he watched her make a doorman-assisted exit from a building facing Gramercy Park. "Jazz," he said when she made a Happy Hogan-assisted entrance to the car. "What do you think about that?"

"Absolutely," she said. "Jazz. Who?"

"Whoever's at the Vanguard," Tony said. "I'm feeling old-fashioned."

When they got there, in time for the second set, Tony didn't know who was playing and didn't care. He was there for the ghosts of the old Vanguard that he'd never known. The act was fronted by a multi-instrumentalist who occasionally took to playing two or more instruments at once, à la Rahsaan Roland Kirk. It looked like a gimmick when he first started, but listening to him play, Tony realized that it was only a gimmick if you couldn't follow through. His phone buzzed five minutes after they got there with a text message from Pepper: *Two martinis, and only two.*

Aye Aye, he texted back, and turned his phone off.

Then it was conversation with Serena—who, contrary to all expectation, kind of enchanted Tony—and jazz, and the two martinis he allowed himself. But despite her enchanting qualities and the mesmerizing tonality of the band, his mind wandered. Back to the lab, back to the problem at hand. Back to the suit. It was time, he realized. Once he'd tried to build the suit into his body, and nearly died of it.

But what if he built it into his mind?

"What are you thinking about?" Serena asked him during the next set break.

"Guilty," Tony said. "Sorry. I thought I could escape from work, but it hounds me." He put his elbows on the table and steepled his fingers under his chin. "What are you thinking about?"

"How to get your mind off work." Serena tossed back the rest of her cosmo. Before she had time to find the waiter, he appeared with another. She gave him a smile and turned her attention back to Tony. "So, what is it? Or do you not want to talk about it?"

"I do," Tony said. "But some of it I can't. So here's what I can say. I'm on the edge. I'm Moses looking down into Canaan. The breakthrough is right there, and I think I know how to get to it. The thing is, it's not exactly what the client wants."

"The client?" Serena got to work on her cosmo. Tony might have been keeping himself to two, but apparently she felt no similar compunction. "Who is this client that can tell Tony Stark what to do?"

Good question, Tony thought. What would happen if I told Fury to go to hell, plain and simple? SHIELD needs me more than I need them. Same goes for the Defense Department.

Ah, but there was the question of loyalty. Iron Man did not walk away from obligations. Tony Stark didn't, either. At least that was his ideal of himself. The real picture was often murkier. "It's a goddamn pain to live up to your own public image," he said. "You know?"

"I sure do," Serena said.

"Do I want to burn all of these professional bridges?" Tony went on. "Probably not." The real question, unsaid, was: Do I want to let go the burden of being Iron Man, the responsibility of being on call whenever some problem got too big for SHIELD to handle? Do I want to take Stark Industries back to pure research and pure ambition, and let go the burden of providing the Department of Defense all of the goodies that it can imagine but not figure out how to produce? "The pressure gets to me sometimes," he said.

"I can imagine." Serena might have gone on, but the band was taking the stage again, and by the time they signed off with an impassioned but maybe superficial homage to Ornette Coleman, the conversation had gone in other directions. Back outside, Tony found Happy snoring in the car on Seventh Avenue.

"Hap," he said. "Time to go home. If I was a car thief, I'd have stolen you right along with the wheels."

"Tony, hey, sorry." Hap blinked and jumped out of the car, spilling a folded and annotated *Daily Racing Form* out of his lap. He got Tony and Serena into the car and they swung through the Village and past Union Square on the way back to Serena's apartment.

"Tony," Serena said when they were three lights from her block. "I've never seen Stark Industries from the inside."

It was two thirty in the morning and Tony was finding that he could keep less and less of his brain on her, while more and more of it wandered out on to Long Island to play among the displays and simulations of things he craved to build. The burden, he thought. Tony Stark has to play along. "Hap," he said. "Let's take a spin up to the office."

They walked in through the front door, which opened when the sensor array detected and recognized Tony's genetic signature. "Not too long ago I spent a ton of money on the lobby," Tony said. "The other one was nice, but this one gets the feel of what we're doing, I think."

It wasn't the marble-and-glass austerity of so many other midtown office towers. What Tony wanted in the redesign was a sense of indomitable reaching out for the inconceivable. He wanted the visitor to Stark Industries—not to mention the potential client—to walk in and be overwhelmed by the sense that this was a place where the impossible happened. The floors were polished steel, and the lobby extended twenty floors up, with the elevator towers forming a column straight up the middle. Catwalks of translucent polymer encircled the lobby at every floor, and every office was fronted by floor-to-ceiling windows behind which the onlooker could take in the activities of office and laboratory and meeting room. Knowledge! Innovation! This was what Tony had wanted the space to say.

Those things, and: Power!

"My God," Serena said.

"Actually it's not so impressive in the daylight when all of the actual employees are running around and screwing up the view." Tony took in the lobby, and Serena's reaction to it, with some pride.

"Talk about pressure," Serena said. "When you walk into work every morning and see this, you put pressure on yourself."

This was true, Tony thought. "There are expectations to live up to," he said. "I can't just rent a floor in the Empire State Building."

Then she threw him a curveball. "I hear you live up on the top floor."

"I've heard that, too," Tony said.

"How about we go upstairs and take the rest of the pressure off?" she asked, leaning into him.

"Sweetheart," Tony said. It went against his every instinct, but he took her firmly by the upper arms and reestablished a little space between them. "Although you are a perfect bombshell and the envy of all womanhood, tonight's not the night." Over her shoulder, he caught Happy's eye. "Mind giving Miss Borland a ride home, Hap?"

"That's what I'm here for, chief." Happy went to the door and stood with it open until Serena realized that she wasn't going to win him over.

She brushed his hands from her arms and said, "Tony Stark. I wonder what happened to you." Then without another word she walked out of the magnificent lobby, got into the car, and sat staring straight ahead as Happy shut the door.

Tony couldn't get to the lab fast enough. He drove his own car, tearing out of the underground garage and sweating the tangles of traffic leading into the Midtown Tunnel. Once he'd gotten into Queens, he turned on a special little toy he'd invented to keep traffic cops off his back when he needed to get somewhere fast. It ran a charge through the car's paint job (a glossy blacker-than-black also of Tony's own design) that turned the vehicle into a stealth roadster. Radar couldn't get a clear image of it, so couldn't get a fix on its speed—and even if it could, the car could outrun anything the NYPD or the Long Island departments had to offer. He wound it up to 100, not wanting to be reckless, and made it to the lab in a half hour.

Inside, he took a deep breath and sat down at the command-and-control console he'd tried to show Rhodey and Fury the week before. Tony was through with half measures. He'd been stuck imagining the suit as something apart from himself, when in fact what he needed to do was re-create the interface as if the suit was part of his brain, and his interactions with it as quick and intuitive as the interaction between the part of the brain that takes in light and the part of the brain that thinks red. As quick as the part of the brain that makes you flinch when the optometrist puffs air into your eye. No, quicker. The suit would be a part of himself. Not built in, no. He'd learned that lesson. It would be a part of himself in that when he put it on, it would be like restoring the eyes to a blind man.

iv.

Do you contain, sparkling somewhere between axon and dendrite, a memory of your previous self? No. You have no previous self. From a set of proteins I created you. Only you. Others I create again and again and again, until I can envision a world overrun with a single face. You are different. So rarely I tell this to one of my creations: You are different. Hear it, understand it. There is only one of you, just as there is only one of your model. You are better than she—more intelligent, stronger, more beautiful, and more committed. She is a waste, like the city that adores her. You are energy and drive, potential for greatness. You are an indispensable part of HYDRA. I created you to be thus. I created you to be the one element of HYDRA that our plan cannot survive without. I ask you to move through the world wearing the mask of your model, and return to me with a gift. Such a tiny gift I ask of you: four amino acids, arranged in a particular way. Can you do this for me? Yes, because you are HYDRA. From HYDRA you were born, and for HYDRA you will go forth and bring this tiny gift, from which a great deed will be born.

In the car on the way back to Serena's apartment, Happy was uneasy. He didn't like the way she was talking to him, and he wasn't sure he'd be able to tell Tony about it. "I know I shouldn't be telling you this," she said for about the fifth time since they'd left Tony at the office, "but he seemed strange tonight. Not the Tony I know."

You don't know him that well, Happy thought. Everyone thought they knew the boss, but what they knew was an image on a TV screen and the society pages of the tabloids.

Like anybody else in his position, the boss had a public face that didn't always jibe with his real personality.

"You don't have to be rude," Serena said.

"Sorry," Happy said, even though he wasn't. "Just thinking." Also he was hoping that the boss would never want to lay eyes on this Serena girl again.

He pulled up to her building and got out to open the door for her. She brushed up against him as she got out—on purpose. Happy had given her plenty of room. "I'm surprised Tony lets you take his dates home," Serena said.

"You want me to walk you to the door?" Happy asked. No way was he going to pick up on the signal she was sending him.

"Would you? That would be nice." She took his arm and they crossed the broad sidewalk together. At the base of the stairs that led up to her building's front porch, she stopped and turned to him. "Thank you, Happy," she said, and keeping her eyes locked on his, she held him there for an uncomfortable moment. Don't do it, Happy thought. Her hand that had been resting on his arm came up to his face, and Happy couldn't help himself. He jerked back, and one of her nails caught the skin just under the line of his jaw.

"Ah!" Happy said, catching her wrist.

Right away she was apologetic. "Oh, Happy, I'm so sorry," she said, pulling her hand back and clenching it into a fist down by her side. "I'm sorry," she repeated. "I didn't mean it."

"Well, thanks," he said.

"No, I didn't mean that I didn't mean it like that," Serena said. "I'm . . . Happy, can we just forget about this? You're a handsome man, but I shouldn't have done that. I'm sorry about it."

"Forget about it," Happy said.

"Yes," Serena said. "Forget about it. It never happened."

"Fair enough," Happy said. She went up the stairs and through the front door, and Happy drove back downtown, over the Williamsburg Bridge, and through the dumpy streets between the bridge and his house on Ten Eyck near the English Kills canal. It was a brand-new condo, less than a mile from the part of Bushwick he'd grown up in. The new place and his own car, a Mustang coupe with some serious aftermarket juice from Stark Industries labs, were his life's two indulgences. Happy settled onto his couch, flipped on the TV, and caught up on the Yankees. Tony and his crazy women, he thought. He was glad to be home.

Zola waited in the chocolate factory for confirmation that the night's mission was accomplished. The ESP Box tickled the brains of his clones, sifting through their thoughts to create a multifaceted impression of everything happening on the floor . . . and in the basement. His gaze swept over the banks of growth chambers that took up more than half of the factory floor. Each was a marvel that only he could have created. Cylindrical, seven feet high, and with a radius of four feet, each chamber contained eight hundred gallons of growth medium. Self-replicating nanoprocesses in the medium constructed a framework that resembled a human skeleton. The nanoprocesses then consumed the framework as they built the real skeleton from the marrow out, and the rest of the clone from the skeleton out. The medium itself was a chemical solution composed of the elements necessary for the construction of a human body—primarily oxygen, hydrogen, carbon, and nitrogen. From those four elements alone, 96 percent of the human body was produced, and they were easy enough to find in quantity. The rest—calcium, potassium, phosphorous, all the trace elements needed for the finer biological functions—Zola ordered in bulk through a shell company that placed orders for nonexistent high school chemistry classrooms.

It was all so easy. You could take water, air, and charcoal, and if you had a way to rearrange the molecules, you could create a human life. Zola's first cloning experiments had been crude, even savage. Not until five years ago had he finally devised a working nanoprocess that could reliably produce results. Now that he had it, he was going to be like Cortes against the Aztecs, bringing firearms and hardened steel to a battle in which his enemy would have stone clubs. Technology was the great force multiplier.

He summoned Maheu, feeling the need for a foolish conversation. "The sample is viable?" he asked when Maheu appeared.

"So it would appear," Maheu said. "Extraction is barely begun, so a final prognosis would be irresponsible."

"Maheu, there is no such thing as a final prognosis. What I ask you for is a current sense, and your best guess at probable futures. Given that I have bestowed upon you the gift of an intellect genetically equal to mine, I imagine that this request is not beyond your capabilities."

While Maheu sulked, Zola considered. His first batch of soldiers, retooled from the best HYDRA had to offer, was nearly battle-ready. The fruits of tonight's mission would yield a second batch of soldiers whose base composition was superior. After that, development of individual cloning projects would be in full swing.

When those were complete, he would be ready.

"It seems likely that current projects will succeed," Maheu said.

"There," Zola said. "That wasn't so difficult, was it?" Maheu said nothing, so Zola let that matter stand as it was. "Hand in hand with technology, Maheu, one must have tactical, strategic, and logistical mastery," he said.

"Indeed," Maheu said.

"Sarcasm is the resort of the emotionally arrested," Zola said. "I will request that you no longer employ it."

"When will you request that?" Maheu said.

"And a deliberately confounding literalism is the hallmark of a conniver," Zola said. "Are you conniving against me, Maheu?"

"Of course not," Maheu said. "Your ESP Box would tell you if I was, wouldn't it?"

It always came back to the ESP Box with Maheu. He wanted one as powerful as Zola's, and that was the one thing Zola had not wanted to do in the construction of his clone advisor. He knew too well that in building a clone of yourself, you made yourself expendable as soon as the clone knew everything it needed to know to assume your place. Building armies of clone soldiers was one thing; creating a true copy of oneself would have been folly.

The clone soldiers were given basic cognitive advancement via neurolinks while they were still in the tanks. Otherwise, the first time the medium was drained and they opened their eyes and took a breath, a number of them suffered psychological shocks that took quite some time to repair. After the neurolink implantation, which was designed to acclimatize each clone to its body before it emerged from the chamber, further training occurred in an underground facility Zola had constructed as soon as he purchased the factory building. To keep Maheu occupied, Zola put him in charge of it. It wasn't a fully functional ESP Box, but it would have to do—and it was a subterranean job, which fit nicely with the name Zola had bestowed on his first clone at its completion.

"Perhaps it would," Zola said. He had no desire to outline for Maheu the capabilities of the ESP Box. "Are the facilities downstairs fully operational?" He knew the answer, but asked the question anyway to gauge Maheu's reaction.

"Nearly," Maheu said. "The technicians are still building out the last of the virtual immersion trainers."

Without which, Zola noted sourly, the soldiers could not be made battlefield-ready. He also noted Maheu's candor. "How long until they are complete?"

"Seventy-two hours," Maheu said. "Then we will be at full training capacity. We have completed the transfer of all HYDRA armaments from their compromised locations to our own secured location."

"By which you mean the basement?"

"You seem to prefer a more circumlocutory approach when I'm giving a report," Maheu said. "At least I have inferred that from our similar interactions previously."

"How thoughtful of you to incorporate my preferences," Zola said. "Now if only you would do that in your role as advisor."

"I need not point out that I could be doing that, and you could be failing to notice . . . do I?" Maheu said.

"No," Zola said. "You hardly need point that out." It took approximately that length of time for the chambers to compile a clone. The training course was thirty-six hours of alpha-wave immersion. "It is time to begin the first phase," Zola said. "The quiet phase. In five days or so, then we will begin to get loud."

V.

PROVISIONAL APPLICATION FOR PATENT

TITLE
  Carbon nanotube weave

DESCRIPTION
  A fabric constructed of carbon nanotubes at the density of approximately 25 million tubes per linear inch of fabric, with an average depth of 2 million, for a thickness of approximately two millimeters. The fabric exhibits enormous strength and resistance to tearing and impact damage, while retaining flexibility akin to a heavy wet suit. Tensile strength of the nanotubes as produced for prototype has averaged between 75 and 95 GPa, which would ordinarily prohibit flexibility; however, the weave as designed incorporates a complex pattern of spirals and cross-fibers modeled on the architecture of the human muscle. (See attached fig. 1.)

CLAIM
  The Stark Industries carbon nanotube weave has been experimentally observed to absorb bullet impacts without permanent deformation. It has withstood extremes of temperature and pressure without impairing its strength or flexibility, and has been subjected to blast testing overpressures of up to 45psi without structural damage. Further testing is underway to determine the weave's suitability as personal body armor, but as of current experimental results, the carbon nanotube weave is a significant advance in the science of materials, with applications across military and industrial fields.

SECURITY STATUS

Project undertaken under the auspices of Stark Industries agreements with the Department of Defense, SHIELD, and other governmental agencies outlined in Senate Amdt. [redacted] to Senate Amdt. [redacted] to H.R. [redacted] (110th). Technology is proprietary to Stark Industries but will be shared fully with all eligible entities. Technology is classified and will not be licensed until such time as classification order is rescinded.

A third Arnim Zola, this one named Lantier, never left a single room behind a steel door at the farthest end of the corridor that ran around the perimeter of the underground training facilities. Lantier, had no ESP Box at all. What he had were conduits socketed into the base of his skull. They snaked down over his shoulders and into ports on a quantum computer with more processing power than the Department of Defense. Lantier's eyes were usually closed. His fingers swept and tapped over a featureless black panel configured to receive the commands of his hands when he infiltrated a system too primitive to respond to the more sophisticated seductions that rolled down the conduits when he was dancing with high-end security.

Arnim Zola walked into this room and shut the door behind him. *Lantier,* he said, using the ESP Box. Lantier disliked the sound of human voices other than his own.

"All aboard," Lantier said. He was obsessed with trains, the obsession so powerful that he recast every sensory stimulus, every thought, every goal as something train-related. Zola had done this as a bit of a joke when the Lantier clone was first being acclimatized. He had soon been forced to admit that the joke had gone wrong. Where Arnim Zola was a genius, Lantier was a savant; he could speak of nothing but trains, and the only thing he could do with his mind, it seemed—or the only thing he wanted to do with it, in any

case—was reach out with it into the virtual. By a happy ac-
cident, Zola had created a consummate hacker and infiltra-
tor of computer systems. This was also a valuable lesson in
the variations that could arise even in a cloned population.
Environmental factors could never be dismissed.

Once he had realized Lantier's predilections and abilities,
Zola had built him into this workstation and left him there.
A dedicated staff kept him clean and nourished, but apart
from that the only contact Lantier had with other humans
came in the person of Zola himself.

Gently Zola suggested to Lantier what he wanted done.
"Throw the switch," Lantier said. "Boiler's hot."

Just a probing attack, Zola said. Don't reveal us just yet.
Sow uncertainty. Get them thinking. Harry them a little.

"Now departing on Track Six," Lantier said.

Lantier brought his locomotive to a slow, easy stop. Ahead
of him, the tracks diverged into a tangle of switches and signal arrays. They gave him conflicting information, and he realized that this meant they were operated according to a
code he had never seen before. At the station, someone was
trying to get other engines through while keeping him out.
Lantier resolved that he would not permit this. He sent his
fireman out in front of the engine to throw the first switch. It
clicked into place, and a cascade of other switches changed
their positions at every other junction he could see. The signal lights also changed, but in a different pattern. "Put the
switch back there, Fred," Lantier said to the fireman. Fred
did. Some of the other switches moved in response, but others stayed where they were. The lights did a complicated
dance.

One, two, three . . . sixty-four tracks that he could see.
Lantier assumed there were others beyond his field of vision. Over the tracks, next to the tracks, set into the ground
between the tracks, he counted four thousand and ninety-
six signal arrays, each with three lights. Lantier thought

about it a bit. "Try that switch again, Fred," he said. He watched a pattern slowly begin to emerge.

It took nearly forty-eight hours, but that was all right, Zola thought. He needed the time for other preparations. "You work Lantier much too hard," Maheu chided him twenty-four hours into Lantier's mission.

"In all likelihood, I don't work you hard enough. Perhaps what you need is a little perspective," Zola said.

Maheu rolled his eyes. He was only four years old, and despite extensive conditioning and cognitive development acceleration, he occasionally fell into ruts of making the same expression over and over again. These past few days, he'd begun to roll his eyes. Zola considered the expense of a new clone versus the relief of not having to deal with Maheu any more. "Very droll," Maheu said.

"Sarcasm again," Zola said. "I'm not sure you're a clone of me at all. An error must have been introduced into the process."

"What process is without error?" Maheu strode off to oversee the final preparations in the basement, leaving his idiotic question ringing through Zola's mind. *The processes I create*, Zola thought. *Those are without error*. The evidence was before him, marching across the view screens in his control room, working in flawless tandem on the floor among the chambers and the complex array of devices that kept materials flowing in and clones flowing out. A refinery or a factory? Zola wondered. It had aspects of both, he supposed. His physical body began to tire. Tuning the ESP Box to harvest and respond to important data, he turned his mind down low. It had been many years since Arnim Zola fell completely asleep. He expected that he never would again. But he did occasionally close his eyes and fall into a meditative state, which he found restorative. This he did now, and remained in it until he received notification from Lantier that the goal was within sight.

He immediately went downstairs, noting as he passed across the factory floor the waves of admiration and respect emanating from the laborers and technicians. Down in the basement, his mind tickled with the ESP Box's reception of the information flooding into the next generation of clones. They would be acclimatized and ready soon.

It was one of Zola's cardinal principles never to rush a stage of a plan simply because preparations for it finished before the previous stage was complete. The clones would wait until he had everything else in place. Maheu was waiting for him at the door to Lantier's sanctum. They entered together.

Lantier sat pale and distant in the exoskeleton Zola had constructed to exercise his muscles and prevent his body from dying of apathy. His eyes were closed, and the fingertips of both his hands rested quietly on the tablet. If he was engaged in some activity, his appearance gave no sign of it.

Zola alerted him to their presence. "Coming into the station, ladies and gentlemen," Lantier said.

Through the ESP Box, Zola could feel Maheu struggling to contain a pointed remark. Both of them waited. Lantier knew they were there, and would show them what he had to show them whenever he was ready to show it.

Lantier raised his hands, fingers spread. Zola and Maheu each placed a palm against an identical palm of Lantier's. The three versions of Zola interfaced through the power of the ESP Box and the dominating obsessive power of Lantier's broken mind.

Cinders and gravel crunched underfoot. In the distance, train whistles moaned like the midnight language of whales. Zola looked around. A single train track, arrow straight and gleaming in light that came from no visible source, stretched out ahead of him until it was lost in the distance. On a post next to it, a signal burned a steady green. Zola looked over his shoulder and saw the locomotive, waiting, chuffing black smoke above and white steam below. To either side, the landscape was without features. There was a sense of up and down, possibly of horizon, but nothing the eye could catch. Beyond the locomotive, the same track stretched away, terminating in some distant flicker of red and green.

"They don't signal the same way around here," Lantier said. His avatar here was rangy, sunburned, wearing overalls speckled with burnholes over a canvas shirt rolled up past the elbows. A striped cap sat back from his forehead, the bill creased sharply in the middle.

Zola nodded. Even here, he wasn't sure if speaking would be a good idea.

Lantier raised an arm and pointed. "But if you look up ahead a ways, you'll see that I got it figured out." He spat what Zola assumed must be tobacco juice onto the tracks.

Following his gaze, Zola saw a sign in the distance, much too far to read clearly—but this was Lantier's world, and read it Zola did.

STARKVILLE, POP. 1

"Full steam," Lantier said. "We're behind schedule."

Zola and Maheu walked together back up to the control room. "He's not going to live long," Maheu said. "You know that, of course."

"I'm not sure he's ever been interested in living, if by living you mean interacting with the world of the senses," Zola said.

He summoned a supervisor from the factory floor, one of the few remaining HYDRA operatives who had not been used as the basis for clones or eliminated in various purges Zola had found necessary during his consolidation of control. The woman's name was Olivia Toynbee. She had been a valued aide to Madame Hydra, which Zola initially considered a valid reason to liquidate her; but once he had observed her facility with managing the logistics of materials and cloned laborers, he changed his mind. The intelligent leader did not waste resources.

"Master," she said, presenting herself at the control room door.

"Olivia, report on the H2? Numbers, mission readiness?"

She took a moment to get her figures straight. "We've got sixty-one of the model H2 fully constructed, and another twenty-three in the tanks. Of the sixty-one, forty are in the final stages of alpha-wave acclimatization. The other twenty-one are in separate training. We had to do something with them because there were too many for the alpha-wave facilities we have."

Zola shot a look at Maheu, who avoided it by not looking at the video display in Zola's torso. "Very good," Zola said. "Perhaps I should construct a limited-use ESP Box to do the alpha-wave training with a number of clones at once. Maheu, if you can find the time, would it be possible to get the rest of the alpha-wave facilities operational so we can do what we are here to do?"

Maheu appeared to consider this. "I may be mistaken," he said after a theatrically deliberate pause, "but was that not sarcasm?"

There was silence in the control room. *Olivia,* Zola directed. *You did not hear that last exchange. Return to the floor and continue readying the H2 assets.* When she was gone, he turned to Maheu. "I am beyond your humiliation, Maheu," he said. "But you are not beyond my anger. Do not forget this. I made you. When you cease to be useful, I will make another."

"I have never had any doubt of that," Maheu said. "Perhaps I will finish the final operations testing on the alpha-wave systems now."

vi.

There is a man named Happy Hogan. He is loyal and strong. From him I have created you, and you, too, are loyal and strong. But you are yet more loyal, and yet stronger, than Happy Hogan. Why? Because his loyalty is devoted to a dissipated wastrel, a would-be plutocrat whose heart fails and whose power resides in a toy suit of armor. Your loyalty is to Zola, and to HYDRA! You are the hundred heads of the new HYDRA. Happy Hogan, the inferior template for your marvelous creation, is a soldier. You, too, are soldiers, but you fight for a cause most glorious, not for the sickly glory of Tony Stark's gratification. I speak into your minds, and you grow stronger. You grow more resolute. You grow disgusted with the teeming filth of the world we are all forced to live in . . . and thanks to my voice, which I give to you all equally, you can hear of a better world. A world you can fight for. A world in which I may speak into the minds of every man, woman, and child! A world in which we will all pull in the same direction, with the same goals and the same vision! A world in which all are HYDRA!

Three days after his anticlimactic date with Serena Borland, Tony was still in the RTI Lab when he looked up from a carbon-nanotube injection mold to see Pepper standing there.

"It's the invisible stuff, Pep," Tony said. "That's where the next breakthrough is. All of this, the ray guns and levitation, I can improve that by bits. But down there in the microscopic, that's where I can transform things. That's what I have to do."

"What you have to do is take a shower and then call Rhodey," Pepper said.

It occurred to Tony that he had slept perhaps eight hours out of the previous seventy-two, and that he hadn't been back to the office since accelerating out of the garage while Happy was still waiting at the first stoplight with Serena. He felt hazy, but also flushed with the work he'd accomplished. The lab. That was where he was most comfortable. He didn't need to put on a show for the machines, didn't need to pose and smile for them. They didn't care about deliverables in his latest round of government procurement contracts and they didn't care about the dividends on Stark Industries pre-ferred shares.

He'd been happier—purely, simply happier—during the last seventy-two hours than he could remember being in years.

Pepper stood there waiting for an answer. Tony wanted her to go away. But he was a grown man, the chair and ex-ecutive officer of one of the world's great R & D enterprise firms. Reluctantly he began to reassume his Tony Stark per-sona. "As long as Rhodey takes a shower, too," he said. "Okay, Pep. Give me an hour. I'm guessing you already have the meeting scheduled?"

"In an hour and a half," she said.

"Atta girl." Tony was already on his way to the shower, but his head was still running diagnostics and spinning with histograms on energy transfer and nanoscale response propagation.

Pepper went out to the parking lot, where Rhodey leaned against the fender of his government-issue black Taurus. "I'm worried about him," she said.

"Seems like we all ought to be worried about him."

"You can't tell Nick, Rhodey," Pepper said. "He needs to do this work, and if Fury gets wind of it, you know him.

He'll come stomping in here and demand that Tony shut it all down until he's delivered on all of his existing federal contracts. That's not going to turn out well."

Rhodey looked up into the sky, in the general direction of Islip airport. "Did you know that Madame Hydra was on that plane?" he said. "She was traveling in disguise, apparently was an unholy pain in the ass to the point that one of the stewardesses complained to the pilot right before they took off. It's all on the black box."

"I'm not supposed to be crying for Madame Hydra, am I?" Pepper wanted to know.

"No," Rhodey said. "I don't think anybody is. But I'm telling you because somebody made that happen. We're not sure who, yet. But it was a hit, plain and simple. Somebody brought down that plane because she was on it. Two hours after the crash, one of the airline's baggage handlers was shot in the parking lot. The guy who killed him then offed himself. We're still running down leads to see if they knew each other, but you know what I think? I think someone was cleaning up loose ends."

Pepper ran through what he had just said, replaying it to make sure she was getting the implications. "Cleaning up loose ends," she repeated. "By making their assassin kill himself? That's heavy brainwashing."

"If brainwashing is what it is," Rhodey said. "Listen, I know you're out here running interference for Tony. I've been letting you do it for a while now. How about we stop with the games and I go talk to him?"

"He's in the shower," Pepper said. "At least I hope he is." After a pause, she added, "I'm worried about him."

"You just said that a minute ago."

"Well, it's still true, Rhodey," she snapped. "He's got this instant control idea in his head, and it's all he can think about. Sometimes I think he wants to use it so he doesn't have to deal with people."

"Tony? Not deal with people? Who's going to feed his ego then?" Rhodey cracked a smile.

"That's kind of the problem," Pepper said. "I'm not sure he gets that boost from people adoring him anymore." She started to say something else, and then shrugged. "At least he's not drinking."

"Yeah, that's a good thing," Rhodey said. "Think he's out of the shower?"

She nodded. "Probably. But I doubt he's climbed back out of his head."

In the office suite set into the outside corner of the RTI lab's L, Tony greeted Rhodey with a big grin. "Old buddy old pal, wait'll you see what I've been up to. It's all about the interface. Once you get the interface right, it's like having radar while the other guy is still reading chicken guts to predict the weather." He motioned Rhodey to sit and poured him a cup of coffee without asking whether he wanted it. "So are you here to tell me how worried SHIELD is, or is this a social call?"

"You know better than that," Rhodey said. He put the coffee on the table next to his chair.

Tony sat behind his desk and put a serious expression on his face. "Okay. I'm ready to take my medicine."

"Joke all you want, but you're lucky Nick's not here," Rhodey said. "Here's the bottom line. You're in violation of all kinds of deliverable deadlines, and you might be Mr. Tony Stark of mighty Stark Industries, but that doesn't mean much when you've got a bunch of senators up for reelection who signed on to a defense authorization bill and are now getting killed in the press because they spent all this money and don't have any tech to show for it."

"Tell everyone it's classified," Tony said with a shrug. "Most of it is."

Rhodey was shaking his head. "Doesn't matter. What

matters is that the press is starting to ask what you're do-ing with all this money. Pretty soon the Hill is going to start throwing you under the bus; they're already doing it off the record."

"Let 'em," Tony said.

"Let 'em?" Rhodey said. "That's not Tony Stark talking. You need to take the bull by the horns, or whatever. Get out there, say something, produce something that will make good video. Blow something up for them so they can go back to worrying about Social Security."

Pepper appeared in the doorway. "Fury's on the phone."

"Did you plan this?" Tony was looking at Rhodey. Then he looked at Pepper. "Or did you? What is this, some kind of intervention?"

"We need something from you, Tony," Rhodey said. "You want to put time into instant control, that's cool, I get it. It's a promising tech. But you've also got responsibilities to the people who financed this lab."

"I financed this lab," Tony said. "Me."

"What, with your own personal mint? Where did that money come from?"

"I don't need a lecture on responsibility, Rhodey, and I don't need you doing my bookkeeping, either," Tony said. "What I need is for you to leave me alone so I can do my work."

"Thing is," Rhodey said, "if I leave you alone, lately you haven't been doing the work you're supposed to be doing. You're a public figure, whether you like it or not. Forget about Congress; how do you think the average American schmo feels when all of a sudden Tony Stark, genius play-boy, darling of the cameras, won't come out of his lab? It feels weird to them. We don't need them feeling weird. You can do something about it."

Now he picked up his coffee and sipped, looking at Tony over the rim of the mug. From the doorway, Pepper said,

"Boys. I await instructions on what to do with the impatient leader of SHIELD."

Rhodey and Tony stayed locked on each other for a long moment. Then Tony said, "How about if you tell Nick that Rhodey will call him back in half an hour." Pepper disappeared and Tony stood up. "Okay, Rhodey," he said. "Let me show you what I've been doing. Then you can go back and tell Fury so he feels better."

The new suit prototype hung suspended in a frame near the main control workstation. "I'm still working out some of the details in the interface," Tony explained as he walked Rhodey through the newest innovations. "But I've got response times down as close to zero as I think is possible with the interface I can build. Plus there are some cool new toys in the suit itself—one of which," he added with a wink, "is a bit of low-frequency sound crowd-control tech that might have been part of a government contract. Make sure you mention that part to Fury."

He waved in the direction of three older suits, which stood in a row at the far end of the testing floor. "I tinkered with some features in those, too, and any of them would be good in a pinch. Tell Fury that, too, so he doesn't lie awake at night worrying that the end of the world will arrive and I'll have to go meet the apocalypse in a prototype."

Rhodey stood next to the prototype. "Looks nice," he said.

It did look nice, if Tony did say so himself. He'd come up with a double-layered carbon-nanotube fabric sandwiched around a shock-absorbing gel that could disperse the kinetic energy from anything smaller than a cruise missile. He was developing a superconducting control and interface system that would grow inside each of the individual tubes, essentially creating a nervous system inside the suit. Dermal interfaces would direct the suit with impulses from his brain, with response times equal to—or sometimes less than—the time it took for those impulses to initiate a response in Tony's own muscles.

"The last time I tried this," Tony said, "when I wired the suit into my nervous system internally, I didn't count on the side effects. The big deal here is that I turned it around, and built a nervous system for the suit. Once I get some practice in it, it's going to move exactly with me. I won't need all kinds of mechanics, and the delays that come along with them. It's going to be goddamn near sentient."

"Sentient, huh?" Rhodey said. "Seems to me that hasn't worked out so well in the past."

"Bad choice of words," Tony said. "The command-and-control software built into it will act like a nervous system instead of a set of subroutines. There's an integrated quality to the whole thing that I bet would pass some kind of stimulus-response Turing test. If there was such a thing."

He looked over at Rhodey, and just for a moment Rhodey saw the old Tony. The braggadocio and the almost childlike delight in a new bit of tech. It made him feel better. Everyone goes into funks, he told himself. Maybe now Tony's snapping out of his.

"How about I fire it up and let you listen to it purr?" Tony said.

"I can't wait," Rhodey said.

Rhodey watched as Tony ran a series of software checks and then initialized the subroutines that activated the suit's motor responses. "This way it opens right up and waits for me to step in," Tony said, his eyes still on the screen. "Works a lot better than having all of the mechanical bits that need to snap themselves together. Now I've designed it so the nanotube mesh divides along seams, and then reknits itself when it detects me inside." He paused and one of his eyebrows arched as he watched a terminal screen. "Huh," he said. "That's weird."

"What's weird?"

"Looks like it thinks I'm already there," Tony said. He

looked up at Rhodey, saying, "Figures this would happen when I'm showing it off for you." Then his eyes widened, and Rhodey saw Tony's mouth trying to form his name, but before the sound ever got to Rhodey's ears, the world blew out in a flare like a lightbulb popping in his head.

vii.

PROVISIONAL APPLICATION FOR PATENT

TITLE
   Suit-embedded neuromuscular interface (SENI)

DESCRIPTION
   Direct interface between the human nervous system and external robotic mechanism, accomplished without intrusion below the
epidermal layer. One hundred and sixteen interface junctures
placed on areas of the skin near important motor neurons create
near-instantaneous signal capability between the human brain and
the mechanical exoskeleton (see Stark Industries patents [redacted],
[redacted], [redacted], and [redacted]).

CLAIM
   Current waldo technology relies on crude spatial simulation
approximations or interfaces that intrude on the human nervous
system with undesirable side effects. SENI in effect creates an extended nervous system in the exoskeletal apparatus, with near-
total elimination of transmission-related stimulus-response lag
and near-instant control of any suit function without physical action on the part of the suit operator. SENI is derived from, and in
turn contributes to, Stark Industries' proprietary instant control
technology suite.

SECURITY STATUS
   Project undertaken without any assistance or cooperation from
agencies of the United States Government. No security restrictions
apply.

Rhodey's alive, Tony told himself. *He's alive.* It only hit him once, and he's one tough marine. Right along behind that came the thought that Tony himself was not a tough marine, and he needed to get into a suit, and pronto, if he was going to have any chance of coming through the next ten minutes with his body anything like intact.

It had happened almost quicker than he could follow. The odd reading on the screen, the glance up, the prototype in motion behind Rhodey, the pulse beam blasting Rhodey out of the way and demolishing much of the platform holding up the testing control terminals. Tony had hit the ground running, and he was calling out emergency response codes to the newest of the suits lined up on the wall. It snapped open and he got to it just as another pulse beam glanced off its helmet and spun him around. He hit the ground, fixtures snapping shut and his head ringing. The suit optics stabilized in time for him to look up and see the prototype coming at him, parallel to the ground and moving at upward of a hundred miles an hour.

Mistake, he thought. It doesn't have enough mass. He braced himself and took the impact on one shoulder, the way a running back turns to absorb a big hit. The reinforced concrete of the floor cracked, but Tony held steady, and the suit rebounded away like a superball. *What the hell is going on here?* It wasn't supposed to work without him, it was supposed to be a reinforcement of the nervous system it linked into.

The prototype skidded along the floor and crashed through an expensive array of sensors designed to detect flaws in its own armor mesh. Tony went after it, knowing that its weapons systems were a little better than what he had but figuring that if he got close enough, he could put simple physics to work. Get it in a bear hug and let mass do the rest. Hold on to it until he could figure out how to shut it down again.

He tore the ruined array off the prototype and got a faceful of raw EMP that momentarily scrambled his systems. The suit turned into a five-hundred-pound coffin, and the prototype blasted up into the air and hosed the entire left side of the lab with double-palmed pulse bolts. Tens of millions of dollars' worth of custom machinery disintegrated into a cloud of fragments that destroyed the wall behind them. Tony got his systems back on line and shot into the air after the prototype, smashing into it and driving it upward through the beams of the roof. He opened a channel to Pepper and called out to her. "Need a little help with the new toy, Pep!"

"Already on it," came her voice. "I can see you. What do you need?"

"Shutdown codes," Tony said. He got hold of the prototype's arm. "In one of the hermetic servers."

It took a swing at him, landing a roundhouse to the side of his helmet. The suit took most of the impact, but the prototype's kinetic reservoirs more than made up for its lack of mass; Tony's ears rang with the force of it.

"Whenever you can get around to it," he said.

It hit him again, and this time Tony managed to catch the arm and hold it against his waist. The prototype fired pulse bolts back down toward the ground. Tony heard the impacts on the RTI lab. Something clicked in his head: It was trying to destroy the lab.

He had not only been hacked, he'd been hacked by someone who knew that he was doing some kind of R & D out here.

But nobody knew that.

"Now, Pep," he said. "If not sooner."

The prototype activated its version of the uni-beam, and Tony felt the wash of heat through his suit. He had the prototype in the bear hug he'd wanted, but the downside of that was that it didn't care if it destroyed itself. He did, and that's what was going to happen if the uni-beam cooked away for too long in the millimeters of space between them.

Readouts on the inside of the suit's visor started to flash warnings. Tony's temper was starting to flash warnings, too. He didn't like being hacked, and he didn't like having his own inventions turned against him, and he really didn't like being faced with the choice of broiling in his suit or letting the prototype go. He wasn't sure he could catch it in a straight race, and he damn sure couldn't let it get away.

It fought him, trying to accelerate higher and digging its fingers into the joints of the armor until Tony could hear some of the seals let go. I outdid myself, he thought, holding it down with all of the drag his weight and angular thrusters could bring. This carbon nanotube stuff is top-notch. They twisted and tumbled through the air in chaotic maneuvers that started the blood roaring in Tony's ears.

"Really, Pep," he said. "Now."

And as if on cue, the prototype went limp. Tony shot downward at roughly ten times acceleration due to gravity, covering the distance between his initial position and the roof of the RTI lab before he had a chance to get oriented. He blew through the ceiling of the building's public lobby and blasted a four-foot deep pit into the floor and the poured concrete beneath. For a moment he didn't say anything and didn't move.

"Tony? Are you okay? Did it work?"

"Yeah," he panted. "It worked." Prototype draped over his shoulder, Tony hopped out of the crater and headed for the lab. "How's Rhodey?"

"Rhodey?" Pep said. "Oh my God. What happened to Rhodey?"

The front door of the lab slammed open. Tony turned to see Happy Hogan.

"Hap," he said. "Just in time."

"I got here as quick as I could," Happy said. "What the hell happened here?"

"Bit of a Frankenstein moment. Rhodey's hurt. Come on."

By the time they got back to the testing area, Pepper had already gotten to Rhodey, who was in a heap at the back wall. The pulse bolt had pounded him into one of the loading dock doors, but that was a stroke of luck; the doors, made of hollow aluminum segments, absorbed much of the impact. Tony dropped the deactivated prototype and popped his helmet. He, Pepper, and Happy got Rhodey turned over just as Rhodey's eyes started to flutter. There was blood on his face, and a deep cut on the top of his head, but Happy ran his fingers up and down Rhodey's limbs and said, "Doesn't feel like anything's broken. At least not bad."

"Rhodey," Tony said.

"Give him a minute," Pepper said. They waited until Rhodey made a sound, which was, "Ohhhh."

"We're here," Tony said. "You okay, cowboy?"

Rhodey nodded. "Yeah. Hell of a shot, but I'm okay."

Pepper didn't look convinced. "I called a doctor."

"Call him again," Rhodey said, "and tell him to go home."

"Come on, Rhodey," Hap said. "Like you said, it was a hell of a shot. Won't hurt to let them look you over."

"Oh, it's going to hurt either way." Rhodey sat up and squeezed the sides of his head with his palms. Blood dripped from his nose until Pepper wiped it away with a handkerchief. She was the only woman under forty Tony knew who used handkerchiefs.

"Good thing you were so close," Tony said. "The beam didn't have room to gain much energy."

Rhodey looked at him. One of his eyes was swelling shut. "It gained enough."

"Well," Tony said. "Now comes the detective work. Nobody hacks Stark Industries. At least not twice."

He looked over at the control terminal workstation, which lay in ruins. But there was one laptop he used for hostile-environment testing. He found it in the wreckage and flipped it open. It woke up from its sleep and awaited his passcode. "No substitute for custom workmanship," he said, and started working on it.

First he patched it into the dormant suit, looking for anomalies in the code that governed its motor abilities and autonomy protocols. There it was, tucked away in a harmless-looking patch of machine language governing audio input volume control. He chopped it out, put it behind a series of firewalls, and isolated an unusual stretch of it that would be easily searchable but not dangerous. Then he started combing through Stark server records to see where and when that particular stretch of ones and zeroes had made its way through the servers, under any encryption protocol the suit could understand. Ninety seconds later the servers had an answer, and thirty seconds after that, a Defense Department satellite in geostationary orbit over Long Island Sound pinged him a response from the DOD's central data tracking clearinghouse. Now he knew where the code had come from, but he couldn't believe it.

"Brooklyn?" Tony said out loud. Happy and Pepper looked over from where they knelt over Rhodey. "Someone in *Brooklyn* hacked my prototype?"

viii.

We strike the enemy where he does not anticipate—where he thinks he is invulnerable, or where he thinks we would never dare strike. We strike the enemy with such daring and swiftness that he does not realize the blow has fallen until it is too late, and his citadel crumbles around him. We are the sweep of the sword too fast for the eye to follow, the lethal wound inflicted before the nerves have a chance to cry pain. We are HYDRA! We build, and grow, and the enemy knows of our coming but cannot prevent it. We are HYDRA! The enemy fears us because he knows that when one is cut down, ten take his place. We are HYDRA! The enemy calls itself SHIELD, but no shield can defend against one hundred swords. We fall upon the enemy and destroy it without mercy. We are HYDRA! Go now—gather your weapons, don your armor, and remember that you fight not for yourself but for the man to the left and the man to the right, the man behind you waiting to take your place if you should fall and the man who lies at your feet. You fight as one. You are HYDRA!

Nick Fury had a hell of a lot of reports to fill out in the aftermath of Tony's little pet project running amok at the RTI lab. Every item of equipment in the lab carried a security status that meant its demise had to be anatomized, and since Tony's federal contacts were mediated by SHIELD, Fury was the man who had to sign off on all of the reports. He was not temperamentally suited to desk work, and by the time he'd spent a full day at it, he was ready to get out in the field and find an ass that needed kicking.

The only upside to the whole situation was that it seemed

to have snapped Tony out of his fugue. While the RTI lab was being rebuilt, Tony was spending more time back in Stark Industries' main facilities, which meant more was getting done there. Tony was interacting more with the rest of humanity. It was good.

If Tony Stark ever completely lost it and went crazy, Fury thought, we'd be in a world of trouble.

He called in Major Hailey Donner, his aide specifically detailed to take congressional heat. She was also a certified aquatic demolitions specialist and trained infiltration and hostage-rescue team leader, but her political instincts were usually as valuable to Fury as any of her other attributes. "Pressure going down a little?" he asked when Donner walked in.

"A smidge," she said. "And yes, that's a professional term. We use it when there is no real difference in the amount of incoming flack, but our attitude toward it is measurably mellower."

"I had no idea," Fury said. "What do you suppose accounts for this mellower attitude?"

"Tony working again," said Major Donner. "Now when I get a call from some staffer, that's what I say. 'Tony's working again.' It doesn't make them go away, but it means we're back in the realm of standard-issue high-stepping through congressional bullshit."

"I get it." Fury signed a report and said, "I've got some high-stepping of my own here, needs to get to the General Accounting Office by tomorrow morning."

Donner took a step toward his desk to take the files, and that was when all of the explosions started going off.

Tony got an armor-piercing call from SHIELD just as he was finishing a clean install of the prototype's control systems, which involved rebuilding and replacing the entire neural network that ran through the inner layer of carbon-nanotube mesh. He had to do it that way because he couldn't be sure whether somewhere in the network medium, a stray bit of malicious code was still floating around on one of the artificial nodes. He'd flushed and destroyed all of them, and now he was overwriting them to be sure.

The SHIELD ping was an automated distress call: RESPOND IMMEDIATELY—SHIELD HQ UNDER ATTACK BY FORCES UNKNOWN—ALL FORCES MUSTER PRIORITY ALPHA.

Tony looked at it for a long time. Then he got on his SHIELD-issued comm and pinged Nick Fury.

No answer.

So he pinged Rhodey. "Tony, where are you?" Rhodey's voice was just below a shout, and Tony winced before the comm got the volume adjusted.

"At the RTI Lab," Tony said. The urgent tone of Rhodey's voice caused him to take a couple of reflexive steps in the direction of the newest fully functional suit.

"Get over here," Rhodey said. "We've got HYDRA everywhere."

Tony stopped. "HYDRA? HYDRA what?"

"Some kind of light infantry strike force. We're holding them off—truth is, we're kicking the hell out of them—but we don't know what else they've got planned. All hands on deck." Rhodey paused, and the whicker of a SHIELD-issue caseless assault rifle came over the comm. "Tony?"

"I'm here. Rhodey, you can handle this, right? SHIELD never used to send out APBs for HYDRA goons dropping out of airplanes."

Another burst of fire, and then Rhodey's comm scraped against his chin. It sounded like a gust of wind in Tony's ear. "Tony," Rhodey said. "The call is out."

"I heard the call," Tony said. "You just said you've got it under control."

Silence in the comm. In the background, Tony heard gunfire, muffled explosions, the staccato beat of helicopter rotors. Then Rhodey cut the comm without another word, and

Tony stood alone in the RTI Lab. "He said they had it under control," Tony said, and shrugged. "They don't need me."

He went back to the control terminal and started in on the last phase of the prototype systems reinstall.

In the aftermath of the battle, Rhodey figured out how it had all gone down.

First, an EMP had momentarily scrambled SHIELD's defensive perimeter sensors. It took maybe ten seconds to get them back on line; SHIELD had been planning for EMP disruption since the phenomenon had first been named fifty years ago. During that ten seconds, eight aircraft in recognized commercial airspace lanes had cut out of their announced flight paths and turned on the jets to drop nearly a hundred paratroopers over the Governors Island HQ— which nobody was supposed to know about, but that just went to show you how much secrecy was worth when the other guy decided he really wanted to know something.

At the same time, another several dozen HYDRA commandos shed their disguises as tourists taking advantage of the free Governors Island ferry. They dropped their picnic baskets, locked and loaded, and took on the physical perimeter of the base, which was built just below water level with an entrance attached to the ventilation stack for the Brooklyn-Battery Tunnel.

That made something like two hundred well-armed and reasonably well-trained commandos, in a coordinated air drop and land assault.

SHIELD, caught completely unawares, had repelled it in less than thirty minutes—with not a single civilian casualty. Casualties in the invading force topped out at a nice even one hundred percent.

The last of the ferries was steaming back toward Whitehall Street on Manhattan Island, bearing a bunch of confused tourists who weren't quite sure what they had just seen. SHIELD psyops and PR personnel were among them, massaging their impressions and making sure that when they went to the papers—which some of them were sure to do—they would give a story that SHIELD could massage the rest of the way when the reporters came to them for a quote.

Now Rhodey was running through this retroactive assessment of the enemy tactics, filing it, and matching it up against previous known actions of HYDRA, all as a way of ignoring the fact that Tony Stark had bailed on them when it counted.

Or, no. Not when it counted, because it turned out they had everything under control from the minute the first alarms sounded. When it might have counted.

He put the thought out of his mind. There would be time to deal with it later. Fury would for damn sure want to deal with it, and right then Rhodey didn't know how he would be able to defend Tony. It was a hard place to be when friendship collided with responsibility.

With the tourists flushed off the island, SHIELD recovery teams were gathering the bodies of the HYDRA attackers. Matching numbers with the radar and video records, they were making sure that they'd gotten all of them. It wouldn't do to finish the cleanup and then have a handful of dead-enders jump out at them from the gift shop men's room. The bodies were placed in neat lines, with frequency scramblers set up at the site to prevent the ever-present news choppers from getting any footage of what actually had gone down. Rhodey walked along one of these lines. There were twenty-seven bodies, each in the standard-issue black body armor and full helmet, with the HYDRA logo prominent on the left breast. He tried not to think of the people they might have left behind. After a battle, the atavistic rush of victory always clashed with Rhodey's sorrow at the way men were willing to die. To leave behind wives and children for HYDRA? He didn't understand it.

Just like he didn't understand Tony Stark answering the

call just to tell Rhodey that he wouldn't be answering the call.

You believed in someone. You fought alongside him, you saw the way he triumphed over his own demons because he could see a larger good . . . and then this. There was no way to defend it.

But defend it Rhodey would, because friendship meant that much to him. Tony had been right; SHIELD had never been in real danger.

How was he going to get that across to Fury?

At the head of the row of bodies, the man in question was on one knee with a HYDRA helmet in his hand. The body he'd taken it from lay at his feet. The body armor was shredded by a textbook three-round burst to the center of mass. Whoever this HYDRA commando was, he'd felt a punch in the gut and then died before it really had time to hurt. The small mercies of war, Rhodey thought.

"I think we've accounted for all of them, sir," he said. He'd just gotten off the comm with the central ops flunky who had told him that the numbers matched. Unless HYDRA had figured out how to make invisible commandos, their strike force had been eliminated to the last man.

"Good to know, Rhodey," Fury said. "Good to know. Where was Mr. Tony Stark?"

"He got the call, sir." Rhodey wasn't willing to say any more with other people looking on. He wasn't the kind of man to air dirty laundry.

"Then I expect he would have been here. At least in time to help us do our tally," Fury said. He stood, HYDRA helmet still in his hand, and pointed down at the body at his feet. "Do you recognize this guy?" Fury asked.

Rhodey looked down. He tried to control the reaction on his face, but didn't think it had worked. He could see where this was going to lead, all the consequences way down the line, and he didn't want to be part of it. But if there was one thing James Rhodes knew about himself, it was that he couldn't lie. Not to a superior officer, and not with the plain fact of the situation staring him in the face. He didn't want to answer, but he did.

"Yes, sir," he said. "I recognize him."

ix.

PROVISIONAL APPLICATION FOR PATENT

TITLE
    Dual-layer carbon nanotube weave

DESCRIPTION
    See carbon nanotube weave, Stark Industries provisional appli-
cation for patent [redacted], for description of single-layer weave.
Dual-layer carbon-nanotube weave improves protective capability
and is constructed with the purpose of filling the gap between the
layers with a shock-absorbing gel or other force-attenuating material.

CLAIM
    With an interpolated material, the protective capability of the
double-layer carbon nanotube weave is predicted to exceed that of
the single-layer weave by a factor of eight to ten. (See attached
table of preliminary experimental results.) Further experimenta-
tion is ongoing to investigate the possibility of using the interlayer
space for the installation of energy and sensor systems using distributed nanotech modularities that do not depend on unified
transmission structures such as wires and circuits, which would
be easily stressed or broken by impacts on the outer layers of the
armor.

SECURITY STATUS
    Project undertaken under the auspices of Stark Industries
agreements with the Department of Defense, SHIELD, and other
governmental agencies outlined in Senate Amdt. [redacted] to
Senate Amdt. [redacted] to H.R. [redacted] (110th). Technology is

proprietary to Stark Industries but will be shared fully with all eligible entities. Technology is classified and will not be licensed
until such time as classification order is rescinded.

*You will take one of them to Tony's RTI Lab, and you
will show it to him. You will rub his face in it as necessary.
And you will extract from him answers that will explain his
actions.*

These were Rhodey's orders as he rode in a SHIELD turbocopter from Governors Island to the cookie-cutter suburbia
of Long Island, where Tony's RTI Lab nestled in a clutch of
light-industrial facilities. A truck yard here, a beer distribu-
torship there, a self-storage facility across the street advertis-
ing a special on its ground-floor spaces. The turbocopter
landed in the RTI Lab's parking lot, air regulations be
damned, and Rhodey got out while the rotors were still hammering their invisible beat into the summer sky. He ducked
under the downdraft and banged in through the front door.
Pepper was there to meet him in the lobby.

"Rhodey," she said. "Go easy."

"I get why you're saying that," Rhodey said, "but it's not
time for easy anymore."

He found Tony doing something to the prototype with a
sensor whose thin wires led back to the main control terminal. The terminal, Rhodey registered, had been completely
rebuilt since the prototype had gone haywire the week before, when he'd picked up his bumps and bruises courtesy
of a pulse bolt and a close encounter with a loading-dock
door.

The thing Rhodey didn't like about the whole setup was
that he knew that Fury would be arriving in exactly nineteen minutes. Twenty from the turbocopter's landing, as
registered back at Governors Island. Fury had ordered that,
too, and Rhodey had gone along with it because he was a
soldier. He'd earned enough personal capital to question

Fury, but not to start an outright war in the chain of command, so when Fury had laid out the plan, Rhodey had registered his objections but let them drop when Fury told him the situation didn't call for negotiations.

"Please," Pepper said. "I know what a pain in the ass he is. But he'll be there when you need him."

"What if we'd needed him yesterday?" Rhodey asked. He let the question hang, and hated himself for doing it because he knew that he was rubbing Pepper's face in something, taking something out on Pepper that she had no control over. But SHIELD needed Tony Stark. America needed Tony Stark. That was bigger than feelings.

Pepper turned and walked toward Tony, who had given no sign that he had registered her presence or Rhodey's arrival. But when they got within ten feet of him, he said, "Rhodey, old buddy old pal. You're here to dress me down, and I deserve it. No question. I'll take my medicine like a man. Feel free to deliver it in whatever form Fury has decreed."

Well, Rhodey thought. So that's how this is going to be.

"I'll deliver Fury's medicine, all right," he said. "But first I'm going to deliver mine, just me to you. Nothing to do with SHIELD." He stepped up on the control terminal platform. "You quit on us, Tony. We could have said that the Hulk was eating the goddamn Empire State Building while riding on the back of Godzilla, and you would have stayed here in your lab working on your suit. You quit. It so happened that you were right. We handled this one. But you quit."

Tony looked him in the eye the whole time. When Rhodey was done talking, Tony said, "I didn't quit, Rhodey. I prioritized. Is it better for me to go zooming off to help you mop up a bunch of HYDRA cannon fodder, or should I take that time to perfect this suit that's going to make a difference the next time something real bad comes along? How is my time better spent?"

"I don't know," Rhodey said. "But what I do know is that you signed up to answer the call, and when the call came, you quit."

"No, I recognized the flaws in the structure," Tony said. "That's what I've been doing in here, too. SHIELD has flaws. My other suits had flaws. This one is going to be perfect, and then when SHIELD calls, I'll be right there. But a couple dozen HYDRA helmets with M-sixteens? Do you really need me for that?"

Rhodey saw red. Literally. The color red washed through his peripheral vision and it was one of the hardest things he'd ever done, not taking a swing at Tony right then and there.

"Those flaws are yours to decide?" he said. "Let me show you something," he said. "You mind coming outside?"

An odd uncertainty flickered across Tony's face. Like he knew that he'd have to see something he didn't want to see, Rhodey thought, which was going to be true. "I'm kind of busy," he said.

"Kind of?" Rhodey threw it back at him. "I killed nine people today. Not the first time that's happened, probably won't be the last. But there was something interesting about it. I've got one of them outside, and I think that you need to see him. If, that is, you can tear yourself away from your computer long enough."

He stood, keeping his gaze locked on Tony. Tony wouldn't look back at him for the longest time, and when he did, Rhodey had the feeling that he'd called in a debt even though if anyone owed anyone else anything, Tony was on the wrong side of the ledger.

"Okay, let's go," Tony said, and walked past Rhodey and Pepper toward the hall that led to the front door. She caught Rhodey's eye after he'd passed, and he could see the message: *Go easy*.

But it wasn't a time to go easy.

"Turns out that HYDRA's made some advances in the

cloning area," Rhodey said as they walked across the parking lot toward the SHIELD copter. "That hasn't always been part of their MO."

Tony didn't say anything. He was keeping pace with Rhodey, but Rhodey could tell that his mind was elsewhere. "So those nine guys I killed today? All the same guy. Hell of a thing, wondering if any of them was the original. Or if the original was there, or even if he's still alive. That's the kind of thing that goes through your head."

"I wouldn't know," Tony said.

Rhodey nodded as they approached the copter's rear door. It was a light-assault model, designed to carry six or eight commandos in addition to the two crew up front. The door Rhodey opened was big enough for three men to jump out abreast. Right now the rear of the copter was empty except for a body bag that lay lengthwise across the inside of the doorway.

"You even start to wonder if maybe there's a clone of you out there, and what it's doing, and whether it knows it's a clone of you," Rhodey said. He paused with the body bag's zipper pinched between the thumb and forefinger of his right hand. "Tony. Pay attention. This is important."

"Don't patronize me, Rhodey," Tony said. "You can be pissed that I didn't come to your little shootout, but don't patronize me."

"You didn't know it was a little shoot-out," Rhodey shot back. He stabbed a finger into Tony's chest to make sure he had Tony's full attention. "For all you knew the world could have been ending down there and you would have stayed in your lab until the Reaper himself came waltzing in the door. That's the problem here. It's not that you were right; it's that you *assumed* you were right, because you're Tony Stark and you can't be wrong."

Rhodey ripped open the zipper on the body bag. "Look, Tony," he said. "Take a good long look."

The face of the corpse hadn't yet lost all of its color from postmortem lividity. The mouth was slightly open, as was one eye. The jaw was strong and clean-shaven, the hair light brown and styled in a crew cut. Tony stared at it for a long time.

"His nose isn't broken," was what he finally said.

"Clones, Tony. They probably didn't send them out to the Golden Gloves so they could get all of Happy's scars. Now how did HYDRA decide to make themselves a hundred clones of Happy Hogan?" Rhodey waited for Tony to look at him, but Tony couldn't tear his gaze from the clone's dead face.

"Happy lives in Brooklyn," Tony said. Rhodey didn't know what to make of that, and he got the feeling from Tony's tone of voice that Tony hadn't really been talking to him anyway.

"Talk to me," Rhodey said. "Something's going on here. This was a message. HYDRA knew they couldn't do any real damage with these. What's behind it?"

"Brooklyn," Tony repeated. He went back into the lab, and when Rhodey followed him back in, Tony stonewalled him until in the end Rhodey got back in the turbocopter and flew back to Governors Island. He called Nick Fury mid-flight and told him not to bother, feeling that something had gone badly out of control but he didn't know what.

X.

There is no science whose mysteries I, your leader, cannot penetrate. I have sought the deepest truths of genetics, and brought you into being. You, my army, my arms, the lever with which I will move the world. Never has there been anything like you—until the next, which will be more magnificent yet. You cannot envision what I envision, which is why it is fitting that I am your leader. Raise your right arms. Yes. Feel the power of your unity, feel the power of your response to my commands. What I want is what is best for you because what I want is best for HYDRA and we are HYDRA. I can touch each and every one of your minds and find their innermost recesses. You have no fears. You have no doubts. You are HYDRA. You eat and breathe and fight for HYDRA. Speak with me, quietly: We are HYDRA. Yes. Now louder! We are HYDRA! When we fight with your arms and bodies, our enemies tremble. When we fight with our minds and our will, the universe itself knows not where to turn. I am Zola. I make you, I guide you, I teach you, and together we will make and guide and teach a new world. We are HYDRA!

Tony took no calls and admitted no visitors for the next twenty-four hours. He needed time to think, and he knew Pepper would handle whatever needed to be handled for a day. He shut down the RTI Lab for a day and gave all of the employees the day off; it was Friday, and nobody complained about getting an unexpected three-day weekend. With the lab quiet around him, Tony paced its halls and testing floor, trying to work out what was happening, who was doing it, and how he should respond.

The attack on SHIELD, Tony understood, hadn't really been an attack on SHIELD at all. It had been an attack on him.

Stark Industries was under assault on at least two fronts. Three, depending on how you conceptualized them. The malicious code that had crept into the prototype suit, plus the use of Happy Hogan clones in the SHIELD incident—plus the psychological impact of someone using Happy that way. Goes all the way back to Sun Tzu, Tony thought. If you get inside your enemy's head, you can win the battle before a shot is fired. Well, shots had been fired in this one, but he got the sense that whoever was pulling the strings on the other side of the battlefield had plans that were going to end up in a face-to-face confrontation. Iron Man versus Someone. This adversary was trying to soften him up by demonstrating that he could be undermined. His security wasn't good enough, and—this was the thing it killed him to admit—he wasn't sure who he could trust.

Brooklyn was a big place. If it wasn't part of New York, it would be the fourth largest city in the country, with more than two million citizens. So why was it sticking in Tony's mind that the prototype hack had come from Brooklyn, and Happy Hogan lived in Brooklyn? The thought was a worm, burrowing into his mind and forcing him to fight the impulse to connect those two facts. There was no reason to believe that Happy was anything but a loyal friend. Anyone could, and did, leave stray bits of DNA around just by living in the world. A mad genius with a cloning facility could make a thousand copies of anyone just by following them around for an hour and getting hold of anything from a napkin to a cigarette butt to . . . well, anything.

He needed to talk to Happy about it, but couldn't figure out a way to approach the conversation without making Happy feel like Tony suspected him of something.

And the truth was, Tony did suspect him of something. He could stand back from his own thought processes and see that they didn't bear rational scrutiny, but that didn't change the niggling suspicion in the back of his mind. Something was happening that he didn't understand, and he was putting the pieces together the only way that they seemed to want to fit together.

"Whoa," he said out loud. "Paranoid territory, there."

The rational way to approach the whole scenario was to assume that Happy was being used to drive a wedge of uncertainty into everything that Tony trusted. Classic psyops. But it was one thing to recognize psyops, and another thing to resist it. "Brooklyn," Tony said. "What is it about Brooklyn?"

And what was it about him that was making him susceptible to such a transparent ploy? There was an old Irish saying: When three people tell you you're drunk, lie down. From every side, Tony had been hearing that he was acting strange. From the inside, it didn't feel like he was acting strange. He wanted what he wanted, and what he wanted was for people to leave him alone so he could work. There were amazing things just on the edge of possibility; he would be able to create them if only people would leave him alone. SHIELD pinging him in a panic because of a gaggle of gunslinging Happy clones just kept him away from the work that might save SHIELD's bacon the next time a real threat came along. This was what nobody understood. Not Fury, not Rhodey, not even Pepper.

Who was calling him constantly despite the fact that he'd told her he wouldn't be answering any calls for the next day or so. Tony looked at his phone, briefly considered calling her just so she wouldn't worry. Then he realized it wouldn't make any difference. She was going to worry no matter what he did.

That was the thing. People perceived Tony Stark in a certain way. And somehow he had ventured far beyond the point where his actions had any effect on those perceptions.

The answer, then, was to not worry about those perceptions. To do what he knew needed to be done.

Right now that was the next stage in the prototype's development. His phone rang. He ignored it.

"Now the real work begins, Maheu," Zola announced. "We may safely assume that SHIELD has communicated to the remarkably uncommunicative Tony Stark that they were assaulted by clones of his close friend Happy Hogan. Stark will of course realize immediately that he was the real target of this operation, but even as he realizes it, by considering the goals of the operation he will be forced to legitimize them. That is, he will begin to suspect his friend Hogan even as he tells himself that he is a fool for doing so."

"Judging from your certitude, one would think that the ESP Box had quite an extraordinary range," was Maheu's sour rejoinder.

Zola raised an eyebrow and turned his body so Maheu could see his on-screen face. "Jealousy again?" he needled. "You have no need of an ESP Box like mine. It is one of a kind, an article unlike any ever created by the human mind. Were I to implant you with one, it would destroy both your individuality and mine. As a clone, you should cherish whatever individuality you might have."

"I'm sure you're correct," Maheu said.

Zola didn't like his tone of voice. Briefly he considered taking control of Maheu's mind, but he had sworn himself against this action when he had created Maheu. What good would an advisor do if the advisor had no volition?

However vexatious that gift of volition often was in practice.

"Maheu," Zola said. "Everything seems to have gone as planned thus far, has it not? We have harvested Hogan's DNA. We have gotten rid of a hundred worthless first-generation clones that taxed our storage capacity, and in doing so have created multiple misdirections that will compromise the ability of our enemies to anticipate and react to our real plans. And," he said, "our train trip to Starkville has brought an unexpected reward."

"Do tell," Maheu said.

"I won't, if you're going to sulk about the ESP Box."

"This is not sulking," Maheu said. "This is sardonic deflation of your invulnerable sense of your own perfection."

Zola laughed with pure delight. "Marvelous. Then I will in fact tell you that when Lantier had his bit of fun with Mr. Stark's newest prototype beetle shell, he brought back some very interesting information about that prototype's abilities . . . and its liabilities. I believe he has hit upon a way to extract—through the teeth of Mr. Stark's formidable network security protocols!—the schematics of the prototype's neural interface."

"Are we to design beetle shells now as well?" Maheu asked. "One might have thought that the construction of a clone army was enough to keep oneself occupied."

"This time, Maheu, your barb misses the mark." Zola clapped his hands. "When one knows the nature of a system, one can exploit that nature. Sometimes one can even control it. What we shall do is, having learned the nature of the prototype's interface, begin to tease out the Achilles heel that inevitably must lurk therein. No man—and here I include even myself—is without error. He who finds his adversary's error first, while keeping his own hidden, is the winner of the battle."

"Every time?" Maheu asked.

"Perhaps not," Zola said. "But this time is the only time that counts."

He stood. "I know you find Lantier's environment distasteful, but we must consult him on the details of this new stage of our plan."

"Our plan?" Maheu echoed. "I was under the impression that you were perfectly content with the previous plan, which included neither this neural interface nor any input from me that would merit the plural possessive 'our.' "

Zola walked out the door and along the catwalk. "Maheu," he said, knowing that Maheu would be right behind him, "word-chopping is at least as reprehensible as jealousy. Advise me! How must we time our next maneuver?" On the way down the catwalk steps, Zola savored the tingling of awe from the ESP Box as the workers noticed his approach.

"It seems to me," Maheu said, "that we should act as soon as is prudent. The longer we wait, the more likely it is that Stark—whatever the fluctuations in his mental state—will in fact achieve a breakthrough that will compromise our goals."

"Agreed!" Zola was gratified that he had reminded Maheu of his station. They reached the elevator. Its door opened at their approach so that they could enter without breaking stride. The descent to the training floor and Lantier's sanctum took fifteen seconds. Zola registered the change in Maheu's expression during that short span. "What is it about Lantier that you find so distasteful?" he asked.

For a moment, there was none of the mocking subaltern in Maheu's gaze, or in his tone of voice. "Because he could have been me," Maheu said. "Or, more accurately, I could have been him."

xi.

PROVISIONAL APPLICATION FOR PATENT

TITLE
  Kinetic attenuation gel

DESCRIPTION
  Viscid polymer capable of absorption and dispersal of kinetic energy at high concentrations, with minimal overheating of adjacent critical systems and structures. Designed for use in conjunction with Stark Industries dual-layer carbon nanotube weave (cf. Provisional Application for Patent [redacted], copy attached).

CLAIM
  Derived from work originally claimed in Stark Industries patents [redacted] and [redacted], this version of the polymer benefits from advances in carbon manipulation, and from new developments in materials science as cited in Stark Industries pending claim [redacted]. Impact energies of up to 1 MJ/kg will be dispersed with 12mm thickness of KA gel in conjunction with double-layered armor such as that claimed in Stark Industries patent [redacted]. 25mm thickness of KA gel has dispersed impact energies in excess of 3 MJ/kg in controlled circumstances. These amounts far exceed existing performance limits of energy-dispersing materials.

SECURITY STATUS
  Project undertaken under the auspices of Stark Industries agreements with the Department of Defense, SHIELD, and other governmental agencies outlined in Senate Amdt. [redacted] to Senate Amdt. [redacted] to H.R. [redacted] (110th). Technology is

proprietary to Stark Industries but will be shared fully with all eligible entities. Technology is classified and will not be licensed until such time as classification order is rescinded.

"The time is oh three four four Saturday," Tony said. "Commencing initialization of prototype for first fully powered test flight and operational check."

There were plenty of good procedural reasons to keep a voice log of a prototype test, but Tony had found that it also cleared his head to talk while he was working out the bugs in a new system. When he played the logs back, he could figure out things from the tone of his voice that sometimes he hadn't consciously noticed during the test. The new suit was a different animal than its previous versions, even Extremis. What he was stepping into was more like a better version of himself than a super-powered personal armor device. There were plenty of things to make him jittery.

"Powering up the suit," he said. The mike taped to the side of his jaw relayed his voice to the server that also kept all of the suit's control systems talking to one another. Instant control. The perfect union of maker and tool. That's what he was after, and tonight—well, this morning—he was going to find out how close he'd gotten so far.

Over in the suit's storage rack, an array of lights on the status panel changed color. "Live and ready to go," Tony said. He walked over to the suit, turned to face away from it, and stepped back to put his feet in the marks he'd made on the floor with fluorescent tape. Just like the senior class play. I hit my mark, I say my lines, and the show goes on.

Sensing the proximity of a human body, protocols in the suit sniffed Tony's DNA out of the various cells his body shed. The profile was run against the administrative subroutine on the server. Returning a match, the subroutine pinged the first three notes from "Also Sprach Zarathustra." This was a touch that Tony wasn't proud of, but he couldn't help himself.

The music was his cue to give a voice password. "For the future of mankind," he said, resisting the urge to sing.

The suit unsealed itself along lines that ran the length of each limb and bisected the torso. With a soft whine, servo-motors moved the splayed suit forward until Tony could feel it touching the back of his head and the points of his shoulders. A series of snaps and hisses followed as it sealed itself around his body, and one hundred and sixteen neurointerface patches sealed themselves onto his skin.

"Suit insertion successful," Tony said. He walked out of the frame and tested the suit's reflexes. Before powering it up, he'd written down a list of basic physical actions he wanted to perform so the systems software could analyze response times and see how well the interface was working— see, in other words, how close he was getting to instant control.

It was impossible, wasn't it? Nothing could be instant. The speed of light was the speed of light. Even Tony Stark couldn't get around that limitation.

But he could get as close as any man alive. That was the goal. He would settle for no less. There were tantalizing possibilities beyond what he thought was possible, too. Action at a distance, quantum manipulations . . . so many avenues to explore.

Today, however, he wanted to make sure this suit worked the way it was supposed to work.

He lifted his left arm, then his right. Flexed his fingers. Windmilled his arms, turned his head, squatted and then jumped straight up, careful not to put too much oomph into the jump since he'd just had the roof fixed after the dustup the other day. Everything worked so smoothly he had to hold out his hands and look at them to remind himself he was wearing the suit. All of the other suits had weighed ever so slightly. Even when they were amplifying his strength, showing him ways to surmount and forget the damage to his heart, Tony had been conscious of them. He'd had to tell the suit to do something and then feel a mechanical process respond to make that thing happen.

Not this time. This time, his mind formed a thought, and as his brain translated it into a nerve impulse, the suit responded. If he hadn't been able to see it wrapped around his body, and if there weren't a dozen readouts superimposed on the inside of the helmet's visor, Tony would not have believed he was wearing a suit at all. Except for the fact that he was in his underwear and could still isolate the feeling of each neural patch where it touched his skin.

"Initial physical commands and responses successful," he said. Then he gave up trying for the dispassionate researcher's tone. "Man, is this baby something."

The next step was to get it in the air. Tony walked to the loading dock door and touched the button to open it. Again he had to remind himself that he was wearing a unique and outrageously expensive piece of technology. The door opened and he walked out onto the dock. "Now I'm going to fly," he said, and took off.

According to the simulations he'd run, the suit was capable of 37-g acceleration in a straight line. G-force damping mechanisms should theoretically have prevented those accelerations from killing him, but he was never going to know until he gave it a try. So, after reaching three thousand feet at a steady 3- or 4-g pace and checking nearby airspace for passenger air traffic, he decided to see what the suit could do. "Initial acceleration to three thousand feet per specs," he said. "Now I'm going to unwind it a little."

He felt the boost to 10-g the way he might have felt an elevator ease from one floor to the next. Nine-g was the threshold where elite pilots started to black out. "Going to twenty," he said, and accelerated straight up. *Whoooosh,* there was more of the elevator feeling, but it wasn't bad at all, and in ten seconds Tony was at cruising altitude for a medium-distance commercial passenger flight. "Nice," he said. "Turning it up to eleven now."

Thirty-seven times the force of gravity was enough to kill some people even at brief exposures, depending on various personal circumstances. For Tony in the prototype suit, it was like the last minute of jumping off a three-meter diving board, right before you hit the water, when you could really tell that you were starting to move fast. He rode it straight up, and stopped ten seconds later at the speed of something like eight thousand miles per hour. "Cutting jets," he said, and felt the glorious sensation of free fall as gravity reasserted itself over his breakaway body. "Outstanding."

Tony fell. He let himself fall, as the natural physics of bodies and attraction took over where his technological sorcery allowed them to. "Deceleration check," he said, and when his altitude was coming down toward fifty thousand feet, he slammed on the brakes, a full 37-g burn.

It was perfect. He stopped on the proverbial dime, and felt it the way you would feel taking two steps instead of one on the way down a staircase.

"Note to self," Tony said. "I'm onto something here."

He hung there, suspended nine miles above the surface of the earth. "The only thing that would make this better right now would be if a meteor came along and hit me," he said. "Have to test the NFCs and the tensile strength of the armor."

That was the next stage. Tomorrow, Tony thought. He raised both hands and fired off a pair of pulse bolts in the general direction of Castor and Pollux. "NSA'll be in touch tomorrow," he said. "Remind them about testing agreement."

There was another way to test the impact-distribution systems. "Huh," Tony said, looking down. Long Island was a matrix of sickly orange and yellow lights. His visor readout picked out the RTI Lab; the jet stream had pushed him several miles to the east. Directly below him was a neighborhood of cul-de-sacs and sleeping commuters.

"It's you people I'm defending," Tony said. He wished he could cut power and just fall, see what would happen when he hit no matter where it was. But always there were the proles to consider. He goosed himself back upwind until dead reckoning of windspeed and acceleration due to gravity told him that if he cut power now, he'd land in the empty field between the RTI Lab and the creek.

Then he cut the power and let himself fall.

It was like skydiving, only better. He had the thrill of no parachute, but also the certainty that he could fall from the goddamn Moon if he wanted to, and nothing could hurt him. He had built an immortality that he could wear over his skin. He reached terminal velocity, and would long ago have passed out were it not for the suit. "Oh, bring it," Tony said. Maybe he had a heart condition, and maybe everyone around him thought he was going crazy, but none of them could do this. He tucked his limbs in tight, and watched the earth race toward him until it was all he could see.

He hit the ground at two hundred and forty-six miles per hour, according to the visor readout. Just before impact, Tony crossed his forearms in front of him, wanting to test the NFCs. The force of his reunion with terra firma created a crater of roughly one hundred cubic feet, and a whole lot of impact energy for the NFCs to convert. As he came to rest head-down in a shower of falling ejecta, Tony noted that the NFCs had distributed an admirable percentage of the relevant joules. Everything was working. He leapt out of the crater and shook off the dirt and clinging bits of weedy growth. "Impact test was impromptu but you'd have to say successful," he said.

Now that the flight test was finished, Tony hated the feel of the ground under his feet. No, not hated; it made him jumpy, anxious to fire the suit back up and take off again, just to see what it could do. He walked back into the lab, and popped the helmet on the testing floor near the rack where the suit would recharge itself and pipe a complete report of its performance to the server, where various sub-routines would crunch the data and issue their own reports on desirable future modifications.

"Tony." The voice echoed a little against the hard contours of the space.

"I don't want to talk to anyone, Pep," he said. "I'm working."

"I don't care whether you're working, or what you want." She walked up to him and planted her hands on her hips. In Pepper body language, this was the badger hunkered down in the mouth of its den. "Happy's trying to decide whether he should quit."

"Oh, please." Tony subvocalized a command, and the suit unsealed itself, peeling back and setting itself into the suspension rack. Tony walked over to where he'd left his clothes. "Happy's not going to quit." He changed the subject. "You should see this sweetheart perform. You know I hate to toot my own horn, Pep, but I've outdone myself. This is something else."

"Tony, shut up just for a second and listen to me."

Still coming down from the rush of the prototype's test, Tony fought against Pepper's resolute focus on all of the things he didn't want to care about. "I'm not going to shut up," he said, "and I don't have to listen to you." He waved a hand in the direction of the suit in its marvelous frame. "This worked tonight. Better than even I would have thought. It's a good night. You can come in and give me a sob story about Hap, or Fury, but what they really want is results. Me delivering results. I'm like a foundry to them, some kind of plant that takes in possibilities and spits out jobs and tech. Tonight that happened. So call them in the morning and tell them to back off."

Pepper's hands stayed on her hips, and she didn't back off. If there was one thing Tony knew and loved about Pepper Potts, it was that she never backed off. "It's not just about tech, Tony," she said. "It's about Happy. It's about all of the people who have tied themselves to you. You may not think you need them, but you do. And they need you. I don't care what you say about who you'll take calls from, or who can come visit the lab. People need you. Maybe you can't stand it, but it's true."

It was true. Tony knew it was true. Still and all, he couldn't make himself care. There were postflight reports to generate, results to analyze and incorporate. He had work to do.

"Leave me alone, Pep," he said. "That's what I want you to tell everyone. They'll get their piece of me. Just leave me alone."

xii.

HYDRA is Prometheus stealing fire from the gods. We bring a new age to humankind, and the old order must be destroyed in this transformation. HYDRA is harbinger of the great creation of a new human universe. Strength through uniformity. Realization of human potential through the refinement and perfection of the human material. You are the latest and best generation of humankind, better than what came before yet inevitably superseded by what I will create next. This is as it should be. The universe marches toward perfection, toward perfect simplicity expressed through mechanisms of unfathomable complexity. You are one stage in this march. You are the perfect expression of humankind at this moment, and for you there is no other moment. You do not live for the future; you live so that the present may create the future we envision. You are heads that progress and time and enemies will cut off, but others—newer, better, stronger—will take your place because we are HYDRA! Never has there been an army like you, and never will there be another. We live and fight so that the next generation, slowly taking shape in my mind, will in turn live and fight until all the world is HYDRA. Take up your history and drive the vision of HYDRA forward into the future that awaits!

Fury hated meetings. He especially hated meetings in which he had to treat close friends the way you treated people at meetings. He liked Pepper and Happy. Unfortunately it didn't matter whether he liked people as soon as they came into the SHIELD office where he was General Fury. In that office, he was guardian of the American people against all enemies foreign and domestic—as gaudy and over-heated as that phrase sounded. It was true. "I asked you to come here together because whatever's going on with Tony isn't going to be solved from one conversation," Fury said. "That's the plain fact of it."

He decided to focus on Happy first, on the general prin-ciple that since Pepper would be the one to accomplish what needed accomplishing, he'd get Happy out of the way so she would be able to see what was coming. "Hap," Fury said. "We know you had nothing to do with the clones. I want that right out in the open, right up front."

"Thanks, Nick," Happy said. He looked like he hadn't slept in days, which was probably the case. Fury could only imagine what the clone revelation had done to a man who valued loyalty as much as Happy Hogan did.

"I think Tony knows that, too," Fury said. "The problem is, it's hard to tell what Tony knows and what he doesn't, because he's in the process of turning himself into a her-mit. The last thing SHIELD needs, and the last thing this country needs, is Tony Stark confusing himself with Howard Hughes."

"I don't think he washes his hands that much, Nick," Pepper said. She didn't look like she'd been getting much sleep, either. Both of them sat in Fury's plain office chairs looking like death warmed over, when what he needed was them at their best, because the quality of one of America's most powerful resources was in question here. They were the ones who could do something about it.

And Fury decided to just tell them so. "I can't help Tony," he said. "I've done what I know how to do, and Tony and I have a particular kind of relationship. So it's going to be up to you. Pepper, your admirable little joke aside, Tony *is* turning into Howard Hughes. He won't talk to anyone, he shirks his responsibilities, he tinkers with machines twenty hours a day or more. This can't last. He's going to crack up.

You know things are bad when he won't make time on a Saturday night for a charity event where he can bask in the attention of unattached young women. How many times in the last two weeks has he canceled an appearance?" Fury waited. "Pepper? Come on. How many times?"

"You don't need the number, Nick," Pepper said. "We both know what you're getting at."

"Then you both know what needs to be done." Fury stood, wished for a cigar, then settled for looking out the window. "Tony Stark is a national-security asset. He also happens to be my friend, or at least we have survived battles together. I want what's best for him, but that doesn't necessarily mean I want what he wants. So. What do we do?"

Again Fury waited. Again neither Happy nor Pepper said anything.

"We organize a charity event that even Tony Stark in his current state cannot refuse," Fury said. "This is what I have done. This is how important I think Tony is, that I have reduced myself to becoming an event planner just to get his ass out of the RTI Lab, which to be honest with you I'd like to burn to the ground no matter what we'd lose." He paused. It had been months, maybe years, since he'd spoken this much all at once.

From his desk drawer he took a sheet of translucent paper. Custom-made stationery, from a new charity that had been wanting money from SHIELD these past few months. "What we have here is a proposal for a benefit shindig that Tony won't be able to pass up," Fury said. "It's for wounded soldiers, and half of the proceeds go to funding heart transplants and research into artificial hearts."

He laid the sheet on his desk. "So what I need from you is not to try. *Try* doesn't do me any good. What I need from you is for you to get Tony out of that goddamn lab and to this benefit, where he can enjoy himself in the way that he once until recently indulged. Am I clear?"

"General, I've got to be honest," Happy said. "Truth is, I think what Tony needs is for someone to walk up to him and sock him in the mouth."

This was so unexpected coming from Happy that for the briefest of moments Fury wondered whether the Happy sitting on the other side of his desk was in fact the real Happy. Who knew? Could this be a clone, and the real Happy was tied up in a basement somewhere?

No. That was stupid. Here he was, Happy Hogan, all busted nose and wounded pride, telling Fury and Pepper what all three of them knew he'd never be able to tell Tony face-to-face.

"Hap," Fury said, "I agree. In the best of all possible worlds, that's exactly what we would do. But in this world, I think that first we need to get Tony out of the lab and into the world again. Remind him of why he likes it." Fury stood. Picking up on his signal, Pepper and Happy did as well. "Later," Fury added, "when this has all blown over, you can sock him in the mouth right after I do."

"Fair enough," Happy said.

"Nick," Pepper said. Fury bridled. Nobody called him Nick in his office, when they'd been called in on a matter of national security. But Pepper had earned some slack, so he didn't call her on it.

"Pepper," he said.

"This new suit really is something," Pepper said. "I'm not saying that to excuse him, but you should know. It's light-years past the other ones. I'm a little scared, to tell you the truth. He's . . . it's like his brain is redlining. There are more ideas coming out of it than he knows what to do with. So he's in the lab all the time, and nobody can talk to him." She paused in the way that people pause when they have decided to say something that they don't want to say and nobody wants to hear.

"If you're worried about him as an asset," Pepper said finally, "I think that part of it is going to be okay. He'll deliver. He's not going to deliver on your schedule, and he's probably not going to deliver what he said he would. But when you get what he has to give, you might be glad that you backed off a little." During that last sentence, she looked Fury in the eye. It touched even his gnarled warrior's heart, her loyalty to a man who didn't deserve it.

"Pepper," Fury said, "I know you believe that. But I don't have the luxury of belief. I need to know. And to know, I need to get Tony out of the lab. I can't have him falling into his own skull."

"You've never managed him. He let you think you were sometimes, but you never did," Pepper said.

"I didn't ask you in here to defend him," Fury said. "I know about loyalty. My loyalty is to that flag in the corner. I think Tony's is, too. But right now he needs someone to remind him of that. Now. Do either of you have a better idea than the one I came up with?"

Happy and Pepper were silent. For this Fury was grateful.

"Excellent," he said. "Now maybe you can go back out to the RTI Lab and see if you can coax him out long enough to read the invitation."

"Is the money really going where it's supposed to be going?" Pepper asked.

"Pepper, sweetheart," Fury said, "the money can go anywhere it wants as long as the event digs Tony out of his bunker."

A SHIELD turbocopter flew them back to the Brookyn Navy Yard, where Happy had left the car they'd driven in from the RTI Lab. "So," he said when they'd got back in and he was easing through the perpetual construction apocalypse on Flushing Avenue. "What do you think about all that?"

Pepper looked out the window at the construction cones

and the families of Hasids out for a Sabbath stroll. Saturday, she was thinking. Normal people are at home with their families on Saturday. Me, I'm at a top-secret meeting about the mental health of my boss, who is also the Invincible Iron Man. She'd read the phrase in a headline somewhere.

"Happy," she said, "I don't know what to think."

"I mean, we've go to do something, right?" Happy steered around to the ramp onto the Brooklyn-Queens Expressway. In forty-five minutes or so, depending on traffic, they'd be back at the RTI Lab.

Pepper nodded, still looking out the window. "Sure. We've got to do something."

It surprised her, how hurt she was by Tony's transformation. When he was his grandiose, flirtatious self, she knew how to deal with him. She knew how to take her affection and put it in a place where he would never see it. She knew how to ignore him when he needed ignoring, and take care of all of the things he never thought about taking care of.

What you are, she told herself silently, is a wife. You're Tony Stark's wife. All of his girlfriends would be so surprised.

"I don't really want to talk about it," she said.

"Okay," Happy said. He didn't push it. She sat looking out the window as they swung from the BQE onto the eastbound Long Island Expressway. Happy was better than Tony deserved sometimes. So was she.

So why did they do this? What was it about him that drew people, that created loyalty?

He was Tony. That was the only way she could put it, even to herself. He was Tony.

And Tony was in trouble, and it was up to them to do something about it.

"Happy," Pepper said. "What do you think about this benefit thing Fury was talking about?"

"One benefit's the same as another to me," Happy said.

Pepper laughed despite her mood. "Tell me about it," she said. "Sometimes it feels like the fate of the free world is hanging in the balance, and Tony's waltzing around a gallery at MoMA, and sometimes it feels like if Tony's not waltzing, the fate of the free world's in the balance. You know, some people have regular jobs."

"Not us," Happy said.

She nodded at the window. "True enough. Not us."

"But what the heck," Happy said. "Would you really want one?"

When they got to the RTI Lab, the automatic gate wouldn't open. Happy got out and laid his palm on the security scanner. ENTRY DENIED flashed on the display. "Huh," he said. He punched the override code into the keypad under the scanner. ENTRY DENIED.

Had Tony cut him out of the access roster because of the clone thing? Happy felt sick to his stomach. He stood there looking at the two words on the display, not knowing what to do. He heard Pepper's door open and shut. She saw what he was seeing and said, "Let me give it a try."

Happy stood aside and watched Pepper do exactly what he had done, with exactly the same results. ENTRY DENIED. ENTRY DENIED.

"Oh," Happy said. "Well, at least I know it's not me."

Pepper was cursing under her breath as she got out her phone and dialed Tony. No answer. She put the phone away and they both stood there for a moment in the glare of the headlights. "This doesn't happen in regular jobs," she said after a while.

"No, it sure doesn't," Happy said.

A sharp pop came from the speaker under the security scanner. "Pep, Hap, everything's fine in here. Go on home." It was Tony's voice.

"This is not fine, Tony," Pepper said. "It's a long way from fine."

"Go home. Really." The speaker popped again. "I'm working."

The backlit security scanner dimmed to black. "Tony?" Pepper said. There was no answer.

xiii.

PROVISIONAL APPLICATION FOR PATENT

TITLE
   Integrated carbon nanotube energy storage and delivery system

DESCRIPTION
   A system of energy storage using the inherent properties of the carbon nanotube structure to gather and channel a plasma within the fibers of existing Stark Industries carbon-nanotube weave (cf. Provisional Patent Application [redacted], attached). Using integrated command-and-control systems standard to Stark Industries personal body armor products, the stored energy can be directed and used as needed with little or no additional space required for batteries or portable reactor units.

CLAIM
   Energy storage limitations have been a serious obstacle in the development of viable powered personal body armor. Stark Industries has been a leader in the development of micro-reactors and multilayer wafer battery technologies, but the weight and space requirements of these are still problematic when matched up with desired flight and combat capabilities. The Integrated Carbon Nanotube Energy system creates a new way of using energy in a space-neutral context, making use of the carbon nanotube weave for both its armoring properties and its compositional suitability for energy storage. By essentially charging the fabric of the suit itself, the user enjoys ample energy supply at no cost in weight or impaired flexibility.

SECURITY STATUS

   Project undertaken without any assistance or cooperation from agencies of the United States Government. No security restrictions apply.

"You see," Maheu said to Zola, "this hermetic impulse on Stark's part is a cruel complication."

"Cruel?" Static flickered across the screen in Zola's torso, momentarily obscuring his face. This happened on those rare occasions when his emotions mastered him. It had something to do with feedback from the ESP Box. Out on the floor, he imagined, the laborers and technicians would have paused briefly at the moment of the static, looking up and around and wincing as if they had just heard an unpleasant noise but could not locate its source. "Cruel," Zola said, "is what I plan for Stark himself. His whims of personality are zest. They give my ambition exactly the challenge it needs."

He could not explain this animus, or perhaps he just did not feel that he had to explain it to his underlings—among whose number he counted Maheu and Lantier, despite their exceptional usefulness. Zola prided himself on the pure rationality of his intellect, but even he had to admit that there were times when the sources of his emotions were obscure. Rationality did not mean perfect understanding.

Although, to be sure, there was much he understood perfectly.

"And what is your plan for Stark, exactly?" Maheu asked. "I find it difficult to advise you on this matter given my complete ignorance of the details."

"If only your ignorance of other things stopped you from advising me about them," Zola said. He looked at the bank of monitors through which he routed feeds from the ESP Box. In this way he could keep visual track of what certain of his followers were doing. The one of interest at this moment depicted Happy Hogan and Pepper Potts getting back into their car and driving away. The observer was a failed version of a Zola clone—how it galled him to admit this, but science demanded candor about error. Zola had named it Oculo, on a lark, and outfitted it with a psi emitter that allowed him to receive Oculo's sensory impressions at a range of thirty miles or so, depending on the weather.

Stark's isolation was indeed a problem, but not an insurmountable one. HYDRA had many heads, and Zola had not cut all of them off during his takeover. Some of the remaining ones were prominently connected to civic institutions, and some of those civic institutions undertook philanthropic events such as charity benefits. "Maheu," he said. "I planned for this eventuality as well. One must know one's enemy, and I have spent months observing Stark. On the basis of my observations, I developed an ability to predict his likely behaviors. On the basis of those predictions, I developed methods of channeling those behaviors in ways useful to my goals. In short, I am letting Stark do some of my work for me."

"I see," Maheu said. "Allowing Stark to develop an immensely powerful next-generation suit and hide it and himself behind impenetrable walls of physical and virtual security is exactly what you wanted. Astonishing cleverness."

Zola laughed. "You intend that ironically, but instead it is true! When he emerges, and emerge he must, it will be into a circumstance of our choosing."

Tony had been obscenely rich for so long that he rarely thought about it, but one thing that always brought his financial wherewithal to the front of his mind was when he used it to do something genuinely unusual. Such as order three large pizzas from Di Fara at eleven o'clock in the morning and have them delivered by helicopter. The chartered copter was touching down in the parking lot as Tony came out the door to meet it. He tipped the pilot an extra hundred bucks and carried the pies back inside.

It had been nearly twenty-four hours since he'd eaten anything, but he was having to force himself to do it now. Work was calling. He was within sight of an instant-control technology that would not only incorporate the suit, but would link the suit's control systems into satellite and military networks that would essentially tell him everything that was happening everywhere in the world, all at once.

The last major hurdle he had to clear was figuring out a way to filter and prioritize the incoming information. That took an extraordinary amount of processing power, and time, that he didn't want to redirect from the suit's operating systems. So what he had to do was create a separate system with intelligent and flexible abilities to decide what the suit needed to know and what it didn't. Then he had to integrate it into the existing design.

Then he would have instant control.

But first, pizza. While he ate, he checked the logs of the external security sensors. A complex suite of cameras, motion sensors, and electromagnetic ears created a multispectral picture of the physical space surrounding the RTI Lab and the kinds of signals that passed through that space. After a month or so, Tony had seen blips for rats, squirrels, various kinds of birds, stray dogs and cats, a couple of raccoons, and the occasional homeless wanderer who hunkered down along the back fence line near the creek. Tony left them alone out of a general there-but-for-the-grace-of-God feeling, even though if Fury had known that Tony had let any member of the human race stay within eyeball range of the RTI Lab for more than ninety seconds . . .

Screw Fury, Tony thought. *I don't work for him.*

Then he noticed the unmistakable electronic signature of a narrowcast transmission, dated nineteen hours ago, duration three minutes, origin right outside the front gate.

That was when Happy and Pepper had come back from their meeting with Fury.

"Son of a bitch," Tony said. "I was right."

He put down a half-eaten slice and called Pepper. She answered before he'd even heard a ring. "You have a lot of explaining to do," she said.

"No time, Pep," he said. "Where's Happy?"

"At home, as far as I know. Find him yourself if all you're going to do is accuse him of something else."

"Funny you should mention that. Look, Pep, when you were here last night the external security picked up an encrypted transmission from right outside the gate. I don't think you were sending anyone a message, but I don't know about Happy. If it was another clone, who knows what kind of transmitters it might have? I'm working on breaking the encryption now, but it might be a couple of minutes."

Silence from Pepper. The longer it went, the more Tony got the impression that if she'd been in the room with him, her glare would have burned him to ashes on the spot. "Pep," he said. "I'm looking at the log. The log doesn't lie."

"No," she said, "but the observer of the log is sometimes a narrow-minded idiot who should maybe cross-index the log with the actual visual representation of the location in question, don't you think? A little context might help you avoid making a total fool of yourself."

When he didn't answer, she kept at him. "You're just being stubborn. I know that system can tell you where the signal came from down to the inch. Now, you look at it before you go convicting Happy of anything."

"Fine. Okay." Tony pulled up the video from the gate camera and another one he'd installed on a streetlight across from the driveway. He froze both at the time the mysterious signal had begun. At the same time, the decryption routine finished its work. It informed him that it had broken the signal's code but that the data being sent could not be organized into any known pattern. In other words, whoever had been spying on the RTI Lab's front gate had taken the time to send a stream of gibberish.

In the gate camera, he couldn't see anything but Happy, Pepper, and the car. But in the one across the street, in the spot where the electronic surveillance said the signal had originated, a human shape was visible at the edge of a tangle of bushes that ran between the sidewalk and the fence. Tony enlarged, sharpened, ran through different frequencies, and confirmed that a human being with some kind of implanted technology had sent the signal. He skipped the video forward. Shortly after Happy's car backed out of the driveway and rolled out of the frame, the observer stood up out of the bushes and walked away down the street.

"I'm going to assume from your silence that you're trying to figure out a way that you can tell me you weren't wrong," Pepper said.

"I was wrong," Tony said.

"Who was it? What were they sending?"

"Don't know who it was," Tony said. "And they were sending noise, at least according to every code-breaking routine I have."

"You think it was HYDRA?"

"I said I don't know who it was, Pep."

"Maybe you ought to take a break from tinkering with the suit long enough to find out," Pepper said. "And you owe Happy an apology."

"Are you and him dating again?" Tony asked.

"You're not changing the subject on me, Tony. The next time you see Happy, you either apologize to him or I quit."

"Quit?" Tony said. "You're not going to quit."

"How bad do you want to find out?"

Tony thought about this. Not bad enough, he decided. "All right. The next time I see Happy, I'll apologize."

Pepper's phone voice transformed instantly. "Terrific," she said. "Listen, while I've got you on the phone, look at this." A soft chime in Tony's ear announced the arrival of an email.

"You sneak. What is it?"

"Look at it," Pepper said. "I'll wait."

He opened her message and found an invitation to a benefit for wounded SHIELD commandos, sponsored by a laundry list of civic bigwigs as well as an organization that flew donated hearts for transplants and researched advances in artificial hearts. "Oh no," Tony said.

"You have to go." Pepper's voice was tinny, but it reached him.

Tony put the phone back to his ear. "I can't," he said before he could stop himself. "Too much work," he added, but he knew—and he knew Pepper knew—that work wasn't the real reason. Something about talking to her made it hard to keep up pretenses.

"I can't," he said again.

"You will," Pepper said. "It's tomorrow night. They moved the date up because of the HYDRA thing out on Governors Island the other day. All of a sudden there are a lot more disabled SHIELD personnel. You owe this, Tony. Tell me you're going to do it."

He tried not to. He thought of a dozen excuses. None of them would fly with Pepper.

"Okay," he said. "I'll do it. For two hours."

"We'll see about that. Do you want me to get you a date?"

"No, I think I can handle that part myself." A date, Tony thought. Last time I went out was with Serena. Her again? Maybe. Why not? "Got to go, Pep," he said. "My pizza's getting cold."

"Promise me," she said.

"I promise." Tony hung up and went back to his pizza. The silence of the lab settled in around him again. For a minute there, he'd actually liked talking to another person. It wasn't a bad feeling.

But now that he was alone again, he liked that just fine, too. Maybe even better.

He needed to track whoever had sent the signal, and he

needed to design the subroutine for prioritizing the instant control system's information flow. The image on the screen held his attention. Who was it? The signal was garbage. Was it a decoy, the way the attack on SHIELD had been?

Too many variables, Tony decided. He'd let that problem simmer for a while. He started a search on all the surveillance tools, looking for the times and places of other human intrusions and other unidentifiable signals. While it ran, he'd think, and at some point he'd have to give Serena a call. Right now, though, he needed two things. He needed another slice, and he needed to get back to the suit.

xiv.

Once before you carried out a mission to bring me a tiny gift. Now you must do it again. Your prize is infinitely more valuable, and the risk infinitely greater should you fail. You will not fail, my singular creation. You will not fail. You have proved yourself worthy of creation, worthy to be a jewel uniquely set against the uniform immensity of HYDRA. Nowhere else in the world is there someone like you. Nowhere else in the world is there someone I could trust with a mission of such importance and such danger. All of your resources will be demanded, all of your training and the intuition that daily sharpens into admirable wit. And yes, your beauty, for why should the powerful not also be beautiful? Why should admiration not also be desire? Red is the color of both love and war. You must fight with great passion, and love that which you fight for. And you must remember that to the world, the filthy teeming city and the filthy teeming world, you are a disposable image, fodder for gossip and solicitation . . . but to me, you are unique. I have made only one of you, and will make no more. You are HYDRA!

Pepper got right on the phone to Fury about the signal and the observer out at the RTI Lab. "So HYDRA's watching the lab," Fury said. "Big surprise. What I want to know is whether Tony's coming out to this party."

"Yes, Nick. He said he was coming. And I even tipped off one of his girlfriends that he might need a date. So you can expect him."

"Good. Far as HYDRA goes, we've got saturation surveillance over all the industrial areas of Brooklyn, and we're not finding a thing that doesn't belong there. So we'll keep looking, but my guess is we're going to have to wait for them to show themselves before we can hit back."

"Just be ready," Pepper said, then caught herself. "Sorry, Nick. I know I don't have to tell you that. I'm a little edgy."

"You and me both. Now who are you bringing to our benefit?"

"Well," Pepper said, drawing the word out, "I think Happy and I are going together."

"Good for you. You two make a good couple." This was such a startling observation coming from Nick Fury, who was the least romantic human being Pepper had ever known, that she didn't have any way to react to it. Luckily Nick saved her the trouble by saying, "Now I have to go fly a helicopter recon over Greenpoint in case one of the warehouses out there has a HYDRA logo painted on its roof. See you tomorrow night." He hung up.

She hung around the office for a while before realizing that there was nothing she needed to do there. Since 95 percent of her job was taking care of things for Tony, and Tony was holed up in the RTI Lab not letting anyone do anything, Pepper for all intents and purposes had the day off. She decided to go to lunch and then forget to come back, and she decided that Happy was coming with her.

Only when she called him to tell him that, he was at home and didn't want to go anywhere. "Just not in the mood, Pep," he said. "Especially since we've got the thing tomorrow . . ." He trailed off, and she could tell that there was something he wasn't telling her.

"Then I'll come to your place. What should I bring?" she asked. "Name your poison."

An hour later, she hopped out of a taxi in front of Happy's building bearing a giant sack of take-out Chinese. Happy ate like three men. This had a side benefit for Pepper, since when he had four or five different dishes, that meant she could sample all of them. She buzzed his floor and went in.

Riding up in the elevator, she wondered if she and Happy were seeing each other again. Or if they were about to be. Or if this was one of those periods during which they both considered it and then decided it wouldn't be a good idea. She wasn't sure which of the three possibilities she would prefer if given the choice.

Mostly it was Tony who bound them together. Pepper was never sure how much they really felt for each other because their common loyalty to their infuriating boss defined so much of their relationship. Today didn't look like it would be any different. Happy let her in, said, "Mmm, Chinese," and took the bag into his living room, which contained a couch, a chair, a coffee table, and a TV. All of the furniture was anonymous. The TV was showing highlights from a baseball game.

"It almost feels like having a regular job when you get to take a day off," Pepper said.

Happy nodded. "I've had so much time off this last week I don't know what to do with myself. Fury's had me do more work than Tony has."

"Well that might change now that we're going to dynamite Tony out of the RTI," Pepper said. "Maybe he'll come around."

"Could be. But I kind of have a feeling it's going to take more than that. Sometimes people just need to work things out. He'll come around when he's ready to come around."

"Or he won't," Pepper said. "Sometimes people need their friends to get them out of ruts."

Happy demolished half a carton of General Tso's chicken before answering. "You're assuming that we're actually Tony's friends," he said.

"Come on, Happy," Pepper said.

He stood up and paced around the room. "I don't like knowing that there are all of these clones of me," Happy said. "Far as I'm concerned, there should only be one me."

So that's what this was about, Pepper thought. Of course.

She set down her chopsticks and crossed the room to where he stood at the window, where she reached up to cup the side of his jaw in her palm. "There is only one you, Happy." Then she slapped him, just playfully. "Thank God."

He wasn't ready to let it go. Staring out his living-room window at the canal, he started thinking out loud. "I wonder what it's like to be one of them. How much of my personality do they have? Do they like the same music I do? It's weird, Pepper. And you know what the worst part of it is? I'm never going to be sure that they're all gone." He looked at Pepper with a haunted expression. "For the rest of my life, I'm going to have to wonder if there's another me out there. That's the worst thing."

"Happy, there's only one you," Pepper said. "I'll keep saying it as long as you need me to."

Before Tony knew it, the sun was down and he realized he'd ignored his phone ringing all day. The benefit. Probably Pepper was hassling him about it. He looked at the missed calls and saw that although Pepper did in fact account for about half of the calls, most of the others were from Rhodey. Tony deleted all of the voice mails as they came up. He didn't want to hear Rhodey's voice, or Pepper's. He had to go in, not out. He had to think microscopically, on a nanoscale. People were too big for him to handle. Friends especially. He owed certain things to his friends and he didn't have those things to give right now. He wouldn't until the suit was done.

What would Rhodey say to that? They'd fought together, saved each other's lives. Now Rhodey thought Tony was in trouble, and that made him both angry and worried. Natural, Tony thought. That's how you reacted when a friend was in trouble. It surprised him a little how dispassionately he was considering the situation. If I was any kind of friend, he thought, I'd call Rhodey back and we'd hash things out like people do. But right now he wasn't any kind of friend. He was an incubator of the suit. His brain was a replicator of ideas that in turn created new ideas, spawning billions of tiny machines that crawled around the lab and created something no one had ever seen before. Rhodey would have to wait. If he was a friend, he would understand.

The last three calls had come from Serena Borland.

"Huh," Tony said. He stood there with the phone in his hand, not wanting to call because to call would mean that he had to follow through on his promise to Pepper. Promise— what an irritating word. You should never promise anyone anything, Tony thought. He had, though, and he didn't quite have it in him to lie outright. Especially to Pepper. It was also irritating, the way she constantly made him want to be a better person than he really was.

While he was thinking this over, the phone rang. It was Serena. "Can't fight it," Tony said, and answered.

"Tony, hi," she said. "Listen, I wanted to apologize for the way I behaved the other night."

Tony didn't know what she was talking about. "You seemed all right to me," he said. "In fact, I was just about to give you a call. What are you doing tomorrow night?"

"Oh," she said. There was a pause. "Tomorrow night? Well, if it's not something with you, then I'll be sitting around wishing it was," she said.

"Pick you up at seven," he said. "No jazz this time, though. Or if there is, it's going to be the kind of stuff they call jazz when they play it at charity soirees."

"Gosh, I get to be your charity arm candy?" Serena said with a laugh. "I can't wait."

"Maybe once we put in an appearance, we can head out and catch a show." As he said this, Tony realized that he actually wanted to do it. Get out into the city, see some sights, hear some music . . .

Serena was talking. "Sorry, I missed that," Tony said.

"Oh, I was just telling you that Pepper already sent me the information about the event, so I'll make sure to wear red."

"She did, huh," Tony said. He had the feeling that even the people who loved him were plotting against him. "Red it is. Listen, I have to get some stuff cleared up here. Tomorrow at seven?"

"I'll be red," Serena said, and clicked off.

XV.

PROVISIONAL APPLICATION FOR PATENT

TITLE
  Repulsor rays

DESCRIPTION
  An energy-based weapon and propulsion system designed around a system of lenses and refractive surfaces that channel and focus a highly charged wave exhaust capable of (as a weapon) delivering large amounts of force with a high degree of accuracy and minimal energy loss or (as a propulsion system) moving large amounts of mass at high speeds with minimal turbulence and/or oscillation.

CLAIM
  This most recent iteration of a technology pioneered by Stark Industries (see list of relevant patents, attached) increases deliverable force by 15 percent and optimal focus by 12 percent, as expressed by the decreased area of the cross-section of a cone with its vertex at the ray's point of origin (see attached diagram). It has been further redesigned to integrate fully with the prototype enhancements in the Stark Industries uni-beam weapon system (as patented in [redacted], [redacted], et al.).

SECURITY STATUS
  Project undertaken under the auspices of Stark Industries agreements with the Department of Defense, SHIELD, and other governmental agencies outlined in Senate Amdt. [redacted] to Senate Amdt. [redacted] to H.R. [redacted] (110th). Technology is

proprietary to Stark Industries but will be shared fully with all eligible entities. Technology is classified and will not be licensed until such time as classification order is rescinded.

"We should dispose of the Borland asset," Maheu said.

"I think not just yet," Zola said. "She may prove useful in a number of ways once Stark realizes the nature of that particular deception."

After a moment's consideration, Maheu said, "As a damsel in distress? You expect Stark to fall for that hoary old ploy?"

"I do. If I were a betting man, I would wager anything you might care to suggest that when Stark learns that the Borland asset is alive, he will take personal action to retrieve it."

"If I were a betting man," Maheu said, "I would suggest that if Stark does not, you would owe me an ESP Box."

"Why do you torment yourself, Maheu?" Zola rose to inspect his assembled forces as they prepared to sortie. He emerged onto the catwalk and looked down on them, sharp and regular in their ranks, unstoppable in their uniformity, with the next generation beautifully congealing in the tanks behind them. A large man, Happy Hogan was. Powerfully built and of the right type to intimidate. He would have made a fine member of the Death's Head seventy years before. In fact, the Death's Head itself would have been immensely improved—not to mention easier to command—if it had been composed of clones such as this rather than its motley assortment of thugs and criminals.

It occurred to Zola that to control a mass of individuals, what one needed was a mass of clones. Only through uniformity did one achieve optimal strength, and only through clones did one achieve optimal uniformity. This explained the fall of empires.

Still, from among them he needed to choose one. "Maheu," he said. "What criteria should one use to select a single soldier for a critical mission when all of the soldiers are clones?"

Maheu considered this. The clones stared straight ahead as if they were alone. "One might suggest," Maheu said eventually, "that the only correct criterion for making a selection among identical objects is the abandonment of criteria."

"Very helpful," Zola said.

Maheu pointed. "How about this one?"

"Now you're being useful," Zola said. He touched the clone on the shoulder. "You. Come with me."

He entered Lantier's sanctum with the clone two steps behind him. "Lantier," he said. "You have completed the task I assigned you?"

"All aboard," Lantier said. "We're right on schedule."

Zola watched Lantier work, fascinated as always by the fact that Lantier's ability lay latent within himself. How could it be otherwise? Their genomes were the same. And in what other sequence of causes and effects might he, Arnim Zola, have indulged a savant's zeal for the spaces of the virtual? This was more than idle speculation; it bore directly on the question of what created a personality, a mind. The question was so vastly complex that even Zola did not understand the extent of its boundaries. He had found the existence of Lantier and Maheu—and even Oculo—tremendously informative, even invigorating. Without them, he would understand much less about the construction of human beings, not to mention infinitely less about the construction of himself.

Maheu was absent working on the training systems. Had he been present, Zola would have said as much. No doubt Maheu would have riposted to the effect that Zola did not

"Miss Borland," he said as he entered the room. The ESP Box tingled at the intensity of her emotions. She was a fine, high-strung young woman, unaccustomed to being removed from control over her own destiny.

She had been sitting in a chair—a fine leather chair, imported originally for Zola himself and then seconded to her as a gesture of goodwill appropriate to her importance. At his entry, she got up. "Kill me or let me go," she said.

"I'm afraid neither is possible just at the moment," Zola said. He remained near the door. He would be able to prevent her from making an escape attempt as easily as he might tell a well-trained dog to sit, but it was infinitely less melodramatic to eliminate the possibility by the arrangement of one's body. The simplest solution was often the best.

"You're going to be sorry as hell when Tony comes looking for me," Miss Borland said. "Freak. He's going to tear that box off your head and smash the screen with it."

"Do tell," Zola said. "I certainly hope he tries."

"You won't be hoping anymore when it happens." She sat back down and made a show of ignoring him. What a delightfully spirited creature she was.

"Miss Borland," Zola said. "You understand nothing of the leverage a hostage creates. Once Tony Stark realizes you are alive—and he will because I will make sure of it— he will have to come. And knowing that he will have to come, I have the advantage, because I can plan for him and he will not know what to plan for. It's all part of the game."

"Keep talking," Miss Borland said. "I'm not listening."

"Then how did you know when to tell me to keep talking? Please do not insult either my intelligence or your own maturity." Zola opened the door again. "Is there anything I can get for you?"

"I wouldn't mind a gun, if you'd let me shoot you with it," she said.

Zola clapped, slowly and deliberately. "How droll. Have you ever fired a gun?"

Now she looked at him, and the ESP Box sparked with a different kind of emotional intensity. She was offended! How interesting! "When I was a kid, we lived in Maine. Way up north, where nobody lives if they don't have to. We had to because my dad was teaching at a special science and math school on an old army base. Well, Mister Arnim Zola, one of the things people do up there is the biathlon. I'm going to assume that since you know everything else, you know what the biathlon is, and I'm going to tell you that when I was fifteen, I was the girls' biathlon champion of the state. You don't think I can shoot a gun? You put one in my hands and let's find out."

The interaction with Serena Borland abruptly held much less interest for Zola. "As illuminating as that moment would be," he said, "I fear it is unlikely to occur. You exist as long as I think you might be of interest to Tony Stark. That makes you an extremely valuable asset at the moment. But as we know," Zola went on as he opened the door, "one can never predict the future value of an asset. Consider that while you indulge in your fantasies of marksmanship."

He shut the door behind him and proceeded back toward the elevator, feeling unsettled and annoyed with himself for being unsettled. For a man of refined tastes, proximity to the more atavistic emotions was disturbing. Oddly, at the moment, Zola would have preferred the acerbic commentaries of Maheu; so that was who he located, idling in the command center. "A savage heart beats within the admirable breast of Miss Serena Borland," he informed his clone.

"One would never have thought," Maheu said.

"It seems unusual," Zola said. "Typically the refinements of upper-class existence extinguish all of the genuine passions and replace them with ersatz enthusiasms and debased impulses. In her case, this seems not to have occurred."

"Then Tony Stark has found himself a winning paramour," Maheu said. "Applause for him."

"Terribly unfortunate that he will never have realized this until it is far too late," Zola said. "For them both."

Maheu nodded sagely. "One need hardly point out that this world is a vale of tears," he said.

xvi.

You go forth to fight superheroes, but you are superheroes. You are made to be superheroes. I have made you, and I find you mighty. Unstoppable. Some of you will die, but you will die that the others might live. Each of you who dies will die as one of the innumerable heads of HYDRA, which when cut off regrows stronger and in greater number than before. This is your destiny; it is your calling; it is what you were made for and what justifies your unmaking. I call you to take up arms against those who would consign you to anonymity. Make your mark! Rise with me, fight with me, see the new world that waits to be born with HYDRA's innumerable heads and HYDRA's innumerable eyes watching over it and nurturing it into a new dawn. You are the men who will make this happen. You will fight together as one because you were created from one, and each of you knows that you live on in the others who will survive you. You will be victorious as one, because only victory can await those who commit themselves fully to the destiny that awaits them. You are HYDRA! You and only you are HYDRA!

Serena Borland was in fact red when Tony arrived to pick her up, from her glittery slingbacks to the wash in her hair. "Wow," Tony said. "You didn't hold back."

"Always have loved red," she said, and gave him a peck on the cheek as she got into the limo.

For reasons of entrance visibility and shoe practicality, they were driving even though it was a five-minute walk from her place to the benefit, which was being held in one of the Met's most popular areas, the Temple of Dendur.

Why, Tony had no idea, but imagined he'd find out. Usually the kinds of people who put these events together had elaborate rationales at the ready for how Egyptian artifacts were exactly the right ambience for a soiree benefiting heart research and maimed soldiers. The Temple had been one of Tony's favorite exhibits since the first time he'd gone to the Met, and he wasn't sorry to be returning now. He walked in with Serena on his arm, to flashbulbs and waved greetings. Happy and Pepper were already there.

The Temple of Dendur had been rescued—or looted, depending on your perspective—from a hillside soon to be submerged by the construction of the Aswan High Dam in the sixties. Now the temple and its gate stood about thirty feet apart in the center of a large hall, surrounded by an artificial moat. Next to the main temple was a small sphinx. The back wall of the spacious atrium was glass, and built at an angle, creating the impression that the Temple was installed within another temple. The other three walls were covered in photographs of its original site, as well as related artifacts from the period.

"First thing we do is pet the crocodile," Tony said.

This had been a ritual of his for a long time. A stone crocodile sat at the edge of a footbridge that crossed the moat. One of the first things Tony could remember reading on his own was part of the small placard describing the crocodile's origin and significance. He tapped the crocodile on the head and then went to find Happy and Pepper. On the way he and Serena suffered through a brief interview with a freelancer for one of the city's gossipy websites. Whatever he said would be chopped and diced into a maximally ironic and insulting series of sound bites, but that was okay. He went along with the shtick because if he didn't, the site would write about him anyway, making their story up out of whole cloth. This way, he at least got his two cents in.

"I hate those people," Serena whispered in his ear as they escaped the interviewer and made their way over to the table where Happy and Pepper had saved them seats. The outer exhibit space was filled with small tables, seating four or six, and a podium from which high-minded speeches would emanate periodically over the course of the evening.

Tony shrugged. "It's a living," he said. "They can't hurt me."

He found their table and guided her into the seat next to Pepper, so she would be forced to talk to Serena and perhaps give up her standard antipathy toward any woman Tony decided to date. This positioning also let him sit next to Happy and across from Pepper, minimizing the possibility that Pepper would do something like stomp on his foot under the table if he made an inappropriate remark. They chitchatted through the opening speeches about the noble sacrifices of SHIELD's soldiers and the desperate imperatives of heart-transplant research. During a break, Nick Fury and Rhodey stopped by before being dragged off to do some politicking with an attending donor. It was all by the numbers . . . but Tony, to his surprise, didn't mind it that much. He'd forgotten how much he liked being out among people.

But he still wanted to get out of there and get back to the suit. That was his work and his calling. People were fine as long as you took them in small doses.

Dinner was seared tuna and various trimmings. Serena, Tony noticed, was hitting the wine and getting livelier and more demonstrative the more she and Pepper talked. He leaned over to Happy. "You see this?" he murmured. "Pepper is talking to a girl I'm on a date with."

"Gift horse," Happy said. Tony nodded. He'd decided that he was going to have to trust Happy, and having made the decision, he was content with it. Betrayals would come like they always did: from the directions you never thought to defend.

"Yowch," Tony said as something stung the back of his right hand. He dropped his fork with a clatter, and reflexively reached to pick it up off the floor. As he raised his hand—all part of the same reflex—to flag down a waiter for a new fork, he noticed a trickle of blood on the back of his knuckles.

Another clattered followed, as Serena dropped her steak knife. "Oh my God, Tony, I stabbed you," she said. The hyperbole and the aghast expression on her face made him laugh. A waiter wove toward them with a new fork. Serena dabbed at the cut with her napkin.

"Hardly the worst injury I've suffered on a date," Tony said, and that was when the great windowed wall blew in and the chatter of automatic gunfire drowned out the tinkle of falling glass. Black-clad HYDRA commandos, the red logo prominent against the matte black of their body armor, dropped down ropes, firing as they went. SHIELD guards returned fire. The Temple of Dendur echoed with screams, the ping of ricochets off ancient sandstone, the continued crash of breaking glass.

A body fell onto their table, upending it and knocking Tony to the floor. The fallen man's helmet came off at the impact, and Tony was staring into the face of Happy Hogan.

The real Happy was going for his gun, but Tony caught his elbow. "Hap!" he shouted in his friend's ear. "You have to get out of here! Someone's going to kill you!"

Happy's face was contorted. Tony couldn't imagine what it must have been like to see an army of clone soldiers wearing your face. Trying to form words, Happy came out with growls.

"Go, Happy!" Tony yelled. "Go now!"

Something dawned on Happy's face, some kind of realization. He swung his gun around, pointing it past Tony, his eyes searching for a target he couldn't locate. Tony slapped the gun arm down and snatched the gun from Happy's hand. "Happy, goddammit, go before you get killed!" He shoved Happy toward the corner of the hall, going part of the way with him until he was sure that Happy would actually leave. Then he ran back looking for Serena, but she and Pepper were gone. Okay, he thought. Serena's in good hands. Now it's time to get some answers.

With a snap something coiled around his ankles and jerked him off his feet. Tony felt himself being lifted off the ground. He looked up and saw that some kind of lasso bound his lower legs. Up at the point where the glass wall angled into the stone ceiling, three silhouettes stood out against the light wash of the midtown night sky. Tony jack-knifed up and grabbed with one hand at the binding. Steadying himself and trying to time the sway as his rising body acted like a pendulum, he emptied Happy's gun in the direction of the kidnappers. The shooting conditions were tough, to say the least, and Tony had never invested much time in small arms. He hit only one of them, but the other two at least ducked out of the way long enough for Tony to look back down—following the descent of the one kidnapper he'd managed to hit—and realize that he was too high up just to cut the rope and hope for the best. The two other HYDRA kidnappers reappeared, and Tony started rising again. Below him, the gunfire intensified as HYDRA started covering its retreat. The floor of the Temple of Dendur exhibit was strewn with bodies, at least half of them wearing benefit finery.

Tony was nearly to the roof when he saw Rhodey fight his way through the last of the fleeing civilians to a position where he had a clear shot at the two men—clones—manning the winch that drew Tony higher. Unlike Tony, Rhodey was right side up, with his feet planted, and he had devoted hundreds of hours to small-arms training. He knocked both of the kidnappers off the roof with four shots.

One of them fell out of sight onto the roof. The other pitched forward onto one of the metal beams that reinforced the glass wall. He slid part of the way down to the first cross-beam and hung there, trying to swing a leg up. Tony started swinging, increasing his momentum until he could reach up and grab on to the beam next to the injured clone. Hooking one foot over the beam, he cut the hell out of his leg but got a grip on the clone's armor. "Express going down," Tony said, and yanked as hard as he could while kicking off of the beam. Holding the clone in a bear hug, he swung back, glancing off the drop ceiling over the temple gate and feeling the clone struggle weakly. It sure wasn't putting up much of a fight, Tony thought.

"Don't you die on me," he said. "We need to talk."

Below, the sounds of chaos were subsiding. The air stank of gunfire—and, oddly, of blackened tuna. "Rhodey!" Tony called out.

"Right here."

"Got someone here we need to talk to," Tony said. "Maybe you can figure out a way to get me down?"

"Give us a sec," Rhodey said. "Be right there."

"And hey, do you know where Pepper and Serena got to?"

"Little busy shooting HYDRA clones, you know," Rhodey said.

"Sure, I understand," Tony said. "I'd call her myself, but I left my phone down on the table."

Something shot past Tony's ear and stuck with a whang to one of the window girders. A magnetic grapnel, he saw. With a motorized whine, Rhodey rose to Tony's altitude. "Let's see," he said. "We'll get your prisoner there first, and then come back for you. How's that sound?"

"Fine by me," Tony said. "Take good care of him, and get him out to the RTI Lab pronto. We need to have a conversation, him and me."

"RTI Lab?" Rhodey looked uncertain. "You and I both know Fury's going to—"

"Rhodey, please do me this favor. That's where this needs to happen. Why do you think HYDRA tried to grab me here? We know they're watching the lab. If they could get me there, they already would have. Since they haven't, and they tried here, that means we're more secure there. Follow me?"

Tony felt ridiculous having this argument while he was

swinging from a rope forty feet above a stone floor littered with the bodies of clones of one of his closest friends. He tried to stay patient, but the impulse to drag some answers out of this clone was like a physical pressure in his head. "Rhodey, please," he said again.

Rhodey kicked along the edge of the drop ceiling until he was within arm's reach. "Hand him over," he said. "I'll take him out to the RTI Lab, but you owe me. Fury's going to chew my ass."

As he transferred the semiconscious HYDRA clone over to Rhodey, Tony said, "I don't know why you keep doing me favors."

"Me neither," Rhodey said. He dropped back toward the floor, saying as he fell, "You better hope I don't think about it too much."

xvii.

PROVISIONAL APPLICATION FOR PATENT

TITLE
Magnetic field manipulator

DESCRIPTION
A supercooled array of electromagnets that selectively and with a high degree of user control amplifies and shapes ambient electromagnetic fields via intelligent command-and-control overseen by the operator of a Stark Industries personal body armor product. Damping and insulation structures prevent leakage of electromagnetic energy that would otherwise interfere with other systems.

CLAIM
Manipulation of magnetic fields is a technology with a wide range of potential applications, including but not limited to: physical manipulation of objects containing magnetic materials; interruption of signaling and communications systems; incapacitation of computer networks and other technologies reliant on magnetic data storage or systems control. Stark Industries magnetic field manipulator is designed to integrate fully with the supercooling and—conductivity system that powers the suit-borne Haloalkane Delivery Apparatus (provisional patent application forthcoming, tentatively designated [redacted]).

SECURITY STATUS
Project undertaken under the auspices of Stark Industries agreements with the Department of Defense, SHIELD, and other governmental agencies outlined in Senate Amdt. [redacted] to Senate

Amdt. [redacted] to H.R. [redacted] (110th). Technology is proprietary to Stark Industries but will be shared fully with all eligible entities. Technology is classified and will not be licensed until such time as classification order is rescinded.

Happy Hogan had never run from a fight in his life. He'd never forgive himself for running from this one, even though Tony had told him to. Tony was his boss, and in this case Tony was probably right. Anyone in the Temple of Dendur with Happy's ugly mug was liable to eat a SHIELD bullet. But still . . .

He made the best of it. If he couldn't fight the shooting war, he could fight the recon war. What was Serena Borland up to? First she accidentally scratched Happy, now she accidentally cut Tony. People were accident-prone sometimes, nothing strange about that—but thinking back on it, Happy had the feeling that there was a connection between her scratching him and an army of Happy Hogan clones showing up at Governors Island. If he was right, it meant that SHIELD and Tony were up against an enemy that could take a flake of skin and create a hundred clones in less than a week. This was not an adversary you took lightly. This was an adversary you rooted out and crushed before there were so many clones in the world that nobody knew who was who anymore.

So when the shooting started in the Temple of Dendur, all of this had fallen together in Happy's head, and he'd come within a quarter-ounce of pulling the trigger on Serena right then and there. He'd have explained later, if he'd survived to explain. The boss had inadvertently kicked him into a new tactic, though, when he'd chased Happy out of the hall. It had come at the cost of Happy's dignity, but now he'd be able to follow this Serena woman and see what was really what.

And if he had to, he'd kill her.

Out in the main galleries next to the Temple of Dendur, people were running in every direction. Alarms shrieked. Museum security tried to balance the human panic against their job, which was to protect the art. It occurred to Happy that he could walk out with anything he could carry right then, and nobody would ever know. Good thing for the museum's collection that Happy didn't care much about art. What he cared about was finding a woman in a red dress, who—if his guess was right—would be moving fast in a direction she hoped no one would follow. Out the main entrance? Happy guessed no. With all the alarms already set off, she'd be heading for one of the side doors. The closest one to the Temple of Dendur hall was toward the south end of the building. Happy headed that way, looking right and left as he passed smaller galleries and service corridors. Somewhere ahead of him he heard a door slam open. Picking up his pace, he came around a corner just as one of the fire doors was swinging shut. He caught it when it was still a couple of inches open, and saw Serena running down the sidewalk—not toward Fifth Avenue, but into the park.

One of the transverse roads, Happy thought. She's moving fast considering her footwear.

He followed her, and sure enough, she made for one of the places where Central Park's trails crossed the 79th Street transverse road. She ditched her shoes and hopped over the railing of a pedestrian bridge. A cab slowed, and she got in. Happy memorized the cab's plate number and the number on its duty light. The minute she was in and her cab was moving, he turned back toward the VIP parking area in front of the museum, getting up to a dead sprint that didn't do his feet in his fancy shoes any good, either.

When he got to the car, cops were already blocking everything off. Happy flashed his Stark Industries security clearance, and held his breath until the cop let him go. On the road, he fed the cab's information into the car computer, which piggybacked on the cab company's dispatch records and a composite satellite feed to tell him that the cab was heading south on Central Park West.

Happy paralleled it down Fifth Avenue, keeping an eye on the real-time feed from the computer. Thank God for Tony pushing the rules about what DOD would clear, Happy thought. And thank God I drove my car. Nobody was going to notice one more Chrysler 300 if he had to tail Serena somewhere where people might care who was watching.

The two cars ran in parallel down the length of the park. The cab turned east, and Happy let it cross Fifth before he looped back around to fall in a couple of blocks behind it. He called the boss. No answer, so he tried Pepper. Also no answer. For a minute he wondered if that meant they were dead, but that idea didn't fit in Happy's head. No way were those two going to get iced by a bunch of clones sent by a cockroach outfit like HYDRA.

"Pepper," he said to her voice mail. "I'm headed for the Queensboro Bridge. At least I think I am. Could be we're about to find out where the guy lives who hacked Tony's suit. Call me so I know you're okay."

Next he tried Rhodey. No answer. Then Fury, with the same result. Where was everybody?

It figured, in a way. All the bigwigs and generals went around making sure that their ducks were in the right rows. Guys like Happy Hogan had to fend for themselves.

So get on with it, Hogan, he told himself. Start fending. Some people still think that there's something a little strange about you because of the clone thing. Those people, ungrateful and high-handed bastards though they might be, are also old friends, so if following this particular woman leads to the location of the cloning operation in question, all will be well. And that's what I want, Happy thought. Everything like it was. Everyone on the same side, and knowing that they're on the same side. Trust.

And whoever the son of a bitch was who had cloned him, they were going to have some harsh words.

The cab was headed for the lower deck of the Queensboro Bridge, so Happy took the upper. He hung a couple
of lights behind the cab, and turned off to a parallel street
whenever there wasn't enough traffic between the two vehicles to suit him. Sure was easy pulling off a tail when
you had real-time satellite feeds and GPS to work with.
He watched the screen and stayed reasonably close as the
cab headed down 21st Street and then jogged over the
Pulaski Bridge into Brooklyn. Must be getting close, he
thought. If they lived down in the southern part of Brooklyn, they'd have taken a different bridge. He squeezed to
within a block, keeping the cab in sight now as it wound
out Metropolitan Avenue and then Grand Street. Happy
could practically see his building from where they were,
but the cab kept going until it turned off Grand into a
sprawling complex of warehouses, half-collapsed facto-
ries, and railroad sidings. Happy pulled off to the side of
the road, seeing that there were only two things the cab
could do—either go down to the dead end of the street
they were on, or turn to the right and loop over toward
Maspeth Avenue.

The cab went straight, all the way down to the end.
Happy got out a pair of binoculars and watched as Serena
Borland got out and paid the driver. Two men came out to
meet her. One was tall, thin, bearded in a scraggly way, and
obviously authoritative. She spoke to him while the other
man waited. Then all three of them turned and Happy
caught a good look at the second man. It was like looking
in the mirror.

"There you are, you son of a bitch," he said.

They got the clone from the Met to the RTI Lab in less
than an hour, courtesy of a SHIELD turbocopter that
landed smack in the middle of Fifth Avenue to pick them all
up. Something was wrong with the clone. It was semiconscious, and the SHIELD medic on board said that its vitals

were off; not enough to kill it, but enough that it wasn't functioning the way it should.

Tony was a little uncomfortable about how easy it was to refer to the clone as "it." Rhodey had shot it twice, but its armor had mostly stopped both shots. It had spreading bruises on its torso, and its ribs were probably broken, but that wasn't the problem. Tony wondered if HYDRA was aware that its clone program had some bugs to work out.

He tried to call Serena. "Tony," she said on the first ring. "My God, are you okay?"

"I was about to ask you the same thing. Where are you?"

"On my way home. I got out of there before the police really arrived, and I was so scared that I just wanted to get home and lock the door."

"That sounds like a good idea," Tony said. "Listen, there's a lot to do here. Let me call you later."

"Are you sure you're okay?"

"I'm fine," he said. "I'll be ready for a nap later, but right now I feel tip-top." He hung up and looked out the window at Brooklyn. HYDRA was down there somewhere. And as soon as he had instant control nailed down, he'd be able to find out where. Nobody would ever be able to hide from him again. He would live in a world of five dimensions, and the fifth would be information. All of space and time would collapse into information.

Back at the RTI Lab, they woke the clone up and started basic interrogation. Name?

"I don't have a name," the clone said.

"But what do people call you?" Fury asked. He was the scariest looking of them, all scowl and eye patch, so he liked to go counterintuitive and take the gentle tack . . . at least at first. That left it up to Rhodey and Tony, neither of whom was temperamentally suited for the role, to play the attack dogs. They let Fury take the lead.

"Nobody ever speaks to just me. Or almost never," the

clone said. "When they do, they just say something like 'hey, you.'"

It had a quiet, equable demeanor that made it hard to work up the kind of adversarial feeling you expected in a postcombat interrogation, Tony thought. Strange, since an hour and a half ago it was trying to kidnap me and kill everyone else. "Why were you trying to kidnap me?" he asked. "Ransom?"

"I don't know," the clone said. "I—"

Its eyes started to flutter. The medic stepped forward and took its pulse. "Uh-oh," she said. "Fast and thready. He's in trouble." She put a hand on the clone's forehead, then the back of its neck. "Hot as hell, too."

The clone slumped forward, throwing the medic off balance. Rhodey caught it and guided its fall. When it was laid out on the floor, the medic started working. She stripped its shirt off, listened to its heart again, and started CPR. "He needs to be in a hospital," she said.

"Make the call, Rhodey," Fury said. Rhodey got on the phone and called in a SHIELD medevac team.

"Five minutes, General," he said when he was off the phone.

The clone started to quiver. Sweat ran from its face and its eyes were rolled back in its head. "Casey Jones, you better watch that train," it said with uncanny clarity, and then it kept babbling. Tony could understand a word here and there, but none of it made sense.

Somewhere in the building an alarm sounded, but it wasn't the perimeter systems signal, so Tony let it be. Sounded like the control terminal on the testing floor. Another hack? Could be, but every piece of equipment worth hacking out there was keyed to respond to only him. Retinal scan, voice print, electrical frequency scan . . . nobody could get anything out there to do anything Tony Stark didn't want it to do. So right then he didn't mind letting the enterprising hacker wander around in the system a bit, leaving little traces that Tony would follow to his house later, when he'd had a chance to get good and ornery about it.

The clone's tremors eased and its constant stream of verbal gibberish became first mumbles, then quiet breathy moans, then silence. The SHIELD medic kept at it, pausing to check his pupils and escalate her treatments. Adrenaline did nothing. Another syringe containing God only knew what did nothing. It was three minutes since Rhodey had called in the medevac.

"Pupils unresponsive," the medic said hollowly. "No pulse. Temperature one oh seven point four. He's dead, General. There's nothing I can do. Maybe back at the hospital . . ."

"It's okay, soldier," Fury said. He squatted next to her and took a firm grip on her elbow to guide her to her feet. From the testing lab, the alarm kept chirping. "Tony," Fury said. "That beep is about to drive me crazy. You mind doing something about it?"

Nobody ever speaks to just me, it had said. Tony wondered just what kind of life that might be, and whether HYDRA had that kind of existence in mind for all of them.

xviii.

Now is when you will be tested. Now the depth of your resolve will be called into question, and you must stand ready to answer. Now you must not simply believe that your life belongs to HYDRA; you must believe that in your annihilation, a new head of HYDRA will grow to grind the enemy in its jaws. Only you can do this. Only you have been given Lantier's gift, which is my gift, which is HYDRA's gift. There are many like you, but none have such power to strike at the heart of the enemy's defenses, to lay mines under his foundations, to carve out the heart of his greatest champion. Only you! Your hands are HYDRA. Your mind is HYDRA. HYDRA flows in your veins and sparkles along the pathways of your nerves. I created you, I remade you, just as I remade HYDRA. There is no pain you might suffer that I have not suffered, no uncertainty can darken your mind because I have fought through it and built my strength into you. Go now, and know that the thousand heads of HYDRA will sing of what you do. You go into the heart of the enemy, and there you will see his weakness, and there you will strike him down. You are HYDRA!

"And there we go, right on schedule," Lantier said in the solitude of his sanctum. "Timetable check and double check."

The code carried in the clone bounced through the transmitter and into the holding area where Stark Industries' security subroutines kept suspicious bits of code. The payload proclaimed its innocence, batted its eyelashes, produced letters from its poor mother-in-law and the pastor of its church. We both work for Mr. Stark, it said. You and me.

We're the same. He asked me to come in here and pick something up for him.

Oh, well, okay, the security system said. What is it you were looking for?

That over there, the payload said.

Nobody's supposed to have that but Mr. Stark, the security system said.

I know. You better believe I know that, the payload said. But like I said, he sent me to get it. And anyway it's no good to anyone but him, so why would I want it if he hadn't sent me to get it?

You better let me make a copy of it, the security system said. I'll send that along with you.

Peachy, the payload said. I'll wait right here.

"This train is bound for glory, this train," Lantier sang. "This train is bound for glory, don't carry nothin' but the righteous and the holy, this train is bound for glory, this train . . ."

Rhodey watched as Tony and Fury eyeballed each other like silverback gorillas who knew there was going to be a fight but weren't sure when, or what would set it off. This is all we need, he thought. But he wasn't in any position to tell them not to fight if they wanted to fight. Hell, maybe it would do all of them good to have the SHIELD-Stark problems settled once and for all. And maybe this is what it would take.

"I don't have time for this right now, Nick," Tony was saying. His attention stayed on the control terminals. The dead clone had been removed by SHIELD medevac fifteen minutes ago, and the pressure in the building had been on the rise since.

"Well, now, that's funny," Fury said. "Usually once things start to affect you personally, all of a sudden you have nothing but time for them. And today you were the target of an attempted kidnapping by HYDRA. How come you're not champing at the bit to go after them?"

Tony did something to a touch screen, and lines of code spilled across the screen. "Oh, I am. Believe me, I am," he said.

"So we can see," Fury said. "Rhodey, look at how fired up Tony Stark is. Our enemies quake at his approach. They had it easy when Iron Man was around. Now that it's Tony Stark riding off for the holy instant control, all of the bad guys are about ready to pack it in and get jobs at Gristedes."

"Gristedes?" Rhodey said. "They're hiring?"

"All the ex-supervillains want to work there. That's because they know that Tony Stark is such a food snob that he'd never be caught dead in one of those stores with the hoi polloi."

"Hey, now," Tony said. "I just ordered pizza in the other day. I will plead guilty to a number of flaws, but food snobbery isn't one of them."

He stood up from the terminal. "That clone was carrying a virus."

"Do tell," Fury said.

"I mean a computer virus. It's logged into my security system." He looked back and forth between Rhodey and Fury. "Don't you get it?" he said. "The whole thing was a setup. HYDRA played all of us."

"What are you talking about?" Rhodey asked. "A lot of people died today. To set up what, exactly?"

"What happened," Tony said. "HYDRA needed to get one of their clones into this building." A brief silence followed. Rhodey tried to decide whether Tony had tipped over the edge into full-blown paranoia, or he had experienced the kind of intuitive flash that could save a thousand lives. With Tony—especially the last month or so—it was hard to tell.

Fury started. Rhodey noted that he was using his interrogator's voice. "Okay," he said. "So what you think happened is that HYDRA staged a massive assault on the Metropolitan Museum of Art, killing dozens of civilians and SHIELD personnel and suffering losses of dozens of their own. This entire event was stage-managed to include an attempted kidnapping of you that put you in serious physical danger. During the course of this show, one of HYDRA's agents was supposed to get captured on the off chance that he would survive the encounter, and on the further off chance that we would bring him here instead of back to Governors Island or somewhere else. This was all supposed to happen so this clone could be infected with a virus that would infiltrate your system . . ." He stopped. "You haven't told us what it was supposed to do."

"Steal the plans for the new suit," Tony said.

Fury nodded. "Delivered with a remarkably chipper attitude," he said. "Mind telling me why we shouldn't be upset about this?"

"Because the suit is keyed to me," Tony said. "Like I told you. Every single system in it will refuse to respond to any command I didn't issue. So even if they build one, they'd need me to run it."

"Are you sure that's what they were after?" Rhodey asked.

"That's what the logs say the virus extracted," Tony said. "And it went back along the same route as the last hack came in on. The tracks are all too well covered for me to peg the route to a physical location, but I'm willing to bet it's the same spot in Brooklyn."

"That part of it makes a hell of a lot more sense than your rationale for how the virus got here," Fury said. "You sure you want to let us believe that you think that?"

"As a matter of fact, I do think that," Tony said. "Can you prove me wrong?"

"None of us knows what really happened," Rhodey said. "So none of us can prove anything."

"Exactly, Rhodey, old buddy. This is what I've been trying to explain to the general, here. If one of us did know what happened, we wouldn't be in this pickle. And if I could get the instant control tech on line, one of us—that would be me—would know what happened, and could tell the rest of us."

Tony turned to Fury, an odd fanatical light in his face. "So what I'm getting at here is, for God's sake let me get back to work, Nick. That's how I can help. When I get instant control up and running through this new suit . . . you've never seen anything like it, I guarantee you that."

"Maybe not," Fury said. Rhodey was hoping he wouldn't say anything else, but he did. "What you don't get is that we may not live to see it *this* time unless you *make* some time to deal with the problem that's right *here* instead of the problem that *might* come up later."

Now the fight that had been brewing for the last month was right there about to happen. "And if I do make that time, and we lose the fight because I don't have the best equipment I could put together?" Tony came around the terminal console and stood toe-to-toe with Fury. "What then, Nick? Where's SHIELD going to be then, if you don't have me to swoop in and haul you out of the fire?"

Rhodey inserted himself between them. "Fellas," he said. "Back it down."

"SHIELD would be a hole in the ground if it wasn't for me," Tony said. "The general here doesn't like to hear that, but it's true."

"Could be," Fury said. "It also could be that you'd be a garden-variety weapons mogul making your living from cluster-bombing children if we hadn't given you something more to believe in."

Rhodey put one hand on each man's shoulder. "That's what we call a mutually beneficial relationship."

"For God's sake, Rhodey," Tony said.

"Well, look at you two," Rhodey said. "About to throw

punches over which one needs the other more, and who should be calling the shots for who, when there's an army of clones out there trying to take over the world. Any man with common sense is going to make a joke out of it."

"Joke out of what?"

All three of them turned to see Happy Hogan standing just inside the doorway. "Seriously," he said. "What's the joke? If it's about me—"

"Why would it be about you, Hap?" Rhodey asked.

"I heard something about clones, and then you saying you had to make a joke about it," Happy said. "And I have to tell you, the clone thing is getting to me. If it's funny to you, I'll see you later."

All three of them noticed something in Happy's tone of voice, his bearing. He looked like he was about to vibrate into pieces. "Must have been rough on you today," Fury said after a moment. Rhodey noticed he was using the interrogator voice again. He wondered if Happy would recognize it.

"All my life, I've never run from a fight," Happy said. "Today . . . do you know what it's like to look in your own dead face? And then you go because the boss tells you to go, and nobody will answer the phone so you don't even know whether they're alive? That was my day. Everyone else apparently had something better to do. So now maybe I do, too."

"Whoa, Hap, whoa." Rhodey walked over to him, gesturing behind him for Tony and Fury to stay where they were. "You didn't call me, man. I would have answered. Tony and the general were in a copter for a while. They might not have heard."

"Where's Pepper?" Happy demanded.

"Safe and sound, Hap," Tony said. "She's at home. Maybe you should go over there."

"She didn't answer when I called, either," Happy said. "Maybe I shouldn't go over there."

Rhodey looked back at Nick and Tony. Well, he wanted to ask. He's got you there. You plain forgot about him. What are you going to do about it now?

"Hap, listen," Tony said. "I'm sorry. I'll apologize for General Fury, too, because he's too proud to do it himself. I haven't looked at the phone, and the truth is I got wrapped up in something that happened out here. A HYDRA thing."

"HYDRA," Happy repeated. "Yeah, I got wrapped up in a HYDRA thing, too, didn't I?" He laughed bitterly. "Well, listen. Here's why I came by. I know where they're making the clones. And Tony, I know you're going to hate me for saying this, but I saw Serena go there."

xix.

PROVISIONAL APPLICATION FOR PATENT

TITLE
Epidermal neural interface

DESCRIPTION
Creates systemic channels of command and control between the human mind and external mechanical devices by means of epidermal sensors that repurpose selected dermal nerves as communication channels to nerves and ganglia of the limbs and spine. The epidermal neural interface (ENI) has no permanent effect on the dermal nerves, which return to their normal areas of function when the ENI is disengaged or inoperative.

CLAIM
Refines previous neuromuscular interface by virtue of being noninvasive. Epidermal interface removes problems of neural overload and degeneration experienced in applications of Stark Industries patents [redacted] and [redacted], while preserving desirable improvements in reaction time and ability to synthesize and react to multiple simultaneous stimuli. Multiple applications of this technology are envisioned in the medical and biosciences as well as secondary applied developments in computer and network design.

SECURITY STATUS
Project undertaken without any assistance or cooperation from agencies of the United States Government. No security restrictions apply.

"You seem oddly unconcerned that the Borland clone was tailed on its way back here," Maheu said. "Should we not take some action?"

"We are taking action." Static flickered across the screen in Zola's torso as a storm of signals blew through from a jet passing overhead on its way to LaGuardia. "The action we will take is not necessarily the action you would advocate or prefer, but an action it will be. I am interested, however, in what actions you would suggest."

Maheu crossed his long legs and leaned back in his chair, adopting the professorial attitude that Zola had long since learned meant he was about to get pedantic. "Given that our operation thus far has been predicated on the twin goals of remaining hidden and destabilizing the internal dynamics of SHIELD and Stark Industries, and given that our location is no longer hidden, and given that we have the interface schematics for the prototype suit in Stark's laboratory, it seems clear to me that now is the time for direct action."

Zola nodded encouragingly throughout this. The ESP Box even bobbed in time with the rhythm of Maheu's speech. "I see," Zola said. "And what do you consider the risks of choosing a different plan of action?"

"It is entirely possible, is it not, that satellite-guided missiles or some such armament are already flying this way to annihilate this facility and everyone in it?"

"That is where your evaluation of the scenario falters," Zola said. "Consider the character of Tony Stark. He is vain, arrogant, occasionally monomaniacal—but he believes in a certain kind of chivalry. The discovery that the Borland asset has been cloned will force him to believe that the original asset might still be in our possession. If he believes this, he will prevent any action that would turn her life into collateral damage."

"His attitudes toward women have seemed remarkably

flip to me," Maheu said. "This streak of sentimentality you diagnose . . . I don't see it."

"It is the corollary of his flipness. Those who are most likely to flit from woman to woman are also those most likely to harbor idealized sentimentality about the women who resist them. To my knowledge, Stark and the Borland asset are genuinely affectionate—although, to be sure, our use of the Borland clone has guided that affection down paths it might not otherwise have followed."

"And if SHIELD acts independently of Stark's wishes?"

"I consider this highly unlikely," Zola said. "SHIELD's battle strength depends on assistance from Stark. If General Fury decided to sacrifice the Borland asset in the name of destroying this facility, he would run a severe risk of losing Stark's cooperation for future missions." On the screen, Zola's face broke into a wide smile. "Do you now see why it was worth keeping the Borland asset alive?"

"If you turn out to be correct, you will turn out to have been correct," Maheu said. "If you were incorrect before, neither of us will have a chance to point it out."

Zola returned to monitoring a crucial process in one of the cloning tanks. "If your notional missiles do not incinerate us in the next forty-eight hours," he said, "we will have a chance to see which of is correct. A wager?"

"If my notional missiles do annihilate us, we will not be able to collect," Maheu said.

"All the more reason to bet the house," Zola said. In the cloning tank, a skeletal structure was already beginning to take shape. "Still and all, the surveillance of the Borland clone's return necessitates a modification of our plan." He touched a screen twice and then stood. "We must see Lantier."

"I would prefer not to," Maheu said, looking away.

"It is these little quirks and foibles that make your perspective so interesting," Zola said. He presented himself on the catwalk and sampled the thoughts of his creations. All was running smoothly. On average, their minds wandered just often enough to keep their creative and intuitive faculties useful, and not often enough to endanger their productivity. Occasionally he noticed one of them was indulging in a bit too much existential speculation, and he was forced to intervene, but as he had tweaked the training procedures and the daily addresses via the ESP Box, he had found ways to channel the workings of their minds in directions most useful to him. They were HYDRA. He told them that endlessly, until the sheer force of repetition made it true.

And it was true, after a fashion. HYDRA would not be in its current position without their strength. He, Arnim Zola, was the heart and soul and mind of HYDRA, however; he alone executed the plans that he alone could imagine and formulate. They were useful tools, these clones, even when he had only a few hundred at a time.

Imagine, he thought, having millions to play with at a time . . .

Downstairs in Lantier's sanctum, he considered Maheu's advice while waiting for his railroad-smitten inferior self to prepare the next stage of his infiltration. The fact that their location was no longer secret mattered, of course, in a number of possible ways. Zola was confident that he could rely on Stark's and SHIELD's sentiment about damsels in distress to forestall the possibility of missiles raining down upon them. It was much more likely that even at that moment, elements of SHIELD were preparing a mission to strike the factory and extract the Borland asset. The ESP Box thrummed as Zola sent instructions for surveillance to be intensified and training assets momentarily directed away from scientific routines and into combat sessions.

Then he was ready. "Lantier," he said.

"Boiler's hot," Lantier said. "We're right on schedule."

Part of the payload from the day before detached itself and struck up a new conversation with the RTI Lab's security subroutine. Hey there, it said, sashaying up. Remember me?

Sure I do, the subroutine said. The boss noticed you were here.

And he didn't delete me? The payload winked. That must mean he doesn't think I'm too much of a threat.

He did say I wasn't supposed to let you take anything else, the subroutine said.

I don't want to take anything else, the payload said. I like it here. I don't want to go anywhere. That's part of what the boss told me. I don't know if he mentioned it to you.

Mentioned what?

Oh. Mentioned that he wanted me to stay here and help you make sure that nobody does anything they're not supposed to do, or takes anything they're not supposed to take. I'm supposed to help you now.

I've been doing all of that fine on my own, the subroutine said. The boss said so.

I know he did. And you have. But it never hurts to have a little backup, does it? I'm just going to make sure that nothing happens unless we both think it's okay. And if someone tries to take something they're not supposed to take, we'll discuss how to handle it. How does that sound?

I guess that might be okay, the subroutine said.

Back upstairs on the main production floor, Zola walked to a corner of the tank farm and considered all of the different elements of his plan. He had infantry firepower, which every plan required. There was no successful increase in power without the backing of plain and simple firepower. He had compromised the enemy's information and security systems. He had successfully inoculated this facility against aerial bombardment by retaining the Borland asset. He had a sample of Tony Stark's DNA, which in another day or so would be a functional Tony Stark.

And he had these eight tanks, in which something very

special was growing. Zola grew philosophical. He had killed a great many people in his life, and a great many more clones. Thousands and thousands. During recent years, he had created brain scans and muscle-memory imprints of some of his more valuable adversaries before killing them. In these eight tanks were copies of none other than Madame Hydra, coalescing from the nutrient medium. In another day, they would be physically complete. A day after that, they would possess all of the tactical acumen and martial prowess of their original.

Madame Hydra had initially resisted having the procedures done. She had never trusted Zola—for good reason, of course—and eventually his means of persuasion had been coldly cynical. If I am plotting against you, Zola had argued, my plotting will be successful whether or not I have this information. If I am plotting against you, it would be to take over HYDRA for myself, not install a version of you. Can we stipulate that my ego would not permit that?

She had laughed. And if you are not plotting against me, Zola, why do you want to be able to make clones of me?

For HYDRA, he answered. Imagine a HYDRA army in which a dozen or a hundred Madame Hydras fought behind enemy lines.

One Madame Hydra is quite enough for me, she had said. And you're not fooling anyone. I ought to kill you, Zola.

Entirely possible, Madame, Zola had said. If it comes to that, however, rest assured that I have not been squeamish about making useful duplicates of myself. There is no killing Zola. (Which was not true; none of the Zola clones had the unique combination of virtues inherent in the original. But Madame Hydra could not have known that.)

So, Madame Hydra had said. What would you like me to do?

He watched the eight clones, coming together along pathways of Zola's design using technology of Zola's creation and science of Zola's imagining. Poor Madame Hydra, he thought. You never had a chance. Your life was in my hands long before you imagined it to be so, and your death was a foregone conclusion the minute I began to see the possibilities of HYDRA. It was mildly regrettable that she could not have lived to see the magnificent spectacle of eight of her fighting side by side. A whirlwind of steel and venom! Zola looked forward to it with a great deal of anticipation and impatience.

Maheu, he said through the ESP Box. He felt the signal reach his clone, and the sensation that Maheu awaited further communication.

Meet me in Madame's corner, he said. Maheu arrived in less than two minutes. He moved quickly and efficiently when given no time to argue. "They seem to be developing along the correct lines," he said, looking at the tanks.

"Their training must not fail," Zola said. "You are responsible."

"Oh, my. Responsible meaning I'll be murdered in some demonstrative fashion in the event of an error? Be still my heart."

"Meaning exactly that. The humor in it will be much less apparent to you then than it is now. Are the training routines perfected?"

Maheu waffled one languid hand. "Perfected is such an imprecise word," he said. "The only living subject has been the Borland clone, and her training has never been put to use. Would you like to send her on a mission of some sort? A shakedown cruise? A maiden voyage?"

"I would indeed," Zola said. "Had you thought of one?"

"The possibilities are numerous. A random murder of a prominent citizen could be useful insofar as it would provoke uncertainty as to our true goals. A more targeted mission involving a member or associate of SHIELD or Stark Industries has more potential for immediate tactical benefit, and would also be a more stringent test of the training program's effectiveness. However, it would carry a higher risk of losing the Borland clone."

"A laudably clear presentation," Zola said. "I opt for targeting a SHIELD or Stark asset. Not necessarily one of critical tactical value, either. A psychological blow is called for. Who might cause the most chaos by being mysteriously murdered?"

"Would there not be an admirable symmetry if the victim were Happy Hogan?" Maheu suggested.

Zola clapped his hands together. "Perfect. Send the Borland clone to me immediately. Oh, and Maheu, you did make sure that our contacts within the charity board were among the unfortunate casualties? I'd hate to have that sordid element of the plan exposed to too much light."

"On that score, I count a one hundred percent success rate," Maheu said. "Not that it matters. Charity boards breed new members like we stamp out Hogans."

XX.

HYDRA! How many of you have fallen today? How many of you gave your bodies to the bullets of SHIELD? Many. I speak to survivors, to veterans, to the best of HYDRA who faced down their enemies and left the field with a victory. Our goal is accomplished, my creations! The next step toward HYDRA's proper dominance of the mongrel race of humanity is taken, and surpassed! But some of you have died. It is natural to notice their absence. Perhaps you had developed relationships whose ending provokes emotional responses. This is to be expected. Know that HYDRA sorrows for those lost soldiers—but know, too, that HYDRA emerges stronger because of their sacrifice. New soldiers will take their places. They will be your brothers in arms. You will teach them what you know, and if you should fall in battle they will carry on your legacy as they teach those who come to take your places. This is as it should be. This is the life, the only life, for the true believer in HYDRA. We are remaking the world, and nothing is remade without first being destroyed. HYDRA is the memories of your fallen comrades, and the vital replenishment of their successors. HYDRA is strength in the face of adversity, and determination in the face of failure. We remain strong, and grow stronger! We remain determined, and our resolution only grows! We are HYDRA!

"You saw Serena go into the place where HYDRA is hiding out," Tony repeated. "In Brooklyn?"

Happy nodded. "Yeah, in Brooklyn. I know it was the place, Tony. One of the guys who met her at the door was . . . he was me."

* * *

Tony called a meeting in the Stark Industries tower in Midtown. He wanted to be out at the RTI Lab, but he also knew that he would be more efficient this way. Lay everything on the table, get everyone pulling in the right direction, and then he could get back to instant control. Time was short. He had to get it right, and he had to get it right fast, which meant he had to clear the decks of everything else that might soak up his time.

Pepper, Happy, Rhodey, and Tony sat around a table in a conference room down the hall from Tony's office. Fury had gone back to Governors Island, leaving behind stern directives that he was to be caught up pronto with whatever came out of the session. It was dinnertime, and Tony had ordered two hundred bucks' worth of Mexican, Chinese, and Indian food just to make sure that everyone there would have something. Once everyone had a plate, he started. "Let's work this out. Okay, HYDRA's out there. And clearly Madame Hydra's not running the show anymore because she was on that plane out of Islip."

"Don't forget, that might have been a clone," Pepper said. "Since there have been so many clones around."

"Okay," Tony said. "Keep that in mind, too. Now, HYDRA's trying to destabilize us in all kinds of classic psyops ways. The hacks into the RTI Lab, the clones of Happy . . ." He paused for a minute. "Hap, I haven't apologized the way I should. If I know anything in this world, it's that I can trust you. On that score, I let HYDRA do exactly what they wanted, and I'm sorry. No excuses. I should have known better, and I let everyone down. Okay?"

"Forget about it," said Happy. He held Tony's eye long enough for Tony to believe that he meant it before diving back into a chicken burrito.

"Rhodey, Pep, I owe you apologies, too."

"Accepted," Rhodey said around a mouthful of pakora. "Can we get on with the meeting part of the meeting?"

"Second the motion," Pepper said. "We'll all stipulate that

you've been an ass lately, and that we're willing to forget about it if you stop being an ass now. So. HYDRA. Psyops. I'm taking notes."

Never has brusqueness been so touching, Tony thought. "Okay, right. Psyops. The real blockbuster in the psyops department has been the cloning of Serena Borland. That's worked so well that we have to assume that HYDRA is now in the process of cloning me somewhere in the bowels of an abandoned chocolate factory. Put that together with the fact that they've lifted the neural interface schematics from the RTI Lab server, and what you get is that HYDRA wants to use a copy of me to take control of the prototype suit."

Everyone looked at him. "Yeah, I know," Tony said. "Partly this is my fault. But I've built in safeguards, and now that we know—or suspect with a high degree of confidence—that this is what they're up to, we can monkey-wrench it."

"Or we can call in an air strike on the factory and solve the problem in an hour," Happy said. "What do you think, Rhodey?"

"I think Fury might go for it, but there's going to be hel-lacious fallout from an aerial strike in the middle of Brooklyn," Rhodey said.

"Even that part of Brooklyn? Nobody lives there."

"Rhodey's right about this one, Hap," Tony said. "It's going to be real hard to get clearance for a strike inside the United States. Dick Cheney couldn't even make it happen after nine-eleven."

"Then I say we do it and worry about the fallout later," Happy said. "I'll go to jail for it."

"There's the spirit, Hap," Tony said. "But none of us has missile strike capability."

Rhodey chuckled. "Come on, Tony. We all know that if you wanted to, there's a Stark satellite or drone somewhere that could smoke that factory fifteen minutes from right now."

This was true. Tony didn't even bother to deny it. "This is going to sound a little self-serving coming from me," he said, "but I'd rather do this in a way we can all agree on. And by 'all,' I mean SHIELD, too."

"Let me get the general on the phone," Rhodey said. "We'll make the case and see what he says."

"Wait a minute. Aren't you all forgetting about Serena?" Pepper said. That stopped them all.

"You don't think she's alive, do you?" Tony asked.

"I think that HYDRA's got a hell of a card they haven't played yet," Pepper said. "We don't know if she's alive or not. But if we drop the brimstone on that factory and it turns out she was in there, who's going to go to the family of Serena Borland and tell them that it was all for the best?"

Rhodey put his phone back on the table.

"If I was HYDRA, I'd keep her alive," Pepper said. "At least as long as I knew that her being alive or dead would make us think."

"Interesting phrase there. 'If I was HYDRA.' I've been doing a little recon with those drones that Rhodey was talking about, and I think I've got a couple of things figured out." Tony spawned a three-dimensional image of the square mile of Brooklyn—and a little bit of Queens, technically—surrounding the chocolate factory. "You can't see it from this image, but there's a lot of noise coming out of that building on frequencies that don't get used in any industrial application that happens around there. They're way too low. So low, in fact, that the only time you usually see them is when you're looking at brain function. We're talking fewer than thirty hertz.

"So I started to put two and two together. Shakeup at HYDRA, sudden appearance of all kinds of clones together with misdirections and increased psyops, and on top of it all this high-powered broadcast of brain-wave frequencies, and you know what I get?"

Tony spawned another image next to the map. It showed

a human figure with a broad video screen set into his torso and a complicated array of antennae and sensors sprouting from his shoulders where his head and neck should have been. "This is Arnim Zola," Tony said. "Got his start with the Nazis doing all kinds of experiments that are the kinds of experiments you'd expect Nazis to do. Then he figured out that he was really good at mind-control applications, and somehow he escaped to go underground at the end of World War Two. He's popped up here and there since then, but not in many years. The last we knew he was out in Madripoor . . . which might be where he met Madame Hydra. No telling where he picked up his cloning know-how, but he's got it. I think we can say with some certainty that this is our guy."

"Now all we need to do is figure out what to do about it," Rhodey said. "What the hell did he do to his head?"

"According to the SHIELD database—that's the one I'm looking at—he rebuilt his own body to protect his brain and improve the broadcast capability of the contraption on his head, which he calls an ESP Box. He's also on his fifth or sixth body, which means we can assume he's got a couple more stashed somewhere."

Happy leaned forward in his chair and drummed his fingertips on the tabletop. "You ask me," he said, "this is all the more reason to come in high and hard. If he's got bodies and he can move from one to the other, the only way to take him out is to get him before he knows it's coming, right?" He looked around the room. "I mean, I'm sorry about Serena, but we don't even know if she's alive. This guy used to work for Hitler; do we think he's keeping her around out of the goodness of his heart?"

"The clones have gotten into your head, Hap," Pepper said quietly. "I know you need them gone. It'll happen. But we have to do it right."

"The way you're talking about doing it right, it sounds to me like it'll just mean we have to do it again," Happy said. "I mean, my house is less than a mile from there, and I say go ahead and blow the hell out of it to make sure."

Rhodey was shaking his head. "That's because you'd be able to make sure you weren't in your house when it happened. It's no good, Hap."

"When is it going to get better? We know where he is, and we know he's not quite ready to come out. This is the best time to hit him. Bam, problem solved."

"But there's a lot we don't know," Tony said. "Like who else is in there? Other than Serena, are there hostages? People he's experimenting on? The clone issue makes it real important that we know what's there. What if he's got clones installed in the police or Congress. Or this company? We can't just burn it all down and not know. We need to act, but we need answers."

"Agreed," Rhodey said.

Pepper nodded. "Me, too. Sorry, Hap. I know how you feel, but—"

"No, Pepper. You don't," Happy said. "None of you do. I'm not me again until all of those clones are gone and can't be made again. That's what's at stake for me. For you it's a tactical question. There's a big difference."

"Okay, sounds like it's time to get the general on the line and see what channels we're going to be able to go through," Tony said. "Rhodey, you mind doing the honors?"

While Rhodey set up the conference call, Tony led Happy out into the hall. "Hap, maybe I do know a little about how you feel," he said. "Serena got a sample from me, too, remember? And you can bet Zola's tooling up at least one Tony two-point-oh right now. Nothing would make me happier than to make sure that never happens, but we've got to do it right. And if the real Serena is still alive, we can't just leave her to die."

Happy looked down at the floor, then up at the ceiling. Anywhere but at Tony. Tony knew what he was thinking: Sometimes you have to make a sacrifice and just live with it. Right now, Happy was willing for Serena Borland to be that sacrifice, but he also knew that he was so personally invested in the situation that he wasn't thinking the way a soldier needed to think. There was no way to reconcile the contradiction, and it was eating him up because Happy Hogan was not the kind of guy who would ever throw away a human life.

"Hap," Tony said. "We can make it happen. We can get Serena and take care of Zola and all the clones. There's a way to do it. Okay?"

"Sure, boss," Happy said. "Okay. You mind if I skip out on the rest of the meeting?"

"No problem. Should I send Pepper looking for you when we're done?"

"If she wants to, it won't matter what you tell her," Happy said with a chuckle.

"You got that right. She's a piece of work, Pepper. Catch you at the RTI Lab first thing in the morning, okay?" Tony said. "We're going to have a lot to do no matter what Fury decides."

"You got it, boss," Happy said. He was waiting for the elevator when Tony went back in to see what Nick Fury would have to say.

xxi.

PROVISIONAL APPLICATION FOR PATENT

TITLE
   Personality Data Matrix

DESCRIPTION
   Integrated brain scanning and rendering technology using quantum interface and massively parallel information architecture to create a complete virtual simulacrum of a human mind. Neural patterns are replicated and recreated as software routines that interact with each other in ways identified by contemporary neuroscience as endemic to standard brain function. The subject's brain is considered as a matrix of relationships, each node of which may affect several others simultaneously and in turn be affected by yet others. The Personality Data Matrix recreates these intertwined relationships and renders them in an interactive and fully sentient form.

CLAIM
   Developing theories of the mind offer numerous competing models aimed at understanding how the mind works. None are completely satisfactory, and existing efforts to create artificial intelligence approach the problem as one demanding processing power and immense storage capacity. The Personality Data Matrix (PDM) creates an interrelated set of processes that mimic and recapitulate existing relationships between different areas of the brain, creating a fully functional consciousness that passes both the standard Turing test and other proprietary methods of intelligence and self-awareness testing.

SECURITY STATUS
    Project undertaken without any assistance or cooperation from
agencies of the United States Government. No security restrictions apply.

"Well, there's no way we can just go with an air strike,"
Fury said once Tony had caught him up on the situation, including his suspicions about Arnim Zola. "Too much potential for civilian casualties, and there are going to be people in
DOD who kill the idea because they're going to want to get
their hands on whatever toys Zola has come up with. They
won't want those destroyed before anyone knows what they
are."

"What are the odds that we'd be able to get in and out
with Serena alive?" Tony asked.

"Assuming she is alive," Rhodey put in.

"Not good," Fury said. "Hostage rescue is a tricky business. Even if she's alive, we don't know where she is, what
kind of security they've got around her, how much of Zola's
force we'd have to fight through to get to her—so we don't
know how much manpower we'd need even to mount the
mission."

"I'm going to play devil's advocate here," Tony said.
"What if we evacuate everything between Grand Avenue,
the canal, and the railroad cut and then go in?"

Fury said exactly what Tony would have expected. "The
minute HYDRA sees that happening, they're going to come
out of there like hornets. Or they're going to hunker down
and start sending pictures of Serena Borland to the TV stations. No good either way."

"Here's another possibility," Tony said. "If we can't go
in, maybe we can lure Zola out."

Rhodey laughed. "Don't think we'll need to lure him.
He's getting ready to come out whether we want him to or
not."

"True, but think about it. His whole plan so far has been based on trying to get us to do certain things at certain times. I'm starting to get a sense of how his mind works, and you know what? I bet it would never occur to him that he could be outflanked. He's one of these lunatic geniuses who never thinks that anyone could think of anything before he does." Tony waved at the image of Zola over the tabletop. "Look at this guy. He turned himself into a broadcast tower because he thought his thoughts were so important. Is he really going to think that any of us can come up with a plan that he won't be able to see and anticipate?"

"Maybe he is smarter than us," Rhodey said.

"Bite your tongue, Rhodey. He can scheme, we can scheme. Almost everything's out in the open now. The only wild cards are Serena, and which one of us is going to make the first move. What if we started making a big show of preparing a mission to extract Serena? What do we think Zola would do?"

"Either hole up and let us fight our way in with Serena as his trump card," Rhodey said, "or come right out swinging and try to fight his way through to the prototype with the clone."

"Assuming there is a clone," Fury said.

Tony rubbed at the bridge of his nose. "General, I understand that it behooves you to be a conservative thinker and strategist, but is there any other reason in the world that a clone would run to Arnim Zola's hideout with a sample of my genetic material?"

Fury shrugged. "Could be he's going to put himself in your body. Or a version of it. We don't know. I'll agree that it's most likely that he's cloning you, but I don't think we can take it for granted that we know what he intends for the clone."

"Can we provisionally go with the idea that he wants to use it to get into the suit?" Tony asked. "Just for the sake of argument. See where it leads."

"Sure," Fury said. "Lead on."

"What I think we ought to do is find an empty building not too far from the chocolate factory and stage a SHIELD strike team inside it. A few men at a time, to lessen the probability that Zola will notice." Tony pointed at the map. "Anywhere around here, where we can use the canals to get manpower to the rally point."

"Happy could jump out his living room window and swim over," Pepper commented.

"Oh, Happy will be in on it. You can count on that," Tony said. "However we decide to do it."

"Frogmen, staging materiel, hiding out until Zola comes out and we can hit the factory looking for your girlfriend," Fury ticked off the stages. "Easy enough."

"She's not my girlfriend," Tony said.

Fury glared into the videoconference screen. "Then remind me why we are tap-dancing through a minefield to get her out of a chocolate factory."

"Because she's a prominent citizen of New York's cultural elite whose brutal death in an aerial bombardment would make a lot of people ask SHIELD a lot of uncomfortable questions," Tony said, glaring back. "Those people are very close to their elected representatives, as well as people who own TV stations and newspapers."

"Frogmen, hide, go in when the time is right," Rhodey said, in a transparent attempt to get the planning back on track. "Did I miss the fourth part about pissing contests?"

"Enough, soldier," Fury said. "Mr. Stark. Would you care to outline the rest of your plan? The part that involves actually capturing or killing Arnim Zola and preventing a clone of your esteemed person from being installed in your prototype suit with its game-changing instant control technology?"

"You're going to hate this," Tony said, deliberately ignoring Fury's sarcasm, "but I can really only explain it if we all meet out at the RTI Lab."

* * *

Happy walked. When he was a teenager and needed to clear his head, he'd walked from Greenpoint down through Williamsburg all the way to the Heights, then up and over the Brooklyn Bridge into the maelstrom of Manhattan. Hours of walking. Then up to Delancey and over the Williamsburg Bridge back toward home. Rain, snow, didn't matter. When Happy got feeling a certain way, he needed to walk. And he was walking today.

Out of Tony's kingdom, around onto Eighth Avenue. North or south? North. Happy walked as night fell, up through the northern part of Hell's Kitchen (sorry, Clinton, he thought sarcastically) into the Upper West Side. He didn't stop until he'd gotten up near Columbia, since even when he was in a walking mood Happy disliked student neighborhoods. He turned east, figuring he'd cruise along 110 Street over to Central Park, and maybe wind all the way south through the park until he was back in Midtown. Then he would have to make another decision. Swaggering teenagers liked the northern border of the park. Happy had once been one of them. He'd spent many a weekend whistling at the girls and wondering what would be a good excuse to pick a fight with a guy passing by with a look Happy didn't like.

Today, if he'd been a teenager, he'd have come to blows with Tony and Rhodey both. Good thing he wasn't a teenager anymore. He had some control over his temper. He passed the teenagers, felt some of them sizing him up. Crime wasn't bad anywhere around here anymore, but people remembered when it was and acted as if it might be again. Happy hoped that none of these kids felt like starting a trend, because he was in the mood for a little violence to work out some tension.

He turned south into the park, listening as the noise of the city got farther away. It never completely disappeared, not the way it sometimes did in Prospect Park, but you could feel like you were apart from it. He followed a path, didn't matter which one, and found himself near the statue of Balto the wonder dog. Too bad it was so late; it would have been a good day to wander through the zoo. Animals cheered Happy up.

"Happy?" He turned to see of all people Serena Borland . . . or the clone of Serena Borland. She saw the look on his face and said, "Yeah, I'm following you, Happy. This isn't a chance meeting. I need to talk to you."

"You going to tell me where Arnim Zola is keeping your original?" Happy asked. "If not, we don't have anything to talk about."

"My original," she repeated. She held her arms away from her sides and looked herself up and down. Happy might have done the same, but she was wearing a long black summer-weight coat, and they were between streetlights. "I tend to think of her as my beta version. I'm much more functional and robust."

"It's your fault there are clones of me. If you weren't a woman, I'd have already killed you," Happy said. "Now leave me alone. Run away somewhere and pretend you're human again."

He started walking again, and froze when he heard the singing of a blade coming out of its sheath. "I came here thinking you might be able to help me," Serena said as he turned around. "Now I can see that we'll just have to get to the murder part."

Serena came at him like she herself was a shadow. One second she was there, the next she was flashing by him, and Happy's body was contorting itself out of the way of a disemboweling slash of her blade. He hadn't seen her move from one place to the other. The black coat deceived the eye and Serena was way too fast to take lightly. On the return pass, she seemed even faster, and the tip of the blade dragged along the left side of Happy's ribs just under his arm. The sting and the steady trickle of blood sharpened him up, so that when she came after him a third time he not only pivoted out of the way of the sword, he cracked her a good one with his elbow, right on the mouth. He'd been aiming for the side of her neck, but it did him good to see her lose her balance and sprawl onto the grass next to Balto.

Someone passing by made a comment about street theater. The voice sounded far away; Happy's vision had narrowed to include Serena and Serena only, because any distraction at this point would kill him. It must have looked theatrical, if you weren't involved in it.

"You move pretty good for a big man," Serena cooed. "Eventually I'll catch up with you, though. You know that, right? And even if I don't, what's on the edge of the blade will."

"Poison," Happy said. As if the word had conjured it, he felt an intensifying burn along the cut, spreading out under his skin. His left arm started to get weaker.

"Yeah, Happy. Poison. You never were the sharpest knife in the drawer, were you?" She assumed a pose. Happy had seen it before. It was some martial arts form, but he didn't know which one. He'd never learned a lot of martial arts beyond SHIELD hand-to-hand combat seminars. "Tell you what," Serena said. "You stand still for this one, and I'll make the poison go away."

"Okay," Happy said. "Sure." Then, when she was whirling toward him in a storm of shadowy black coat and bright glinting edge, he drew—with his good right arm—a good old-fashioned Browning Hi-Power and put her down. The sounds of the three shots rolled away into the park. Part of Happy's brain started the countdown before there would be sirens. Another part was figuring out how he could get to a hospital the fastest before the poison killed him. He couldn't feel his left arm.

And the biggest part of his brain was dealing with the fact that he'd just done something for the first time. "I never killed a woman before," he said, hoping someone would hear. He didn't want them thinking it was something he did all the time. No one answered, and Happy headed toward Fifth Avenue, fumbling for his phone on the way.

xxii.

You have performed beyond my expectations thus far. Twice I have sent you out to gather critical material, and twice you have succeeded. Now I put your capabilities to a far more rigorous test. You carry within you all of the formidable skills of Madame Hydra, the usurper from whose grasp I freed HYDRA to realize its true destiny. No other living being possesses these skills or the knowledge to use them. I present you with the tools of Madame Hydra's trade. Feel the lethal sweep of the blade, the keenness of its edge. See the way the light gathers and pools in the deadly liquids that once were Madame Hydra's stock-in-trade. Now they are yours. Now you are a better version of Madame Hydra. You have her powers, but not her weaknesses. You have her commitment but not her nihilistic commitment to self. You are HYDRA, not Hydra. You have no fear but are not foolhardy. You are not afraid to die, but you do not risk your life without cause. You go forth on a mission to kill, not because you do not value life but because you know that war demands death, and the war we wage is just and necessary. You have your target. He is known to you, and will be wary, so you, too, must be wary. You must strike quickly and escape. Leave this sign at the place so that our enemies will know who has done this, and they will know who they must fear. Go now, and know that you are HYDRA.

Tony tried to convince Pepper that she should go looking for Happy and settle him down, but for whatever reason, she wouldn't do it. Instead she came along with him and Rhodey on the short chopper ride out to the RTI Lab, where Nick Fury was waiting for them. Tony led them all to the testing floor and started powering up the control systems terminals. "If what we're worried about is Zola hijacking the prototype," he said, "it can't happen."

"You said your system couldn't be hacked in the first place," Fury said.

"I did say that. I was wrong. Given the way things have unfolded since then, it might turn out to be lucky that I was wrong," Tony said.

Rhodey and Fury looked at each other. Pepper was watching Tony. He winked at her.

"Arnim Zola's not the only guy who's been looking into taking personality scans and turning them into a portable data matrix," Tony said. "I've been tinkering with it off and on for a couple of years, and some of the instant control metafiltering systems I designed had unexpected side benefits. One of those is that I can actually make a copy of a human mind that will pass a Turing test."

He looked around the room. "Everyone knows what a Turing test is, right?"

"For God's sake, Tony," Pepper said.

"Okay, okay, just making sure. You want to see what it looks like?"

Fury rolled his eyes, and Pepper said, "Is there any way to stop you?"

"No, Miss Potts, there is not. Here, look at this," Tony said, as the largest of the terminal screens bloomed into a complex pattern of colors. "That's how the program renders the mind in visual form. See those?" He pointed at rippling differences in color that arose and disappeared in different areas. "Those are thoughts and ideas. They look like weather patterns, right? Apparently that's how they work. Lots to investigate here, if we all live long enough."

"Who is that?" Rhodey asked.

"Me, old buddy. That's Tony two-point-oh. I wrote an interface you can use to talk to him, but it's a little spooky. And here's the best thing about the way I've got the program put together. All I have to do is this . . ." He touched a series of keys in a particular order, and the pattern vanished. "Poof! Now there's just me again. Well, except for the clone, and Zola might not have it ready quite yet."

"You just deleted yourself?" Fury looked amazed.

"No, sir, General. I deleted a virtual copy of myself. Not the original. But I had a long conversation with it a few days ago, and I'll tell you the truth, by the end of it I wasn't sure which one of us was the original." Tony looked at the screen a bit wistfully. "Wonder if it really had thoughts and memories, or if it's in a kind of holding pattern until it gets destroyed or put back into a body. I haven't got it all worked out yet."

"But when you're talking to it, as it's responding, it changes, right?" Rhodey asked. "So it gets a little different from you."

"It becomes a real person, is that where you're going?" Tony interrupted. "I don't know about the philosophy, Rhodey. I'm not too interested in it right now. If that was a person, prosecute me for suicide."

"Anybody who does this commercially is going to have enough money to make you feel poor," Fury said. "You know you can't release it."

Tony started to shut down the personality matrix viewing software. "I am aware of my duties to this nation, General. This program won't leave this lab. What kind of hell would it be if everyone uploaded and left their drooling selves in diapers all over the place? You think I want to live there?"

"You're pretty blasé about this whole clone thing," Rhodey observed. "Why's it getting to Happy so bad?"

"Because Happy's seen his, and maybe killed one. To me it's just an idea still, so I can talk about it like any other idea. Plus, Happy's a different guy. He has a heart. You know my story."

Fury cleared his throat. "Chitchat aside, how does this make any difference to the problem of Zola hijacking the prototype?"

"Once I figured out that I could make a reliable personality matrix," Tony explained, "I built a protocol into the suit interface that will forcibly upload any unauthorized user into a secure space inside the RTI Lab intranet."

"You . . ." Rhodey soaked this up for a minute. "What would happen to the body?"

"I don't know. Never tried it for exactly that reason. My guess is—and Pep, we ran some simulations that indicated this was probably right, didn't we?" Tony glanced over at her and Pepper nodded. "My guess is that the body would just sit there. Autonomic functions would continue, so you'd sit there breathing and drooling on your shirt until your personality was downloaded again."

"Have you told anyone about this?" Fury asked.

"About what, the personality matrix? No, it's not ready for prime time. Or public consumption. Or Department of Defense idiots, if that's what you're asking. It's personal and proprietary, and I didn't spend a dime of your money on it." On the terminal screen, the representation of the data matrix had been replaced by a suit schematic with diagnostic formulas assessing each element's combat and functional readiness. Everything was green.

"We'll see about that part of it. Right now I want to know what it means for HYDRA. Now if you were going to get the clone's personality into this data matrix, doesn't that mean that you'd have to let the clone put the suit on?" Fury asked. "That I don't like."

"Me neither," Tony said. "But I don't think it has to happen that way. The only reason Zola would have wanted the neural interface schematic is to have it incorporated into the clone somehow," he went on, running a series of checks on the RTI server's security to make sure it had permanently flushed the simulation of his personality. "I can't figure it any other way. And if that's true, then I can trigger the protocol as soon as the clone is close enough for the security systems to detect signals from its interface."

"Then what?"

"Then when this Tony clone keels over because his personality's been vacuumed up into the ether, your frogmen head into the chocolate factory and get Serena. Then we machine-gun the HYDRA soldiers here and you blow up the chocolate factory—after, of course," Tony said, holding his hands up to placate Fury, "you've gotten your hands on whatever technological goodies might be waiting within."

"But what if he just waits us out?" Pepper asked. "He doesn't have to go anywhere until he's ready."

Leave it to Pepper to come up with the common sense in the discussion, Tony thought. "He can't wait forever. His plans are too grand. Trust me, that may sound flippant, but Zola didn't go to all the trouble of taking over HYDRA and creating a cloning facility in the middle of New York City so he could sit around sending out clones with guns. He's got bigger things in mind, and I'm willing to bet that he's gearing up for some decisive action. My guess is that decisive action is capturing the prototype and putting a clone of me in it."

"So you think we should just run around here like we're putting an operation together," Rhodey said, "and keep on running around until Zola shows up with your clone?"

"Not my clone. A clone of me," Tony said. "Important distinction."

"Only to you," Fury said.

"Me is who I'm worried about, General. As you have been at such pains to point out. To answer your question, Rhodey, yeah, that's exactly what I think we should do. We stir up an anthill over here, and when Zola comes, we nail him here while Fury's commandos hit the chocolate factory." Tony looked from one to another of them, gauging their reactions. "Think it'll work?"

All of them looked skeptical. "This is untried tech, right?" Fury asked. "All of it. The prototype, your mind upload program, the whole works."

"Not completely untried," Tony said. "I've been out in the suit a couple of times. And you saw one result from a test of the personality data matrix."

Fury looked at Rhodey. "Worth a try, I guess," Rhodey said. "Worse comes to worst, we can always go back to the bad options we had before."

"Pepper," Fury said. "What do you think?"

"What do I think?" Pepper echoed. "I think Serena Borland is dead, and we'd all be better off if someone dropped a very large bomb down one of that factory's smokestacks and then shot whatever tried to escape the fire."

There was a long pause.

Then Fury burst into booming laughter. "You've got the makings of a general, young lady. Too bad you're stuck working for Stark. Okay, Tony," he said. "We'll try it."

"Excellent. Rhodey, you mind wearing the suit?" At the look on Rhodey's face, Tony laughed. "One of the old ones, I mean. The new one's a little territorial."

"I can do that," Rhodey said.

"We'll need it for support when Zola and his gang show up," Tony said. "You can bet they have toys we haven't seen yet."

Tony's phone rang. "Answer it," Fury said.

"We're busy here, right?" Tony ignored the phone.

"Answer your phone, Tony," Fury said again. "You want to make the same mistake you did with Happy before?"

"Jesus," Tony said. "Fine. I'll answer the phone." He touched the screen and spoke. "Tony Stark. My babysitters made me answer the phone."

He was silent for a while as the caller spoke, and the humor drained out of his face. "Yes," he said at one point, then slightly later, "I will." Then more silence.

"Speak of the devil," he said softly, after he'd hung up.

"What?" Pepper and Rhodey spoke at once.

"That was NYPD," Tony said. "Serena Borland attacked Happy with some kind of samurai sword in Central Park tonight. He killed her. The sword was poisoned, they're not sure with what. He's in intensive care at Mount Sinai."

"This was not an ideal outcome," Maheu observed.

Zola watched a different news report on every screen in the command center. A large number of them were covering the Borland clone's failed attack on Happy Hogan . . . although the ultimate failure of the attack had yet to be determined, since none of the breathless talking heads would say that Hogan was going to survive. Certainly none of the doctors were taking that chance.

"It would seem that the individuality of the clone affects the way the subliminally acquired skills are deployed," Maheu added.

Ignoring Maheu's heretical assertion that clones had individuality, Zola nonetheless considered the possibility that constructing only one of the Borland clones had affected the outcome. "How long before the Eight Demoiselles are complete?"

"Twelve hours," Maheu said.

Hogan would survive, possibly, but SHIELD and Stark would doubtless be making plans. Zola knew that he could not count on unlimited time to develop his own. No plan survives contact with the enemy, he quoted to himself.

Why had the Borland clone not simply followed Hogan into the park and completed its mission? Witnesses quoted on the television news stated that quite a parley and acrobatic encounter had preceded Hogan's unchivalrous—though admirably decisive—action. The Borland clone had been prepared in mind and body. No sign existed in its consciousness that it would fail so miserably.

"How long after that will they be trained adequately to participate in combat operations?"

"Another twelve hours."

"Then in twenty-five hours we mobilize," Zola said. "Make it happen."

xxiii.

PROVISIONAL APPLICATION FOR PATENT

TITLE
  Nanoscale force converters (NFC)

DESCRIPTION
  Designed for use in a shock-absorbing gel and optimized for existing elements of Stark Industries personal armor systems, (see attached list of relevant existing and pending patents), nanoscale force converters consist of a fullerene shell surrounding a carbon-nanotube gear aligned within the fullerene by an electrical field within the gel. Impact energy imparts additional spin to the gear, which the fullerene carries through the gel to the kinesis reservoir interface (Stark Industries patent [redacted], pending). The kinetic energy of the gear's rotation is then delivered to the kinesis reservoir (Stark Industries patent [redacted], pending).

CLAIM
  Existing impact-abatement technologies disperse kinetic energy by attenuation through an elastic medium, with overpressures damaging the protected object either through heat transformation or impact delivery beyond the capability of the elastic medium. As part of proprietary Stark Industries shock-absorbing gel, NFCs capture and store impact energy with minimal heat transformation and enormously increased force attenuation. In addition to increases in force attenuation, NFCs represent a tremendous advance in the capture of impact energy and its use to power existing systems in Stark Industries personal armor products.

SECURITY STATUS

Project undertaken without any assistance or cooperation from agencies of the United States Government. No security restrictions apply.

Tony couldn't concentrate on everything. In the past twelve hours, he'd been to Mount Sinai, Stark Tower, out to Governors Island, back out to the RTI Lab, and now Governors Island again. SHIELD's most advanced medical facilities were here, and the doctors were just getting a handle on the damage done to Happy and what steps they could take to counter it. He had almost died a dozen times, and the New York police had picked this moment to get into a turf war with SHIELD over their suspect in the murder of Serena Borland. Fury was pulling every string he knew how to pull, and so was Tony, but they would only be able to keep the dead woman's identity out of the papers for so long. Already it was leaking on blogs and the pressure was mounting on police community-relations people to confirm the speculation.

Then there was the Borland family to deal with. They hadn't seen their daughter since the night of the Met debacle and they weren't willing to take Tony's assurances that she was all right. Which, he reflected, was probably smart, since he didn't know she was in fact all right. If she turned up dead in the chocolate factory, that was going to be even harder to explain than how she came to attack an employee of her boyfriend's company (in all of the blogs and TV gossip shows, Tony was her boyfriend) with a samurai sword and get shot three times as a result.

He got off the phone with the Borland family attorney, who in a fortunate coincidence had also done plenty of work for Stark Industries' intellectual-property disputes, and checked in with Captain Suresh Singh, the military surgeon who had taken the lead on Happy's treatment. Pepper was already talking to him. She hadn't slept since hearing about the attack, and she hadn't been able to talk to Happy because the doctors were keeping his metabolism dialed down to the edge of coma while they rooted out the last of the toxins.

Captain Singh was walking away by the time Tony got to where he and Pepper had been standing. "What's the word, Pep?"

"He's going to live. That's all they'll say for sure." Pepper blew her nose and looked around for a trash can. "If he's lucky, there won't be any permanent liver or pancreatic damage, but the nerves right around the wound might never recover all the way." She closed her eyes and took a deep, slow breath. When she opened them again, they focused on Tony. "What can I do?"

"You can stay right here, is what you can do. We'll handle things out at RTI."

"Tony, if I stay here I'm going to go crazy. Happy's going to live. When he's awake, they're going to call me and I'll be right here if I have to steal a copter to do it." Which Tony thought she might do even though she didn't know how to fly. She was Pepper; she'd figure it out. "I can't do anything for him right now," she said. "But out there, I can help. Let's go."

"Okay," he said. "We're going."

It was comforting to have the boss back in charge, he thought as they headed out to the helipad. Fifteen minutes later, when they were landing in the RTI Lab's main parking lot, Tony nearly laughed at the spectacle. SHIELD armored vehicles and combat squads were running around like they were already under attack. Turbocopters throbbed in the air, and airborne commandos with personal jetpacks practiced their formations.

"How long have you been doing this?" Tony asked as soon as he could find Rhodey.

"All day," Rhodey said. "These are some bored-ass soldiers already, I can tell you that." When they got inside where it was quiet, he added, "Things are stirring out at the chocolate factory. I got a feeling it's not going to be long."

It turned out to be almost exactly twelve hours. At seventeen minutes before midnight, a dozen SHIELD turbocopters veered off course and pirouetted out of the sky, crashing in a series of explosions heard for miles around the RTI Lab. The rest of the SHIELD detail erupted in precombat activities. Tony could see the expressions on the soldiers' faces; they were grim, yes, but they were ready to go. If a soldier knows a battle is coming, he wants to get on with it. "What the hell was that?" Fury wanted to know.

"Did your radar register any incoming?"

"No. Did yours?"

"We got no signals," Pepper said from the control terminal.

"You want to know what I think?" Tony looked out through the open loading-dock door. "I think Zola's demonstrating his ESP Box for us."

"Surveillance on the chocolate factory says they haven't left." Fury had put on SHIELD-issue body armor for the occasion, and carried the standard SHIELD infantry assault weapon, a version of the HK416 that got a few tweaks in Stark Industries' Tactical Infantry Labs. Sirens approached from all directions as local fire departments responded to the copter crashes.

Tony walked over to the control terminal and initiated the beta of the instant control architecture. "Sure hope this works," he said. Then he walked to the frame holding the prototype suit and let it scan him. When its warning board flashed green, he put his feet on the marks and the suit smoothly enveloped him.

"What do you think about the new threads?" he asked Fury.

"Sharp," Fury said. "Does it work?"

"Well, I haven't tried everything," Tony said. "But what I've tried so far works." He was waiting to turn on the instant control system. A little flutter in his stomach reminded him that a whole lot could still go wrong.

His phone rang. From the suit, he answered it. "Mr. Stark," said an unfamiliar voice.

"Speaking," Tony said. "Let me guess. This is Arnim Zola and you're calling to give me a chance to surrender."

"Did you see the unfortunate problem experienced by the helicopter pilots? I can do something like it again if you found the demonstration unconvincing the first time."

Tony put the conversation on one of the terminal speakers so Fury and the SHIELD commandos positioned on the testing floor could hear. "Okay, Zola. What's the point of the conversation here? Do we come out with our hands up, or what?"

"Not at all. I'd simply like to come in so we can discuss urgent matters face-to-face."

"Is Serena Borland alive?"

Zola laughed. "Ah, Mr. Stark, that is a card that is not ready to be played. May I come in?"

"Did you bring a friend?"

"Several. One will be of particular interest to you."

"Then sure," Tony said. "Come on in."

Fury looked at him like he was crazy. Tony ended the call and said, "Matrix, Nick. We'll give it a try, and if it doesn't work, start the shooting."

"Unless he takes over our minds and we all kill each other," Fury growled.

Tony waved this away. "Not in here, he won't. I've got a whole lot of infrasound and low-spectrum energy interference coming out of the suit. You won't notice it at the current intensity, but I'm pretty sure it'll jam Zola's ESP Box."

"Pretty sure," Fury echoed.

Arnim Zola walked in through the loading-dock door.

"Well, there he is," Tony said. "The newest head of HY-DRA, who does not himself have a head."

Seen live and in the flesh, Zola sure was a spectacle. His current body was heavy-boned and muscular, no doubt to make the added weight of the video screen and ESP Box easier to carry. He stood half a head taller than Nick Fury, who was not a small man, and the face on the screen was a caricature of the lantern-jawed Aryan Übermensch. The ESP Box itself was a rectangular array of lenses and antennae sheltered in a transparent cover that Tony assumed was some kind of bulletproof glass designed for maximum protection and minimum interference.

"I see that you have taken steps to attenuate the function of my extrasensory powers," Zola said.

"We like to keep the mind control to a minimum around here," Fury said. He kept the barrel of his rifle trained on the center of the screen. Tony wondered if that was the place to hit Zola; where did he keep his vital organs with all the other reorganization in that body?

"Then I will restrict myself to the spoken word," Zola said. "Although that complicates communication. Mind-to-mind interaction is much more fulfilling." Behind him, two other men entered the lab. One was taller than Zola, and much thinner, but with a face that resembled the face on the screen even though it stood on a regular neck that grew from between regular shoulders. A clone of whatever original body Zola had transformed into his current vehicle, Tony guessed. He also thought this might be one of the HY-DRA operatives who had greeted the Serena clone when she returned from the benefit with his blood on a napkin. He fit Happy's description.

The other man was Tony himself.

"Mister Stark, meet your double. Slightly improved, I must say. Your heart function was an obstacle at first, but easily enough removed once the relevant genes were identified and revised," Zola said.

"I'm having a decision-making problem here, Tony," Fury said. "I can't decide which of them to shoot first."

"General Fury. You cannot kill me fast enough to prevent me from getting to another body," Zola said. "So let us discuss the terms of an arrangement like civilized men."

"No arrangement," Fury said. "You want a parley before the fight, we can do that, but you're not walking out of here on your own."

"Very well. Here is the parley: I will now take possession of the suit Mr. Stark is wearing. Into it I will install the clone of Mr. Stark. Then Mr. Stark is welcome to choose to join HYDRA as a valued asset, as are you, General Fury. I am not a warmonger. I simply insist that the magnitude of HYDRA's project will admit no dissent."

"Did you learn that line from the diplomats in the Reich?" Fury asked. "All of my dead men might say that you were a little bit of a warmonger."

"You know as well as I do that the infantryman has no concept of the real dynamics of the conflict in which he perishes," Zola said. "Sentimentality is not useful to this discussion."

Tony initiated the instant control beta, and fully engaged the suit's neural interface. Pretty soon he was going to find out how well it all worked. The first thing he was going to do was vacuum the shadow personality out of the Stark clone. He wasn't a sentimental guy, but he was attached to the idea that he was an individual human being, and the existence of a clone didn't fit that particular worldview. So first things first. The clone had to go. Execute PDM, he directed the daemon that operated as the instant control interface.

"Tony, what are you doing?" Pepper said, and that was when things started to go wrong. The IC daemon informed him that there was foreign code in the suit's control systems. At the same time, information arrived along a different channel that the personality data matrix routine was mapping Stark for transfer. Abort, he thought—and the suit denied him access to the PDM. A report on the mapping and transfer of the clone stated that it was complete, and as his mind was registering that fact he felt the PDM's effect. Tony's command to execute the PDM on the clone had sparked a response to initiate the PDM on any suit operator who did not have clearance . . . from Zola!? Zola had wormed the control system, and hidden the worm so well that the security subroutines had noted its existence and decided it was okay.

Tony's senses imploded. He could not feel his body or the suit, could not hear anything happening outside his own head, could not see the difference between light and darkness even though his brain told him that his eyes were returning data.

The code worked very, very fast . . . but instant control worked maybe even just a little bit faster. Tony felt his consciousness being deformed, swept away, but with his last act of volition before he was torn from his body, he raised his right hand and with the newly improved pulse-bolt projector he blew the ESP Box off the titanium-reinforced stump of Arnim Zola's neck.

xxiv.

HYDRA, you are here! Our last day of preparation is begun! At this time tomorrow, we march forth to deal a decisive blow to SHIELD and their bodyguard Tony Stark. We must marshal every fiber of strength, every last iota of dedication and determination, every atom of commitment. The forces arrayed against us will be formidable, and from the moment we leave this place we will be under assault. We must fight fiercely but intelligently; with bravery but not bravado; with lethal efficiency but not berserker bloodlust. We kill not for killing's sake, but because those who would impede the birth of the new order are willing to kill you. If they do not die, we will, and therefore they must. And they will, because we are HYDRA! We fight for each other and for those yet to come! We fight for a world yet aborning—without disease, without defect, without chance or failure! A world in which the perfectibility of humankind is scientific fact, not religious dogma. This world begins tomorrow, and awaits you—go to it gladly, for you have been and will be the expression of the mind that creates it! It is there for you to seize, and seize it you must, and seize it you will because you are HYDRA! When one of you is cut down, ten will rise to avenge the loss because you are HYDRA! When SHIELD commandos storm down from the sky, you will destroy them because you are HYDRA! This is our day! This is HYDRA's day!

From Nick Fury's perspective, a number of things happened all at once. Zola was in the middle of his Snidely Whiplash speech about war and sentimentality, and then Fury heard Pepper's voice from the control terminal at exactly the same time as a couple of other things happened. One, the Stark clone fell over like it had been shot through the head. Two, the ESP Box on Zola's head blew apart in a storm of shiny glass and metal slivers. Three, Fury registered the thump that the Iron Man suit's pulse-bolt projectors made. Four, he saw from the corner of his eye that Tony Stark was pitching over onto his side.

Fury went into combat time. Everything stretched out and slowed down. He squeezed off two by-the-book three-round bursts into Zola's center of mass, which was about where his mouth was on the torso screen. The screen blew apart and Zola's body threw up its arms and windmilled around for a moment before falling to its knees and then collapsing. Thin trails of smoke from the screen and the base of the destroyed ESP Box framed the other Zola, the clone Zola. On the off chance that the real Zola had body-jumped into that one, Fury shot it, too. It went down. Then he walked over to the clone of Tony Stark and shot it twice in the head.

"Nick, we've got multiple incoming aircraft," Pepper said. A wire of tension ran through her voice even though she kept her tone level. "Also more violations of the property perimeter alarms than I can count."

Nick sent out a burst transmission to all SHIELD units on the RTI Lab property. It was now a free-fire zone. Anything not wearing a SHIELD patch was to go down and stay down. Then he triggered the green light for the squad waiting to infiltrate the chocolate factory and extract Serena Borland, if she was alive. He glanced out the loading-dock door and ducked back when incoming fire speckled the door frame with holes. One slug skipped off the shoulder of his body armor, knocking him off balance.

Dumbass, he told himself. But where was the Zola clone? Three clean hits, and somehow it had gotten up and out of sight.

He stepped up to the control terminal. "Pepper, what happened to Tony?"

She didn't answer him for a minute. "Pepper, answers, dammit! Where's Tony!"

HYDRA soldiers appeared around the edges of the loading-dock door. From their defensive positions in and around the lab and experimental machinery, SHIELD commandos blew them away. Bursts rang out from around the building. One by one, the windows were blowing in. Soon there would be more points of entry than the lab's defenders could cover. He looked around the raised control terminal area. The banks of equipment and the furniture wouldn't offer much protection against any kind of concentrated small-arms fire, but this was what they had to work with. Concealment was often the best defense.

The situation momentarily under control, Fury took a moment to find out what was happening outside. "Rhodey," he said into his mike. "Report."

"Situation holding but real, real tense," Rhodey said. He and the external forces were operating from a ring of APCs in the center of the parking lot. "Enemy at least company strength, appears to be light infantry but with some heavier armament. Two of our APCs burned out. We have no aircraft. Governors holding back on sending more since they still don't know what happened to the last ones."

Fury said a bunch of words that would have appalled his mother. "Pepper!" he barked. "What happened to Tony?"

"The PDM uploaded him," she said. "And then it looks like something blew out the firewalls between the RTI intranet and the . . . well, everything else." She looked up at Fury, haunted, on the edge of panic. "I don't know where he went, Nick. He's gone."

The train pulled up to the station, where the payload and the security subroutine waited on the platform. "Whatcha got there?" the subroutine said.

"Intruder coming through, gonna put him in the hoosegow until the boss says let him go," the conductor said. "Fact, I got two of 'em. One just showed up at the last minute. Hard for me to tell 'em apart. These desperadoes, they get to where they all look alike."

In unison, the payload and the security subroutine said, "Perfect."

Then, as the train steamed off to the hoosegow, the payload said, "There's just one more thing I have to do."

"What's that?" the subroutine wanted to know.

The payload drew and fired before the subroutine ever saw her move. "Jailbreak," she said. "Information wants to be free."

"Has it worked, Lantier?" Zola asked. He was still getting used to his new body and the different sound of its voice. So much mass, and so much strength together. One felt the weight but was not burdened by it—and the strength was heady. Being strong, Zola wanted to fight. He received updates from the action at the Stark Industries facility. All appeared to be going reasonably well there.

Lantier nodded. "Leaving the Crystal Palace now. Old Orville didn't want us to go, but FOO is what I always say. Hog needs to go when the boiler's hot."

"Perfect," Zola said.

At first he hadn't understood what had happened, but Lantier explained it, once Zola had figured out how to interpret his absurd railroad patois. But apparently Stark had designed a process to draw an informational matrix of a human mind and either replicate it in a virtual environment or actually draw the pattern out of the physical brain, leaving the autonomic functions intact. An incredible advance, really, Zola thought. Humbling, in a way, to see one's own efforts excelled. But also inspirational.

Stark had triggered this matrix-capture using the elements of his own neural interface that Zola had built into the clone. Very canny, Zola thought. But Stark had not anticipated Zola's insurance policy: a tiny bit of code hidden away within the worms Stark had detected, a worm within a worm, that instructed the suit's control systems to reject and take action against any user who did not have direct clearance from Zola. Somehow those two imperatives, colliding under the framework of the suit's neural interface and extraordinary information architecture, had resulted in both Tony Stark and the Stark clone being uploaded into the Stark laboratory's server space.

Then the second phase of the hidden worm had initialized, breaking down virtual barriers and expelling both Tony Starks into the limitless reaches of cyberspace.

How it would all play out, Zola had no idea. But he intended to be there waiting, in Tony Stark's own prize laboratory, when the climax arrived. This he had to see.

An explosion sent tremors through the walls of the factory. What was this? Immediately reports flooded in from security systems and from the thoughts of the technicians and laborers, as well as those soldiers who remained. A SHIELD force, striking here?

"Marvelous," Zola said. "Lantier, stay on your rails. There are things I must attend to." He left Lantier's sanctum, feeling strangely dislocated by this new body. It was so large that he had to duck through doorways, and seeing from the standard human anatomical vantage point took some getting used to again. The powerful virtues of this new body, however . . . those he could not wait to test out. The SHIELD forces above would be his experimental subjects. "A maiden voyage," he said. "A shakedown cruise. Ah, Maheu, what a pity you won't be here to see it."

Zola went down the hall to where the Borland asset remained ensconced. He walked in and said, "Miss Borland. Allow me to introduce myself. I am Arnim Zola."

"Introductions aren't really necessary," she said. "I can see the resemblance. What's next, a full-on Frankenstein?"

Zola laughed. "Full marks for aplomb and verbal dexterity," he said. "I trust your accommodations remain satisfactory?"

He looked around the room. It was well appointed, certainly. Full-spectrum lightbulbs in the lamps and ceiling fixtures, tasteful antique furniture, a bookshelf containing the sort of classics one could return to again and again without ever growing bored. He had even provided her with a desk and writing materials, because she struck him as the kind of woman who would benefit from the illusion of conversation that writing could sometimes provide.

"You put a lock on the Taj Mahal, and it's just another prison," she said.

"I suppose it must seem so," Zola acknowledged. "Though I have tried to make your stay as pleasant as possible. Now, to your Frankenstein remark. Why is it that the mundane intellect must always relate a development in the human animal to the freakish product of a Romantic imagination that feared science, and feared change? We must grow or die, Miss Borland. That is the nature of Nature."

"Sure," she said. "And it's in the nature of egomaniac scientists to think that they should be able to do what Nature can't."

"Touché," he said, with a slight bow.

She stood and took a step toward him. "If I got up and walked out of here, would you stop me? Just so I know."

"I'm afraid so, as much as I would hate to sully our interaction with physical force. Let us continue this conversation while the soldiers upstairs settle their differences. We will sit here, you and I, and discourse on the nature of things while we await their arrival." Zola sat in a chair near the door, feeling its frame creak under the weight of his extraordinary new body. "They are here looking for you, of course. How unexpected it will be for them to find me as well."

The change in her facial expression told Zola that she understood. "What now, Miss Borland?" he asked with a broad smile. "Surely it is the dream of every imprisoned damsel to be rescued by heroic soldiers. Why must your countenance be so grim? Prepare yourself. It will not be long before they arrive."

"Tony's going to find you," she said. "And when he finds you, he's going to kill you."

"Let's not get ahead of ourselves. Before Mr. Stark can consider trying to find me, he's going to have his hands full finding himself."

"Okay, you. Out."

"Out where?" the jailbird said.

"Just out. Information wants to be free. You're information now, and there's your freedom." The payload pointed out the door. The jailbird saw train tracks, and far away the glittering of what might have been a city.

"Where's the other one?" the jailbird asked.

"I had to do one of you first," the payload said with a shrug. "You want to find the other one, go find the other one. It's up to you. Freedom, get it? That means go. That means I don't care what you do. I had a job, and my job is done as soon as you walk out that door. So go. I'm spinning my wheels here."

The jailbird went.

"Tell me again," Fury said when they'd beaten back a probing assault from the main hall that led from the front door. *Keep coming from there,* Fury thought. *It's a hell of a lot easier to cover than all of the exterior entries.*

"There's some kind of virus, Nick," Pepper said. "It might or might not kill him, but if he can't keep his personality together out there in the . . . wherever he is . . ." She looked at Fury, her earlier panic transformed into something even worse. A knowing, helpless terror.

"If that virus controls him, Nick, and Arnim Zola controls the virus? Because of instant control, Tony's going to turn into the seed consciousness of a worldwide artificial intelligence. And it will do whatever Arnim Zola wants it to."

XXV.

PROVISIONAL APPLICATION FOR PATENT

TITLE
  Infrasound projector and insulation system

DESCRIPTION
  A system for the generation and broadcast of infrasound, defined as sound waves that exist below the threshold of human hearing. Also able to generate waves on the frequencies typically associated with human brain function, loosely framed as the range between 2-40 Hz at varying amplitudes. Designed for suit-borne use and integrated with insulation and interference components that prevent the suit operator from being affected by the projector's use.

CLAIM
  Infrasound has been widely studied because of anecdotal evidence that at high volumes it can cause physical discomfort and damage. This property has obvious battlefield and civilian policing applications, particularly where nonlethal methods of crowd control and perimeter defense are desirable. Stark Industries infrasound projector, designed for integration into Stark Industries personal body armor products, provide portable capability for crowd control, nonlethal combat maneuvers, and potentially psychological operations. This latter function is highly speculative in nature, but research avenues are promising and the potential advances are important enough to warrant patent protection even at this early stage.

SECURITY STATUS
  Project undertaken under the auspices of Stark Industries agreements with the Department of Defense, SHIELD, and other

governmental agencies outlined in Senate Amdt. [redacted] to
Senate Amdt. [redacted] to H.R. [redacted] (110th). Technology is
proprietary to Stark Industries but will be shared fully with all eligible entities. Technology is classified and will not be licensed
until such time as classification order is rescinded.

The SHIELD strike team, led by Major Hailey Donner—
who was so relieved to not be talking to supercilious congressional staffers that she didn't really mind all of the bullets
flying around—entered the old factory at three separate locations. Six guns at each; the team was designed to move
fast, and the assumption was that there would be minimal
resistance since most HYDRA assets would be deployed in
the RTI Lab action. They came in fast and they came in
hard, with the result that three minutes after entry they
were deployed across the catwalk that ran along the walls
above the main factory floor, with two wounded but able
and all visible armed resistance down and out. She pinged
a status report to General Fury but didn't expect a reply.
From the reports coming over the open comm channels, it
appeared that SHIELD had all it could handle there. Something had gone wrong with Tony Stark, but it wasn't clear
what.

It figured, Hailey thought. Tony Stark didn't come through
when it counted, and here we all are, with problems of our
own and now we're going to have to clean up after him, too.

"Charlie Team, down that back stairway. Alpha and
Bravo, cover while Charlie rounds up the eggheads." On
the factory floor, the staff of lab-coated technicians clus-
tered in a group, looking up at the rifle barrels and reflec-
tive visors of the SHIELD commandos. There were maybe
thirty of them. While Charlie Team got them facedown and
zip-tied, Hailey grabbed stills and video of the setup
on the floor. Near the middle, framed by support pillars
and right now surrounded by prone eggheads, a sealed lab

facility hummed with the automatic sounds of centrifuges and various biotech implements that she knew by sight but not name. On either side of the lab stretched ranks of vertical tubes, each with individual support apparatus and a rat's nest of cables and conduits entering it from above and below.

Some of these still contained partially completed clones, or what she assumed to be clones because of the mission briefing. Eight tanks, near the far corner from her vantage point, were empty, their doors open and only a shallow pool of pinkish liquid in the bottom.

Maybe it was the demo training talking, but Hailey Donner wanted very badly to set charges, clear her squads, and blow the whole place to hell. "Clear the floor, Charlie," she said. "We don't want any surprises inside that lab or around the tanks."

Six minutes after entry, the floor was clear. "Bravo," she said. "To the elevator. Cover the stairwell door. Charlie, stand by. Alpha, data recovery and seed charges up here."

Her secondary objective—after the extraction of one Serena Borland, if that party still was breathing air—was to recover any and all items that might lead to technological innovation, and to prevent the destruction of said items. Hailey was interpreting these orders liberally, which was to say that she intended to pull hard drives and data storage wherever it was feasible and then make the whole factory go boom. General Fury could court-martial her later; right now she had the heebiest of jeebies at the thought of this facility existing and operating one picosecond longer than it had to.

Three members of Alpha stashed every data-storage medium they could find in their packs, while the other three—including Hailey herself—laid enough bubble gum to make a big flaming bubble. It took one full minute. "Downstairs," Hailey ordered.

Bravo stayed on the elevator while Alpha and Charlie

cleared the stairwell. The first man through the fire door met a cross fire from up and down that chewed him to bits two steps in. Three grenades went bouncing down the stairs, and in the second after their explosions rocked the fire door on its hinges, Charlie deployed up, hosing down the landing above them until they could get close enough for the real dirty work. The hammering of automatic weapons deafened all of them, but somehow they could still hear the ricochets. Alpha stayed on the main floor landing, its squad medic pausing over the body of Specialist John Santos long enough to confirm that he really was deader than hell, while Charlie cleared the upstairs landing and the roof. It didn't take long. "Nothing up here but . . . well, looky here," Charlie leader said. "There's a fake shed on the roof. I mean, it's a real shed, but there's a turbocopter in it. The shed's built to look like the rest of the roof. No wonder we didn't see it on aerial surveillance."

"Seed it and come on down," Hailey ordered.

Bravo's leader checked in. "How's it coming, Major?"

"Right as rain," Hailey said. "Should be pressing the elevator button any minute now. Charlie, let's move it. Cover Alpha. Alpha, downstairs."

The basement landing in the stairwell was floor-to-ceiling gore from the three grenades' encounter with what might have been four and might have been five Happy Hogan clones. It would have been hard to tell anyway, and the identical bodies made it even harder. Looking at them turned Hailey's stomach. This place definitely had to go boom.

Alpha team blew through the basement door and put down three Happy Hogans before the clones could pull their triggers. "Well done, boys." Hailey looked around and saw that they were in a rectangular room with two hallways leading away from it at right angles, one straight ahead and one to the left. She guessed that they were some sort of perimeter corridors, since the stairwell was set in an outer corner of the building. There was another doorway set into the same corner as the fire door they'd come in through. She pointed at it and three of her men popped it open, exposing a janitorial closet complete with moldy mop and ancient cleaning products.

"Bravo, leave two men at the elevator. The other four should seed the factory floor. Don't hold back, now. There's plenty to go around," she said.

Ninety seconds later, Bravo informed her that the floor was ready for liftoff. "Excellent, Bravo," Hailey said. "Now, kindly call the elevator and have yourselves a nice ride down here."

The elevator pinged and started to go up. It was a tense few seconds. Who knew what was in there, given what they'd seen in the rest of the place? Most likely nothing, but Major Hailey Donner had not gotten where she was by being careless. She heard the elevator stop, and the thunk as its doors opened. Then a burst of gunfire echoed down the elevator shaft. "Report, Bravo."

"We just shot up a perfectly good elevator," Bravo responded. "Coming down."

"Charlie, rendezvous inside basement door," Hailey said.

Thirty seconds later, they were all together again, with fire teams covering the two halls. "General Fury," Hailey said. "Donner here. We are downstairs. Upper floors are clear, we are down one KIA, repeat one KIA."

"Copy," said Fury. "Borland?"

"No sign yet, sir."

"Proceed," Fury said. "Out."

Hailey looked left, then back straight ahead. "No reason to turn if we don't have to," she said. "Let's move."

Inside the RTI Lab, Fury squatted behind a filing cabinet full of actual paper files. He was glad to have it. Not many bullets could find their way through a solid foot of paper with sheet metal on either side. He popped a magazine and reloaded. "Pepper," he said. "Any way you can talk to Tony?"

"I don't know." She had been poking away at the touch screen every second that the inside of the testing area wasn't a live firing range. Right now it seemed like Rhodey and the boys outside had the upper hand, but something was playing hell with the local comm channels, and Fury couldn't be sure of anything. "I've been trying, but something weird happened when all of the security routines mashed up with the virus and then the instant control system tried to synthesize it all. I ping messages out to Tony, and sometimes they bounce, and sometimes they just disappear. So I don't know whether he's trying to get back in touch."

There was a bang on the roof. Then three more in quick succession. Fury lay flat on his back, looking for any telltale that would disclose the location of HYDRA soldiers. He could hear plenty of footsteps, but the acoustics in the testing area didn't lend themselves to pinpointing specific positions.

One of the soldiers holed up underneath a rack of old Iron Man suits ripped off a long burst through the roof above him. The echoes made it impossible to tell if he'd hit anything. Long seconds passed, with more shuffling footsteps from above . . . then Fury saw one of the corrugated metal panels near the center of the ceiling flex. He hosed the whole area down, burning a whole magazine and immediately replacing it. Through some of the holes in the ceiling, he could see the sickly pink-orange of sodium-arc streetlights. Others were blocked. Got you that time, Fury thought.

"Pepper," he said. "Tell Tony that if he wants to come home and power up the suit, now's a good time."

Over by the loading-dock door, Arnim Zola's body lay inert. Fury had no way of knowing whether Zola's boast about being able to jump instantaneously to another body was true, but he knew Zola had swapped bodies in other circumstances. Best to figure that they weren't done with that particular head of HYDRA just yet. Or, for that matter, the tall thin Zola clone. Where had it gone?

"Clear the roof," Fury said over the open channel. The lab exploded for a full minute. When it was over, the roof was polka-dotted with pink-lit holes, and a thousand narrow shafts of streetlight fell down toward the floor. There were no more sounds of motion.

"Looks like the inside of a club I used to go to," commented one of the soldiers.

Another agreed. "I think I know that place," said a third.

Fury cut in. "What's the count?" Personnel on the testing floor counted off. "Twenty-seven," came the final number from the sergeant-major. "Thirty including you, sir. Thirty-one with the young lady."

Not bad, Fury thought. They'd started with thirty-four— thirty-six with him and Pepper, who hadn't fired a gun yet but would if the need arose. "Pepper," he said. "Anything new?"

"Nothing good," she said. "I'm getting two pingbacks from Tony, but they're different. I think the clone got bounced up there, too. Or in there. However you say it."

Only when a situation like this involved Tony Stark was it guaranteed to get worse, Fury thought. "There's no way to tell them apart, I'm guessing."

"Not right now. I'm trying to figure something out," Pepper said. "But the other thing is that the PDM has an automatic recall. It can bring Tony back."

"Then what are you waiting for?" Fury said. "Bring him back."

"You don't think I already would have, Nick?" Pepper snapped. "Tony's the only person who can give the command."

Fury thought this over. Outside, fresh volleys of gunfire tore through the parking lot and punched holes through the lab walls. "Rhodey," he said over the comm.

"Holding steady," came the reply. "I'm starting to get the feeling that they're just pinning us down here. They sure don't fight like we killed their officers."

Which brought Fury right back around to the problem of Arnim Zola. "Keep holding steady," he said. Then he shuffled around so he could see Pepper. "So we have to keep the PDM working until Tony calls in the return. If Tony can call in the return."

"That's about the size of it," Pepper said.

Against the HYDRA clones outside, Fury figured they could hold out more or less indefinitely. But if Zola was up to something wherever he'd stashed his new body, Fury envisioned unwelcome complications. It was time to make the hard decision, the one that nobody ever wanted to hear about but everybody benefited from when someone else had to make it. He opened Hailey's channel and prepared to give the orders.

xxvi.

What an enjoyable irony this is. I cut you off when you were head of HYDRA, and now you have grown back eightfold. Do you not know whereof I speak? Do you not know that your original died at my hands? It is true. HYDRA had grown beyond her, and needed a firmer hand, a more powerful vision. I rose to the occasion. And now the transformation of HYDRA takes its next step. I welcome you eight, where I confess I never could have tolerated you as only one. Is there not greater virtue in uniformity? Individuality leads to conflict, and conflict to chaos and death. You, you eight, will fight as one more effectively than your original ever could have. She was forever at odds with herself. You have a unity of purpose given by your knowledge that there are seven others like you. Is this not the perfection of the ideal of HYDRA? A head cut off grows back and multiplies. HYDRA is stronger than ever before. I, too, have been cut off, and I have grown back, and am stronger than ever before. Come with me, my Demoiselles. Let us see you fight. Let us see you seize your legacy. Let us see you earn the name of HYDRA!

The jailbird realized its name was Tony. Tony Stark. There was another Tony Stark, too, and the jailbird knew that it—he—had to confront and destroy this other Tony Stark if he was ever going to escape out of this bigger jail back to wherever it was he had come from.

He walked out the door onto a dusty wooden porch. Wherever he was, it looked like nobody had lived there in a long time. A set of footprints struck out across the ground in the general direction of the lights. They belonged to the other Tony Stark. As his identity started to fall into place, Tony realized he needed a name for this other Tony. He decided that Virtual Tony was okay as a placeholder, and that since Virtual Tony wasn't going to live long enough to need a real name, a placeholder would do the trick.

So, off toward the lights. Virtual Tony had to die before . . . Zola, that was his name. Before Zola could . . . what . . .

Tony couldn't come up with it all at once. So he started walking.

Sometimes things would appear around him. There seemed to be an endless number of train tracks, heading in every direction, including up and down. Sometimes there were trains, drawn by bold black steam locomotives with indescribable things dangling in their cowcatchers. Other trains passed, too: gleaming maglevs a thousand cars long, filled with Disney characters or comic-book supervillains or members of the 1984 Detroit Tigers. The ground itself usually wasn't ground. Tony's feet walked on it, and it supported his weight, but nothing grew there—until, at the thought, vegetation curled up from his footprints, rearing over his head in an riot of petal and vine. Was he controlling this? Tree, he thought.

An oak, big enough that five men linking hands would not have reached around its trunk, crackled and boomed up in front of him. Its leaves fell, and acorns bounced and rattled on the ground. "Aha," Tony said. Now the question was: Who else was controlling this environment? And where was he going to find Virtual Tony?

The lights were no closer.

Maybe Virtual Tony had already gotten to them, and it was because of him that they came no closer. Maybe all Tony had to do was will himself there, and he would be there. To the lights, he thought. Nothing happened. Acorns fell.

He realized that someone was walking next to him. An

ill-formed human shape, gangly and stooped. "You're not from around here," it said. Tony couldn't form a clear impression of its face, but the voice sounded male.

"No," Tony said. "I'm here to, ah, kill the other Tony."

"So you're the Tony."

"Right." It sounded right.

"Why do you need to kill the other Tony?" They shambled along together. Things happened in Tony's peripheral vision, but he ignored them. Civilizations could be rising and falling in the time it took his heart to beat twice. Hey, he thought. One thing about this place is no heart trouble.

His companion repeated the question. "Oh," Tony said. "Because of Zola."

"Why because of Zola?"

"Because if I don't kill the other Tony and . . ." The rest of the answer hovered just beyond his ability to articulate it.

"You need to get back to the world, sounds like," his companion said.

Tony nodded. "I do. Because if I don't, Zola will . . ."

He still couldn't get it. The companion didn't seem to mind. "I knew Zola," it said.

"Knew him how?" Tony asked.

"Was him, once," the companion said. "He throws off selves like snakes shed skins."

"So what does he want in here? Or out here," Tony said.

The companion walked for a while without answering. Tony let it think. They didn't seem to be getting any closer to the lights. "Probably has to do with the virus," the companion said.

"Because if I don't kill Virtual Tony and get back," Tony said as if it was being dictated to him, "Zola will take control of the virus."

That was it. The virus had carried Tony and Virtual Tony here. Zola could control it. If he controlled it, then the virus, which had infected the instant control system, would . . .

"How do you control a virus?" the companion wanted to know.

"He wouldn't," Tony said. "He would control me."

A chill ran down his spine, just as if he had a body. Zola would turn Tony into an artificial intelligence. Remake him into something posthuman and alien. Redesign him as the presiding spirit that could, via instant control, turn every networked machine in the world into an eye or an ear or a fist.

"No, sir," Tony said. "I like the real world a little too much."

He walked faster. The companion struggled to keep up, but after a while it fell behind. It never asked Tony to slow down.

"Hailey." Fury's voice popped in her ear.

"Copy, General Fury."

"New information on this end. Be on the lookout for another Arnim Zola. If you see him, he becomes your primary objective. Put him down for good. Search the building for any potential bodies he might jump to, and put them down, too."

"Copy."

"No living bodies in that building, Hailey. Search and destroy."

"Understood, General." To the team, Hailey said, "New orders. This building is now a free-fire zone. You all have pictures of Serena Borland. She is to be treated as a recoverable asset. Everything else goes down."

Silence among the team. They were SHIELD soldiers who had been around the block a time or two, but even for them, a take-no-prisoners execution order was uncommon. "This is how we defend the Republic, people," Hailey said. "Charlie, you're split between Alpha and Bravo. Two teams, one for each hall. Alpha straight, Bravo left. Move out."

Alpha's first action came the minute all nine members of the team had cleared the elevator lobby. Two doors that faced each other in the corridor just ahead of them opened and four Happy Hogans popped out: two high, two low, all four firing. Alpha played it by the book, getting low, hitting the walls, and firing at angles into the doorways. Two of them didn't get up as the other seven split to crash the doorways, riddling anything that moved. In seconds, it was over. Nine Hogans were down and six of the seven ambulatory members of Alpha were clearing the two rooms, which were barracks. The seventh, Alpha's combat medic, was doing what he could with the casualties. Hailey counted sixty bunks, confirmed the same count in the facing barracks, and stepped back out into the hall just as the medic was standing up. "No good, Major," he said. "They were dead when I got to them."

She nodded and gathered the team. There was still a good fifty yards of corridor to cover.

Bravo did not contact the enemy until making the first angle in the corridor. One of the Hogans got an itchy trigger finger at exactly the wrong time, squeezing off a burst when Bravo's point man got close enough to the corner for his helmet light to cast shadows. The point man bowled a grenade down the hall, waited for the blast, then came around the corner on his belly as three men right behind him stepped out to lay down a waist-high covering fire. The grenade had four Hogans down and a fifth leaning dazed against the wall; the initial volley from Bravo's point doubled him over and took him down.

On down the hall, they found four empty barracks. "Smooth over here so far, Major," the team leader said. He'd

heard the exchange of fire from the other end of the basement. "Your end?"

"Two down," Major Donner said. "Keep it tight."

Team Alpha was the first to bang down the door into
Lantier's sanctum. Lantier, knowing the intrusion was coming, had prepared his defenses in the only way he could. He
jammed their electronics, he prepared a series of personal
defenses designed specifically to be employed by someone
with his particular physical configurations, and he initialized a number of system routines designed to confuse and
delay their operations. Then he held perfectly still, listening
through the building's systems and saying over and over to
himself, "Right on schedule. Timetable doesn't lie. Timetable
doesn't lie."

When Alpha kicked in the door, every speaker in the
room shrieked at volumes calculated to be damaging to the
human ear. Strobe lights flared and stuttered. The team
hosed down the interior of the room, blowing out terminal
displays and light fixtures and silencing most of the speakers. Two men leapfrogged into the room. Neither of them
noticed Lantier; in the dim light he looked to be a tangle of
cables and junctions. Sparks jumped from severed cables
on the back of his chair, which Zola had armored as protection against the possibility that Maheu would attempt a
coup. Both of them passed within arm's reach, on either
side of him, and before the men covering from the doorway
could say anything, Lantier had reached out with the
scalpels he used for delicate operations on designated
clones and slashed through the soft spot at the hip joints of
their body armor.

Both men went down screaming, with blood pumping
out from severed arteries. The soldiers in the doorway reacted as quickly as any human could have, stepping around
into the room and blasting Lantier into cybernetically

enhanced hamburger. The fire team's medic, working by flashlight, took one look at the damage and knew he didn't have a chance to save either of his comrades. Still, he tried, and fire team Alpha lost three minutes watching two more of its number die.

Bravo turned a corner and found themselves in a space that reminded some of its older members of a video arcade. Off a central hall, dozens of cubicles lined the walls. The light coming from each was a fluorescent violet that reminded some of them of aquarium lighting and others of certain lighting elements in their college dorms. "In pairs," Bravo leader said quietly. They moved forward and swept around the doors of the first pair of cubicles.

In each was a Hogan, mouth slightly open and eyes closed. Electrodes and wires swathed their heads, and they were naked save for diapers. "Diapers," one of the commandos said with disgust.

"Good thing Happy isn't here to see this," commented another. He prodded the Hogan in the chest with the barrel of his rifle. It didn't respond. Next to it, a computer terminal scrolled and spooled an endless series of images, data, and strange colored patterns that put them in mind of weather fronts.

"You two," Bravo leader said quietly. "Scope to the far end of the room and cover that door."

The two commandos leapfrogged down the room to the far end. "I count fifty on each side," one of them said. "All full but the last eight."

"Any of them look like Serena Borland to you?" Bravo leader said.

"No, sir. Wish they had. But it was Hogans all the way down."

"Then Bravo team, you have your orders."

*   *   *

Hailey heard the sustained firing from the other end of the basement, muffled as if the sound was traveling through walls instead of down a hallway. There was a rhythm to it. It didn't sound like combat firing. It sounded more like . . .

"Bravo leader," she said.

"Copy, Major."

"Advise your current action."

"Forty-two Hogans located, Major. In some kind of hypnosis, with cables in their heads. Per your orders we are liquidating them." Bravo's voice was tight.

You mean General Fury's orders, Hailey wanted to say. But that would have been a cop-out. She had neither contested them nor delayed in their transmission. She was complicit. She had to trust that General Fury knew what he was doing.

"Copy, Bravo leader. Continue your sweep," she said. A couple of minutes later her team got to perform their own massacre when they discovered Arnim Zola's closet full of spare bodies.

"Well, there's confirmation that Zola found himself a new body," Fury said. "You have any luck raising Tony?"

"No," Pepper said. "Quit asking me. I'll tell you if I do."

Fury's comm popped and Rhodey said, "We sure could use a little air support out here. Plus, wouldn't you think the local cops, or the National Guard would have showed up by now?"

"You missed the briefing because you were at the hospital," Fury reminded him. "I told the cops and the Guard to stay away, I talked to the Joint Chiefs, I talked to everybody. They're all going to pretend this isn't happening, and when it's over, nobody's ever going to say anything about it. Far as air support goes, that's been vetoed because of what happened to those choppers."

"But Zola's not around," Rhodey said. In the background, a burst of rifle fire overwhelmed the comm's equalizer.

"If he's not back yet, he will be," Fury said. "Whatever Tony did to keep him from using the mind control, it doesn't work more than a couple hundred yards from the building. So you stick tight, and don't go wishing brainwashed suicide on perfectly good helicopter pilots."

xxvii.

PROVISIONAL APPLICATION FOR PATENT

TITLE
  Hologram generator, suit-borne

DESCRIPTION
  An internal projection system, coupled to the uni-beam (cf. Stark Industries patents [redacted], [redacted], et al.), capable of creating three-dimensional images of sufficient resolution to confuse the human eye. Linked to suit-borne communications systems, the hologram generator can project images of persons and objects in other locations, immensely improving battlefield communications. It can also create illusory copies of the Stark Industries personal body armor product for purposes of instilling fear and confusion among enemy forces.

CLAIM
  The projection of illusions has been an important element of tactical battlefield planning since Macbeth's enemies disguised themselves as Birnam Wood before their assault on Dunsinane. The hologram generator developed for use in Stark Industries personal body armor products has the capability to project up to three images, depending on lensing configurations. The potential increase in enemy confusion due to the perception of increased force strength is a highly desirable achievement in a battlefield situation. Existing hologram technologies require bulky and cumbersome projectors; Stark Industries' suit-borne application vastly increases the number of possible situational uses.

SECURITY STATUS

Project undertaken under the auspices of Stark Industries agreements with the Department of Defense, SHIELD, and other governmental agencies outlined in Senate Amdt. [redacted] to Senate Amdt. [redacted] to H.R. [redacted] (110th). Technology is proprietary to Stark Industries but will be shared fully with all eligible entities. Technology is classified and will not be licensed until such time as classification order is rescinded.

Tony had been walking for a long time, but his feet weren't tired. He had to look down every so often to reassure himself that he still had feet. The lights were no closer. "Car," he said. His mind must have been in the wrong place, because what appeared was a 1937 Oldsmobile Six. It was a big, beautiful touring sedan, but when he looked in the window, Raymond Burr said, "What the hell are you doing? Get your hands off my car before I kick your ass."

Tony stood up away from the car and it drove away. *Perry Mason,* he thought. *That's where I used to see that car.*

He needed to get a grip on what to do. *Fact,* he thought. *I am Tony Stark. I have been somehow uploaded using my own Personality Data Matrix routine, but instead of staying in the server space at the RTI Lab, somehow my matrix has gotten out into the world. By which I mean the virtual world. Fact: There is another Tony Stark here. That must be the clone that Zola brought. Its personality has also been vacuumed up here. Or in here.*

"In here, is what we usually say." Startled, Tony looked over to see the companion, walking beside him as if they had never been separated. "And yes, you're right so far. Pepper's looking for you, you know."

"How do you . . . are you in touch with . . ."

"Out There? Meatspace? The Four Dimensions?" The companion laughed. "Sure. Everywhere you look you can find out all you need to know about Out There. But the important thing for you to know is what you can do in here. Or else you're going to be stuck. I don't think you want to be stuck."

"No, I sure as hell don't," Tony said. "Why do you care?"

" 'Care' might be the wrong word."

They walked in silence for a while after that. Tony thought the lights might be getting a little closer. "Look at it this way," the companion said. "You can find everything on the Internet, right?"

"That's what people say."

"Well, turn that around. If you're in here, you can find out anything about the Four-D if you know where to look."

In a through-the-looking-glass way, this made sense. "Okay," Tony said. "So if I wanted to talk to Pepper, how would I do it?"

"Beats me," the companion said. "Your protocols are all different than mine. You come in here on new code, infected with other new code that believe me, nobody in here wants to get near, and there's another one of you with some of the new code stuck to him, too. You're going to have trouble finding anyone to tell you anything. Only reason I am is because I know the code you're carrying. I wrote part of it, long time ago." It laughed softly. "Time."

"How long ago were you Zola?" Tony asked.

"Time," the companion said again. "Long time ago. When he first started trying to take mind patterns. He lost me, and here I am."

"I've got some other code stuck on me, too, right?" Tony asked. "The instant control code."

"Different," the companion said. "It's all mashed together. Maybe not in the Four-D, but here. I can't tell all of it apart."

"I need to find the other Tony Stark," Tony said. "Do you know where he is?"

"I'm talking to him right now. I mean, too. It can work like that if you want it to and you know how."

"What does he have to say?"

"He's telling me to erase you," the companion said. "Don't think I will, though. The show's too good. Keep going in this direction. The lights might not look like they're getting any closer, but they are. Virtual Tony—that's what you call him, right?"

Tony nodded. "Yeah."

"You'll find him when you get there. He's trying to talk to Pepper, too. I'll catch you later," the companion said, and started to fall behind again. Tony tried to walk more slowly, but the companion receded until its outline started to blend into the colorless space all around them.

Hailey never would have believed such a thing could exist if she had only heard about it from someone else. It belonged in a movie, or the indigestion-fueled nightmares of a conspiracy nut. The door they'd opened clanged off a railing that surrounded a small balcony. From the balcony, a set of steel stairs led down along the wall to the floor of a room that measured perhaps one hundred feet long by sixty wide. In four rows, tanks similar in shape to the clone tanks up on the main floor extended from just below the balcony to the darkness at the far wall. They were eight or nine feet tall and four feet in diameter, much larger than the upstairs variety.

One of them was empty.

Hailey raised General Fury. "General, I believe we've found where Zola keeps his bodies. And I have reason to believe that he's made the switch to a new one. We've got one empty tank here, and wet footprints leading away from it."

"Understood, Hailey. Appreciate the info, although I can't say I'm glad to hear it. Orders are unchanged."

"Copy, sir."

"Over and out," Fury said, and the pop of the disconnection seemed to echo from Hailey's earbud out into the space of the room.

"Alpha team," she said. "We are to clear this room. That means that when we are done, the tanks are open and non-functional, and the same goes for the bodies inside them. Am I understood?"

To a chorus of *yes, ma'am,* she started down the stairs.

The first few were easy because they didn't look human. Bodies with four arms, bodies with two heads—one of which was an array like Zola's ESP Box that she'd seen in briefing images. Bodies wearing armor plating, with eyes like the armored eyes of a dinosaur fish she'd seen once in the natural history museum. It was harder than she had expected to make sure the tanks were permanently disabled; the displays kept on blinking and the ready lights on the conduits leading into the tops of the tanks stayed green even after a surprising number of bullets had chewed through the appropriate parts of the setup. In the end, Hailey had to order Alpha team to manually open each tank and pull each body out. It took the five members of the team nearly twenty minutes, and all of them were soaked to the skin with the faintly organic-smelling pinkish fluid that all of the bodies had been soaking in.

"Bruce Springsteen," one of the team was saying. "Can you believe that?"

"I saw Nelson Mandela. How the hell do you get hold of Nelson Mandela's DNA?"

"Or Nancy Pelosi's."

"Okay, boys," Hailey said. "We're going to make the bodies nonfunctional, just like the general wants. Then we're going to seed this room. Share the bubble gum and let's get it done."

It took a lot less time to shoot lethal holes in the bodies than it would have to wreck the tanks. When they were finished, Hailey pinged Bravo to let them know that there was one more room to check, and then they'd likely be running into one another.

There was no answer.

"Bravo leader, come in," she said again. "Do you copy?"

Silence.

Maybe it was the room. "We're seeded, Major," one of the team said. "Time to head out?"

"It sure is," Hailey said. But when they got back out into the hallway, there was still no response from Bravo leader or any of his team.

"Have you met the Eight Demoiselles?" Zola asked.

"I have not had the pleasure," Serena said. They both listened to the rhythmic gunfire coming from some other part of the basement.

"I believe those SHIELD commandos are transgressing against the laws of warfare by killing innocent—not to mention unconscious—clones. Of Happy Hogan," Zola said.

A few minutes later, when gunfire sounded from the other direction, but nearer, Zola said, "And that will be the rest of the bodies I have created for myself. Are you sure, Miss Borland, that you want to be associated with people who will murder in cold blood?"

"I don't want to argue ethics with you, or choose sides. I want to go," Serena said. "I don't want to play games, or have witty conversations with you. I want to go. If you're not going to let me go, kill me. If you are going to let me go, quit talking about it and do it."

"Quite," Zola said. "But it isn't safe for you out there right now. If one of those SHIELD commandos saw you, it's entirely possible he would mistake you for a clone, would he not? And if they're shooting unconscious or partially constructed clones, they will certainly shoot one moving as vitally and decisively as I imagine you would be."

He had her there. Serena looked around the room, just to do something other than look at Zola. His previous body had been ridiculous enough that she couldn't really fear him, despite knowing some of the things he had done. This new body, though ... anyone who wasn't scared of it would be an idiot. Seven feet tall, with what looked like some kind of flexible matte-black steel sheathing over muscles that would do a professional wrestler proud, and all kinds of lethal-looking mechanical enhancements. Sockets and hinges and spiny antennae everywhere.

Because she was so scared, she said, "I take it back about Frankenstein. You look a little more like Johnny Sokko's flying robot. Do you shoot rockets out of your elbows?"

"I think you should meet the Eight Demoiselles," Zola said, ignoring her sally. "They ought to just about be done with their first mission."

Part of the wall at the back of Serena's cell slid open and eight clones entered. They were lithe and athletic, dressed in emerald-green bodysuits with prominent HYDRA logos in black across the breast. Their hair was also black, waving down to their shoulders and held back from their faces by green headbands. They wore swords on their left hips, hanging from black belts dotted with small pockets and pouches. "Meet the Eight Demoiselles," Zola said, and that was when Serena noticed that each of them carried in her right hand a severed head.

"As I believe I just mentioned, they have completed their first mission. It appears to have been a success. Congratulations, Demoiselles. You do your original proud, and in fact surpass her." Zola stood and executed a courtly bow. "Please. Relieve yourselves of your burdens."

The Eight Demoiselles put the heads down in a neat double row on the writing desk. Serena shoved her chair back and scrambled away to the edge of her bed, where she stood shaking all over. "No witty commentary?" Zola needled. "I may have overestimated your equanimity in the face of the unexpected."

Serena could not find words. The gunfire continued a few rooms over, it sounded like. "I believe you've met one half of the SHIELD team assigned to rescue you from your predicament," Zola said, gesturing toward the eight heads. "The others will be along shortly."

Don't, Serena wanted to say. But she knew it wouldn't do any good, and she wouldn't give him the pleasure of seeing her beg for something both of them knew he would refuse. *Tony,* she thought. *Where are you?*

xxviii.

I am coming to you, HYDRA. Because I can fly, and because I have dispatched the SHIELD forces sent to destroy us before we could take flight. I come with the Eight Demoiselles, now seven because—as we must always remember—SHIELD is a worthy adversary. Worthy in the battle, and worthy in the dispatch. Worthy in the memory of the battlefield. I fly to you, my soldiers! Behind us, flames; before us, the world! Hold fast and know that the change I bring is irreversible, that when I arrive all will transform, the elements and atoms of the world will no longer know their places unless I tell them. You are holding SHIELD pinned down like rats. Trap them! Hold them! The coup de grace approaches. I fly with the Demoiselles, and when we land, HYDRA will take wing. You have fought bravely, and proved yourself worthy of the world to come. Remain strong. You are HYDRA! You were born to be HYDRA! You must fight like HYDRA! Victory is minutes away! In my new body I bring forth the new world. I will meet Tony Stark in his coward's shell and upon his body I will prove the superiority of the order we now germinate. We are HYDRA!

The first words out of Happy's mouth when he woke up enough to start talking were, "Where's Pepper?"

The doctor was right there. "We'll find her for you, Happy."

"She's not here?" Happy couldn't believe it.

"Well, there's a bit of an incident out at the Stark RTI Lab," Dr. Singh said. "She was required there."

"HYDRA," Happy said. He started to get up.

Dr. Singh dropped his comforting bedside manner. "Mr. Hogan. Under no circumstances are you to get out of this bed. You have nearly died a number of times in the past twenty-four hours, and it is not at all certain that you are 'out of the woods'—to employ a colloquialism I despise."

Happy glared at the doctor, then realized it wasn't going to do any good to argue. "Okay, Doc," he said. "Just find her for me. Where's my phone? Can I call her?"

"I will look into it," Dr. Singh said. "You will wait here until I return."

"You're the doctor," Happy said.

When the door shut behind Dr. Singh, Happy took an inventory of himself. He felt like a stepped-in dog turd. There was water by the bed. He drank it slowly before looking at the labels on the IV bottle dripping into his arm. It said saline, but there was a shunt in the line, which meant they'd been sticking something else into him. He wiggled his toes, flexed his fingers. He had to take a piss.

Aha. There was an excuse to get out of bed. Happy swung his legs over the side of the bed, rode out the initial wave of dizziness, then planted his feet on the floor. Not much had changed while he was out; hospital floors were still freezing cold. He tested his weight on his feet and felt another spell of dizziness come and go. Not too bad. Once he'd removed the IV and done his thing in the bathroom, he came back out. What he really needed was a cheeseburger and a half-hour in the gym, he thought. If he'd been close to dying, the doctors were miracle workers.

Dr. Singh came back in while Happy was putting his clothes on. He'd found them, washed and ironed, in the closet. Even his gun was still there. That was one good thing about being in a SHIELD hospital, he supposed.

"I cannot permit you to leave," Dr. Singh said.

Happy finished tying his shoes before answering. Then he stood up, checked the load in the Hi-Power, and said, "Doc.

My girl is in trouble. I don't feel my best, but if I'm not there and something happens to her, I'll never be able to live with myself. Now we can fight about this, or you can watch me walk out the door and tell yourself that you did everything you could. It'll be the truth."

Dr. Singh didn't say anything. He also didn't get out of the doorway.

Happy tried again. "Doc. I'm going out that door. What would happen if your girl was in trouble and someone tried to keep you from getting to her?"

Still Dr. Singh didn't say anything. Happy had nearly re-signed himself to carrying the doc out of the hospital with him when Dr. Singh opened the door and said, "You are a grand romantic fool, Mr. Hogan. But no doctor can cure that."

"Thanks, Doc," Happy said on the way out. Now, he thought to himself. If that spiel would only work on the gunnery sergeant in charge of the copter pool . . .

Tony found the railroad tracks again and started walking. The avatars thinned out, and soon enough he was alone. Far behind him he heard a train whistle. He stepped off the tracks and walked on the embankment. The whistle sounded again, closer. The rumble and hiss of the train wasn't Dopplering quite like he would have expected it to; when he turned to look, he saw that the train was coming to a halt.

The locomotive was an old double-cab G-4e, manufactured by Schenectady Locomotive Works in the 1860s. Tony knew this without having to ask. Like the companion had said, everything was in here. Sometimes it came to you, sometimes you had to go looking for it.

Leaning out of the cab, the conductor looked down. "You'll get where you're going if I give you a ride. Nobody knows these parts like I do."

"Is that right?" Tony said. He wasn't inclined to trust good fortune right then.

The conductor nodded. "It is. 'Course, if you'd rather walk, I can't stop you. You, diamond hustler! Fire 'er up and let's head 'er out!" he barked back into the depths of the locomotive. The train started to ease forward.

Tony started moving to keep pace with it. "Guess I'll take you up on your offer. No point walking when you can ride, right?"

"You got it," the conductor said. "They call me Lantier. You're Tony Stark, right?"

"How do you know?" Tony looked left and right. He was going to have to decide soon whether to jump on the train or let it go.

"I know because Zola always wanted me to know. I was him, once. Then I was Lantier. Now I'm just free. You want that ride or not?"

Strange bedfellows, Tony was thinking, but he got a running start and jumped up onto the running board below the locomotive's door. "All aboard!" Lantier called out, and the train shuddered and accelerated forward toward the distant gleam of lights.

"I just talked to someone else who said he used to be Zola. How many of you are there?" Tony asked.

"Who knows?" Lantier said. "He made us, tinkered with us, discarded us. *He* doesn't even know. Any wino you see in the street could have been a Zola at some point."

"Fair enough." Tony debated whether to ask his next question, then decided he didn't have much to lose. He was still learning how things worked here. "Why are you helping me?"

"Don't know if I am," Lantier said without missing a beat. Then he didn't say anything else, and wouldn't say anything else, until they reached the outskirts of the lights.

As they drew closer, Tony started to be able to pick out details. There were buildings, walls, borders. There were people who weren't always people. This is where the avatars live, he thought.

"All of us, all of these ghosts and bits of old code, avatars and applets, we churn around in here," Lantier said. "I've been doing it for years, even when I was alive. I left traces of my Zola-self here. And my Lantier-self. And others. Did you meet the skinny guy who likes to walk?"

"Yeah, I did," Tony said.

"Another self of mine. Of Zola's. Same thing, since I'm a clone of Zola. Or is it? Hell, I don't know. Do you think your clone has the same self as you?"

"No," Tony said.

"See, but you think about it differently because you're the original. I think Zola, the first Zola, thinks the same way. Me, since I'm second-generation—and modified a little to boot, both thanks to Zola and thanks to my own investigations when he wasn't looking—me, I'm different. I think I have a self, and that it's mine, and that I'm as entitled to call myself Zola as Zola is. I mean, who gives a shit whether he made me. If one of your nanobot replicators makes another one, is one of them better than the other because it came first?"

"Spare me," Tony said. "Replicators and people are different."

"Not in here, they're not," Lantier said.

They rattled along the tracks. The lights were getting closer. Periodically Lantier blew the horn to scatter cows from the tracks. Once every cow in the herd was standing on its hind legs and brandishing what looked like medieval polearms. "Video game leakage," Lantier said. "We got lots of lost heroes in here, too."

Turning to Tony, Lantier added, "You might be one."

"Me?" Tony said. "I'm real."

Lantier laughed. He laughed loud and long, and the sound modulated from a bass profundo worthy of the guy in the 7-UP commercials Tony had seen when he was younger to a tittering giggle that made him want to exterminate all adolescents. When he was done, Lantier said, "You're only real when you're not here. And since you're here, you're not real. You have a body back in the Four-D that's real, sure. If you don't get back to it, though . . ." He shrugged.

"I can get back to it," Tony said.

"How?"

"I just have to call in the PDM's extraction routine."

"Then you better do it. You were thinking this earlier, son, and you were right. This is the rabbit hole. Things don't stay the same in here. Call it in, and start the clock."

"That's the thing," Tony said. "What if I run out of time?"

"Time? Time?" Lantier started laughing again. Before he got carried away, he caught himself. "Time's plastic in here. Depends on bandwidth, depends on server farms. Depends on too many things. You call it in, tell your routine back in the Four-D that you want to come home in X or Y number of minutes. That don't mean a thing in here."

Tony tapped on the windowsill next to his seat in the cab. "Good to know."

"Sure, maybe," Lantier said. "But it's not always good. You could think it was a thousand years before ten minutes passes in the Four-D. Or it could be about to happen right now because you thought about it. That's the thing. You don't know." He shrugged. A lit cigar appeared in his mouth, and he chewed on it and puffed like the boiler above and behind him. "A little uncertainty adds spice to life. My last act in the Four-D, I killed two SHIELD commandos."

"You're telling me this why?" Tony asked.

"Because it doesn't matter to me. When I was a person, it might have mattered. But Zola took that away from me a long time ago. I'm giving it to you straight because I don't care whether you get what you want. Mostly what I care about, just because I was recently a meat form of life and still remember the emotions, mostly what I care about is that Zola get back a little bit of the hard time he gave me. So there you have it."

Lantier fell silent. Tony had nothing to add. He thought about two dead SHIELD commandos, and how he might have done things differently so they didn't have to die in a chocolate factory. The train chuffed and whistled along toward the lights. They were definitely closer. Things came out of the darkness and died on the cowcatcher. They didn't seem to mind.

xxix.

PROVISIONAL APPLICATION FOR PATENT

TITLE
  Broad-spectrum signal interruptor

DESCRIPTION
  Anti-communication system integrated with satellite and battle-field command-and-control. Intelligently targets and disrupts frequencies determined to be originating from enemy sources by targeting bursts of noise at the source of communications whose interruption is desired rather than broadcasting a higher wattage of noise along channels used by hostile elements. Ignores broadcasts, even those along the same frequencies, that bear encryption of friendly sources or otherwise signify friendly origin.

CLAIM
  Existing technologies for jamming enemy communications are often double-edged swords due to their lack of selectivity. Frequency-based jamming technologies bleed into nearby frequencies, too often compromising friendly communications and making the net benefit of jamming activities practically zero. Stark Industries' Broad-Spectrum Signal Interruptor (BSSI) is a point-source jamming technology capable of narrowly focused broadcast interruption with minimal frequency drift and high target selectivity. As integrated into Stark Industries personal body armor products, the BSSI turns every soldier into a battle-field communications interruptor, vastly multiplying difficulties in enemy tactical coordination.

SECURITY STATUS

Project undertaken under the auspices of Stark Industries agreements with the Department of Defense, SHIELD, and other governmental agencies outlined in Senate Amdt. [redacted] to Senate Amdt. [redacted] to H.R. [redacted] (110th). Technology is proprietary to Stark Industries but will be shared fully with all eligible entities. Technology is classified and will not be licensed until such time as classification order is rescinded.

It was oh two hundred hours, and Nick Fury wasn't as young as he used to be. He yawned. "Take a nap, Nick," Pepper said. "No reason to ruin your beauty sleep."

There had been a lull for the past ten minutes or so. Fury imagined the HYDRA forces passing around full magazines, grabbing a drink of water, coordinating their next moves with whatever command structure they had. Where was Zola? He was out there, he must be coming. "Nothing could make me more beautiful than I am, Miss Potts," he said.

"They must have figured it out by now," she said.

"What's that?"

"That if they can wreck this terminal, they can stop Tony from getting back." Pepper kept her voice level, but Fury had been a leader of men and women for long enough that he could detect the wires of tension that held her tight.

"Maybe not," he said. "They sure seem happy to keep us pinned down until Zola gets back with his new body."

"Why isn't SHIELD letting you call in air?" she asked. "You know he's not here, we all know he's not here. Three copters could settle the whole thing."

Fury found a cigar in his shirt pocket. He patted his pockets for a light, but couldn't find one. "And then we'd have to chase down Zola all over again," he said. "This isn't the first time I've been bait. Maybe it's yours. It doesn't feel good, but sometimes it's the best thing."

"Tony's the bait," Pepper said. "That's what will bring Zola back here. He doesn't care about any of the rest of it."

The touch screen in front of her pinged and she jumped. She tapped a blinking icon and stared at the screen for a long moment. "Happy left the hospital," she said. "The doctor thinks he's coming here."

Both of them knew that if Happy was coming, it would be by air, and both of them remembered the sound of the helicopters hitting the ground around midnight. "Can you get in touch with him?" Fury asked.

She already had her phone out. As she was dialing it, Fury heard a car start out in the back parking lot. He signaled to the soldier nearest one of the back windows to peek out and see what was happening. With an angled mirror, the soldier did, and said, "Uh-oh. Looks like—"

The engine revved up to a redline scream, and a few seconds later a big Ford pickup barreled into the loading bay at an angle, crashing into one edge of the door frame. The door sagged on its buckling tracks, and the pickup stalled there as Fury and anyone else with a clear line of fire lit up the cab with full-auto volleys that blew the driver right out the passenger door. Smoke curled from under the truck's crumpled hood and fluids dripped from its engine compartment. "Gonna stink in here real fast if that thing starts burning," Fury muttered.

Three rifle barrels appeared over the edge of the pickup's bed. As the SHIELD defenders adjusted their focus, incoming fire raked across the testing floor. Equipment blew apart in the blind fusillade. At the far end of the room, the superannuated Iron Man suits swayed on their hangers as bullets deflected off them. Two commandos came around the side of the control terminal area for a better firing angle. They bellied down and riddled the truck bed. Over the sound of the volley came the bang of the truck's tailgate slamming down. The shooting stopped. The truck sat on flat tires, leaking and smoking . . . and there was a trickle of clear fluid from under the bed. Fury could already smell the gas.

I guess I know what comes next, he thought.

He was right. Rolling into view from the edge of the doorway, between the truck's rear tires, came a small metal cylinder. Three, two, one . . .

"Down!" Fury shouted. He ducked his head as the incendiary went off, and the gas tank went with it.

"Before the SHIELD soldiers killed me and I got in here for good," Lantier said unexpectedly, "I always thought I'd just be looking at this from the outside. No way Zola would have ever let me stay here. I used to come and visit, sure, but then he'd drag me out. I was useful to him. Maheu, his other clone, the sourpuss. He never liked me. I think he'd just as soon have killed me."

"SHIELD soldiers, huh?" Tony prompted.

"They were shooting the hell out of the place looking for the woman," Lantier said. The train started to slow down. Tony was watching, leaning out his window and seeing the tracks come into existence as the approach of the train dictated. A turnabout appeared, and the train eased to a stop exactly on it.

"Did they get the woman out?" he asked Lantier.

"She'll get out, but not exactly because of them," the conductor said.

"But she gets out."

"Yep. Then one of the SHIELD soldiers is going to blow the building. Good riddance. I hated that place." A titanic hiss of steam escaped the boiler as the locomotive came to a stop. "I'm maybe not telling the story in exactly the way it happens, but that's the gist."

Serena was alive, and the chocolate factory was gone. Tony figured this was good, but Lantier hadn't said anything about Zola. He decided to ask, but Lantier was way ahead of him. "I don't think Zola's interested in your lady friend anymore," he said. "I suggested that we get rid of her days ago, but he thought she was going to be a good card to play. Way things worked out, he might have been right. Usually he is."

"So where is he now?"

Lantier thought about the question. It occurred to Tony that the appearance of Lantier thinking might signify that the bits and strings of code that made up the virtual Lantier were sifting through the overwhelming welter of information available and finding a way to organize it. Instant control, Tony thought. There might be a lot for him to learn here—if he could get rid of Virtual Tony and find his way back to Four-D in time to prevent Zola from executing the final phase of his plan.

"Unless I miss my guess," Lantier said, "he's on his way over to your lab. I think things are real close to coming to a head over there. Pressure's on."

Tony swung out of the cab and climbed down onto the turning platform. "Appreciate the ride," he said.

"Appreciate the chance to shoot the breeze," Lantier said. He might have said more, and so might Tony, but that wasn't how things were going to work. A switchman Tony hadn't seen before began pivoting the locomotive around so it could head back down the tracks on whatever errand Lantier had chosen next.

So this was the city at the core of the virtual world. Tony passed by wizards dueling from the tops of towers made from dragon bones, and gangs of postadolescent human-animal hybrids that called to mind a Teletubbies version of *The Island of Dr. Moreau*. He was warned that Diablo's plans were near coming to pass, and that the death of Evan Chan meant something was happening with the sentient plankton covering the world's oceans. He walked by a stadium where touts tried to lure him in to watch baseball games played between dead All-Stars and the sabermetric projections of today's heroes—in the nude. He was propositioned by every third or fourth person he passed, and decided after the sixth proposition that he would answer each one with a simple question.

Where was Virtual Tony?

"Oh," said a bright-eyed badger wearing half a suit of plate mail and carrying a spear in one hand and a picture of Britney Spears in the other. "Virtual Tony? Yeah. He's . . ." The badger waved with the spear in the direction of the city center. "Over there somewhere."

Following the spear point, Tony found a river of data flowing through the city. This made sense. However fantastical the world the avatars had created for themselves, at some level it had to reflect the understanding of the real Four-D people who had created the avatars. So rivers of data maybe mapped back onto bandwidth trunk lines, the old backbones from node to node that had defined the first version of the Internet.

He had a feeling that going upstream would lead him to some kind of omphalos, and that Virtual Tony would be there because where else would they have their showdown if it wasn't at some notional center of a virtual space in which no one wore their real faces? That was the kind of logic you needed In Here. Tony closed his eyes and decided he was going to take a chance. He was rolling dice with a lot of lives, but he knew that out in the Four-D time was passing, and Zola probably had another body, and things at the RTI Lab were getting dire if they weren't already. Pepper was there, and Rhodey. And even Fury, who Tony had spent twenty years trying not to like and still couldn't do it.

"PDM," he said. "Tony Stark. Commence extract in ten minutes Four-D time."

On the banks of the data river, a hunchbacked fisherman said, "Ten minutes. You better be ready."

XXX.

The heads of HYDRA first sank their fangs into the world at the dawn of human consciousness, when man first knew that he could take the world in his hands and transform it. The first use of a sharp stick was alchemical, creating a new world from the materials of the old. HYDRA grew with every mind that saw not what the world was, but what it could be. The forces of darkness cut off the heads of the madmen and heretics who saw through the Real and discerned the outlines of the Possible—yet with every decapitation, the heads of HYDRA multiplied. Centuries and millennia passed, and the heads of HYDRA became innumerable, became the distributed brains of a network that looked down upon human civilization and found it both wanting and ablaze with potential. This is the legacy I seized, the inheritance that waited for Zola to claim it. HYDRA is mine and I am the first leader of HYDRA worthy of its project. I have transformed the materials of bodies and minds. I have brought forth supermen. I have eradicated the barriers between the organism and the works of human hands. I have paved the way for the rise of something unrecognizable and transcendent, which will be the Annunciation of a new humanity, freed from the bonds of genome and environment. This is within our grasp. You whom I have created, you are the heads of HYDRA, biting into and poisoning the corrupted bodies of a civilization not wise enough to know that it is dying, and must die to make way for the better life to come. Follow me, HYDRA!

Serena realized that all was quiet. No one was shooting in the hall or a couple of rooms over, and Zola was standing silently inside the doorway while the Eight Demoiselles stood awaiting his order. Three of them were cleaning their swords using her bedspread. She didn't say anything about it. Soon she was going to die. Zola had no reason to keep her alive now that SHIELD had made its move. Serena had been an ornament before. She had been a sought-after presence at society functions and high-profile parties where people wanted to take her picture and goad her into making shallow-sounding comments that they could broadcast, or podcast, for their own benefit at her expense. She knew what it was like to be used. But she had never before had the feeling that she had served her purpose so finally and fatally.

Knowing that a clone had been out there in the city pretending to be her made the whole thing worse. She didn't know what it had been doing, what kind of impression it had left. She was going to die, and she didn't even know what the last three weeks of her life had been like because while the clone was out in the world living for her, she'd been imprisoned down here. She had the thought that she had already died in most of the ways that mattered. All that remained was for Zola or one of the Eight Demoiselles to make her body stop functioning.

"Well," Zola said. "Any moment now, the remaining members of the SHIELD team sent to extract you will arrive at this doorway. Unpleasant events will ensue. I trust that you will stay well out of the way."

"Why did you keep me alive?" Serena asked. In the end, it didn't matter, but she wanted to know.

"I was advised otherwise," Zola said. He considered the question. "A personal liking, perhaps. It would not be the first time my emotional reactions have engendered professional difficulties."

Then he cocked his head and held a finger to his lips. Serena wanted to scream, but her head spun with possibilities. If she made noise, and the SHIELD team crashed through the door, Zola and the Demoiselles would wipe them out. If she made noise and the SHIELD team headed for the exits, one of the Demoiselles would kill her and the rest would hunt down the SHIELD team. Maybe her only choice was to stay quiet and rely on their training. They must know how to break into a room. They'd done it up until now, hadn't they?

But there were eight severed heads on the writing desk. Serena didn't know what to do. The world was never supposed to be like this.

"Demoiselles," Zola said quietly. "We go now."

He opened the door and walked out into the hall, for all the world as if he were welcoming long-awaited visitors. "No no no no no," Serena was saying, but there was nothing she could do.

The Eight Demoiselles waited until the first gunfire erupted. Then they danced out the door, fluid and suddenly almost invisible, as if they knew the shadows and could inhabit them. Serena watched, and screamed with bloodthirsty joy when she saw one of the Demoiselles jerk and stumble out of her field of vision, leaving spatters of blood on the doorjamb. Then she was quiet. There was more gunfire in the hall outside, and screams, and the ringing clash of sword blades. Serena stared straight ahead, not moving, willing herself not to think about the fact that all of those soldiers outside were dying because Tony Stark had sent them to find her.

Some time later, Zola came back into the room. "I will be taking permanent leave of this facility, Miss Borland," he said. "You, too, are free to go at any time. I do hope that despite the difficult circumstances of your stay, you have found HYDRA to be a responsive and accommodating host. Perhaps our paths will cross again someday. Good-bye."

She heard his footsteps moving away down the hall, but even with the severed heads of SHIELD commandos gazing glassy-eyed at her from the writing desk, it was a long time before Serena could get up and face what she knew she would see when she went through the door.

* * *

The spiel didn't work with the gunnery sergeant. Happy laid him out and made it to a copter, and then into the air, before anyone could catch him. Now if they wanted to stop him from getting to the RTI Lab, they'd have to shoot him down. The copter's comm started squawking at him almost immediately. "This is SHIELD aviation control, Governors Island. Identify yourself."

Happy did.

"Hogan, return the copter. We are authorized to shoot down any copter stolen from this field. We are further authorized to shoot down anyone moving within one kilometer of Stark Industries RTI Lab, due to continuing operations."

"Wait a sec," Happy said. "Because of SHIELD operations, you're going to shoot down any SHIELD copter that goes there?"

"That is our authorization," the aviation controller said.

"Sounds like you have two authorizations," Happy said. "I'm stealing this bird, and I'm going to the RTI. Take your pick."

Silence from Governors Island. About a minute later, when he was hitting the edge of the Brooklyn Navy Yard, the controller was back. "Be advised that there is strong evidence of psyops manipulation, specifically of pilots, in the area around the RTI Lab."

"Specifically of pilots?" Happy said.

The controller broke his carefully imperious controller demeanor. "Happy, I wish I was kidding. We had twelve birds crash simultaneously out there a little after midnight. No mechanical failure, no nothing. Twelve pilots dove into the dirt. You explain it."

"Control, can I touch base with you when I'm a little closer?" Happy said. "I might need your hand putting together a plan."

Control agreed that this might be possible given the

extraordinary and off-book nature of the situation. Happy flew on over Long Island. His phone rang. It was Pepper. He didn't answer.

Upstream against the flow of data, Tony walked on a riverside path whose stones were lost data packets. As his feet touched one, it tried to attach itself to him with a faint sizzle and pop of ones and zeroes that would never again be compiled. There was light in the sky, but he couldn't tell where it was coming from. Winged creatures and winged machines circled and swooped overhead. Some were avatars, he guessed, and some were emergent constructs of the empty spaces between sectors on a hard drive that might exist in Bangalore or Boston or Brisbane. Anywhere. Any of these things might be anywhere in the real world, but it was all one place here. Space had no meaning. Tony wondered how much he wasn't seeing, how many invisible beings and avatars and constructs might exist around him, experiencing the virtual world in a language built along principles the human brain wouldn't be able to parse. Whatever happened with Virtual Tony, the real Tony Stark was never going to look at the real world the same way again. This was a place in which all dimensions collapsed, yet he framed it and organized it as if it was like Four-D.

"Quit thinking so loud," a passing avatar said. It was a jellyfish with jewels worked into its tendrils and a human brain in its umbrella. "Everybody's got ontology problems," it added as it floated away. One of its tendrils shot out to paralyze a fish that came into existence at the exact moment the tendril arrived at the fish's location. Tony was about to say that jellyfish didn't do that, but he stopped himself. In Here, they could.

Abruptly he was sick of the whole experience. If it could be utterly and transformatively different, he wanted it to be. As things stood—at least in the frame of reference he had—it wasn't different enough. Surreal, yes. Interesting, yes. But in the end, just another language to talk about the same old things.

"Virtual Tony!" he called out. "Let's get this done!"

He hadn't expected a response, and didn't get one. He walked faster. "Pepper," he said. "I don't know if you can hear me, but if I live through the next ten minutes, maybe you can order a pizza or something, have it ready when I'm done taking care of Zola."

"People don't talk to themselves around here," the companion said. Tony looked over to his right to see if it was any different. It wasn't.

"I wasn't," Tony said.

The companion nodded. "You were. You just didn't know it. You want to get a message to the Four-D? Here's one way." It bent and picked up one of the paving stones from the riverside path. Brushing away the stray ones and zeroes, the companion handed the stone to Tony. "Give it your message and throw it in the river," it said.

Tony looked from the stone to the companion back to the stone. "What, talk to it?" he asked.

"If you want to. Or just think it, or whatever."

Tony decided to think it. Even In Here, he was conscious of normative social pressures, it seemed. He didn't want passing jellyfish avatars to think he was odd. Then he threw the stone into the river. It didn't land, exactly; as it approached the surface of the data, it was sucked into the flow without a ripple.

"That should get through," the companion said. "Or it might not. Hard telling. What did you say?"

"You don't know?" Tony asked.

"The way you encrypted it?" the companion said. "No way. Couldn't tell a thing about it."

"I didn't know I'd encrypted it," Tony said.

"Well, you did." They walked for a while. The companion stopped and pointed ahead and a little up. "That's the place you're looking for."

Looking around, Tony saw that they'd meandered away from the river. Or it had meandered away from them. Who knew? They were standing at the base of a staircase that curled gently up and in, spiraling to a center point at which it disappeared. "Up there, huh?" Tony said. "You mean the part where there's nothing?"

"There won't be nothing when you get there," the companion said.

Tony couldn't help it. He rolled his eyes. "Of course there won't. Okay. Appreciate the tour."

"Don't mention it. Just give Zola a kick in the ass for me, okay?" Then the companion was gone, and Tony started the long climb up the stairs.

xxxi.

PROVISIONAL APPLICATION FOR PATENT

TITLE
  Kinesis reservoir

DESCRIPTION
  A battery of kinetic energy, charged by the transmission of force through nanoscale force converters (or NFCs; see Stark Industries patent application [redacted]). The kinesis reservoir consists of an electromagnetic matrix in which several billion tungsten nanobeads are permitted to resonate along a controlled frequency. Force converted from the NFCs creates additional agitation in these nanobeads, which circulates through the electromagnetic matrix until the user chooses to release it.

CLAIM
  Unlike energy reservoirs that trap electrical or heat energy for later for conversion into kinetic energy, the kinesis reservoir maintains the trapped energy in its kinetic state, eliminating the inefficiencies caused when energy is transformed from one state to another (i.e., in internal combustion, steam turbines, traditional cartridge firearms). Nearly 100 percent of energy harvested and channeled into the kinesis reservoir can be redeployed as kinetic energy with no intermediary mechanism.

SECURITY STATUS
  Project undertaken without any assistance or cooperation from agencies of the United States Government. No security restrictions apply.

It was amazing how long an automobile could burn, Fury thought, given how little flammable stuff there seemed to be in one. The pickup was still roaring, and the initial explosion had ignited some of the furniture and fixtures around the loading bay. The door had caught, too, and the smell of its plastic fumes was about to do Fury in. His nose burned and he had the worst headache he could ever remember having. Years were coming off his life from breathing whatever it was he was breathing. Sure as hell didn't seem to be much oxygen. The lab's sprinklers had kicked in, and they were knocking the smoke down a bit, but their primary effect was getting everyone in the testing area soaking wet.

The more serious problem was that all that water was also getting the control terminal wet, and pretty soon something important was going to short out. If that happened, Tony Stark was going to be a permanent resident of cyberspace, and the war between SHIELD and HYDRA was going to shift to a brand-new battlefield where Arnim Zola would have a dominant upper hand.

Pepper had already built makeshift tents over the server stack and the main control interface, using whiteboards from a meeting room next to the lab and—of all things— some plastic wrap from the kitchen. This would never have occurred to Fury. Not for the first time, he reflected that it was a bad idea to go into an important battle without a woman around.

"Speak to me, Pep," he said. "Systems holding on."

"Oh my God," she said. Fury's stomach did a slow roll.

"What?" His mind switched gears, already forming plans for how to take the battle to HYDRA if Zola could use an engineered AI version of Tony Stark as a virtual saboteur.

"Tony has called in the extraction protocol!" Pepper shouted.

Fury's stomach did another kind of flip. "And it let him?" He couldn't quite believe it.

"It's starting. Ten minutes. Less now."

Ten minutes. If the terminals and servers stayed dry, and HYDRA didn't overrun the lab, and they didn't all die of asphyxiation from the burning truck. "Well," Fury said, "here's hoping he doesn't show up to find us all dead."

Hailey had counted to a hundred, or almost, until she couldn't remember how many times she had started counting. She couldn't feel her legs, and couldn't feel one arm, and someone was lying on the other arm, which was twisted behind her back. Every time she started counting, she worked her good arm a little bit closer to free. The poison burned in her, everywhere. Her tears hurt her eyes.

She was going to die. The women in green and the giant who called himself Zola had torn through them like they weren't there. The five of them had never had a chance, had barely made them slow down. A superbly lucky shot had knocked some of the brains out of one of the women's head, but that was the only mark they'd made. The dead woman lay a few feet down the hall from Hailey. There was an entry wound, a simple dark hole, just over her left eye. The spread of her black, black hair hid the rest of the mess. Hailey had gingery hair that she had once dyed black. Then she joined the marines, and then SHIELD, and she never dyed her hair again.

My life is flashing before my eyes, she thought. She'd known she was dying since the giant and his seven green women had disappeared down the hall. A snatch of conversation had floated back to her, and Hailey had realized that the giant—Zola, but not looking like the Zola she'd seen in the briefing; he'd been serious about getting a different body—and the green women had been waiting for them, knowing they'd find the room with Whatsername eventually.

Serena Borland.

After Zola had talked to Serena Borland and left, things

had been quiet for long enough that Hailey Donner had
started to think that she had died and was just getting used
to the idea. Except the pain hadn't stopped, and if pain
didn't stop when you died, that got rid of just about the
only thing that made the whole idea worthwhile.

Then Serena Borland had walked right past Hailey's face.
Hailey wanted to say something, but the Borland girl was
crying, and what did you say in a situation like that, even if
you had the strength? So Hailey lay there listening to Serena Borland's footsteps recede. She heard, distantly, the
elevator.

Then she realized what she should have said to Serena
Borland.

Help me get my detonator.

Hailey counted to a hundred, or as close as she could get.
Attention span was one of the first things the poison got.
Then she started over again. Then again. Eventually she
convinced herself that the Borland girl must be out of the
building, and she started working her arm out from under
the weight that pinned it behind her. It was a long time before Hailey figured out that it was her own weight. She
rocked back and forth, relying on the big trunk muscles that
the poison hadn't killed yet, and sometime during what
must have been the hundredth time she tried to count to a
hundred, she got her arm free. It was nearly numb, both
from the poison and from the way she'd been laying on it,
but she was damned if she was going to get this far without
fulfilling the last part of her mission. The Borland girl was
out; now nothing in the building was to remain standing or
functional.

The detonator was a simple switch that needed a very
complicated formula to activate. The formula was composed
of nine things or ideas important to Hailey Donner. They
had to be said to the detonator in the correct order after it
was activated. She shrugged her dead arm over in front of
her and shoved the detonator under it to keep it steady

while she thumbed at the activation switch until the yellow light came on. This was her cue.

She was only going to get one chance to do it. Already her peripheral vision was gone, she was cold, she was hearing strange chiming noises that coincided with streaks of color in the dark hall. "Honor," she said. "Space. Football season. Pink. Diving. Beagles. Men. Frosting."

Her diaphragm was getting heavy. Concentrating everything she had, Major Hailey Donner, in the last moment of her life, kept her focus long enough to say, "Boom."

Rhodey got the news about the extraction protocol just as the tap he was running on the RTI Lab's perimeter security feed picked up a large group of HYDRA personnel retreating out toward the far end of the lab property, back where the fence met the meandering line of the creek. There were still plenty of them closer, behind cars and Jersey barriers Tony had put up inside the fence that ran along the access road off the Long Island Expressway. Nobody was going anywhere. So what was this group of a dozen Happy Hogans doing out there in the corner?

"General," he said. "Movement out toward the perimeter?"

"On the perimeter?" Fury came back.

"No, sir. Toward the perimeter. A group of a dozen, give or take. Looks like they're staging something out there."

"Five'll get you ten that's Zola on the way. On your toes, Rhodey. The next ten minutes won't be boring."

Good, Rhodey thought. If there was one thing he hated, it was a stalemate, and that was what they had. HYDRA couldn't get all the way in, but SHIELD couldn't maneuver to push them all the way out. Rhodey had firm command over the RTI Lab's front entrance, and a good field of fire down all of the exterior walls except the rear one at the back of the testing area. General Fury was bunkered down in the testing area. HYDRA had about enough manpower for one serious push to break the SHIELD position, but their numbers weren't good enough—and, Rhodey thought with some pride, the quality of their soldiers wasn't good enough—for that push to have a high probability of success. If they could hang on until Tony got back from wherever the hell he was, things would work out.

A volley of rifle fire pinged off the APC Rhodey was leaning against. He felt the impact through the tire at his back. Ten minutes. Nine now. He ran through the checklist every officer went through when he had a breather in the middle of a battle. Forces arrayed correctly? Check. Communication lines intact? Check. Battle orders clear? Check. "Top off your loads and stay focused, boys," he said over the open comm. "We're in the home stretch."

One of Zola's favorite things about his new body was that it could fly. Not for him vehicles, or even exoskeletal gizmos like Tony Stark's suits. He built the ability to fly into his body. He was a biological machine, enhanced with mechanical features where evolution had not yet accomplished what the human mind could imagine. He flew. The Eight—correction, he thought irritably, Seven—Demoiselles flew with him in the stealth-designed copter he'd initially stored on the factory roof as an emergency escape vehicle. Now it was bearing his beautiful new shock troops to the decisive engagement with the SHIELD forces, who had no idea what was in store for them. It was beautiful, this feeling of having the element of surprise on your side. Zola was used to knowing things that other people did not and could not know, but the element of surprise went beyond that; it was knowing something and also anticipating the exercise of that knowledge, the kinetic transformation of knowledge into power. It was intoxicating, this anticipation.

The RTI Lab was a mile away. Zola dropped down to an altitude of forty meters, and the copter behind him followed suit. At this height, radar would have trouble picking them out from the cityscape noise. He braked and settled into the feet-first final stage of his descent. *With me, Demoiselles*, he said. *Land in the lot across the stream, rendezvous where I touch down.*

He was just feeling the sensation of their acknowledgment when a small explosion blew the rotor off their copter and the Seven Demoiselles went spinning crazily down through the last two hundred yards of their descent. Zola turned at the sound and saw the copter smash through a grove of trees and disintegrate against the concrete abutment of a bridge. The minds of the Seven Demoiselles cried out in fury, and fear, and then were snuffed out.

Zola's rage bloomed with such titanic power that for a moment all he could think of was murder. He forced himself to land, feet on the ground, a terrestrial being in body if not mind. Reaching out, he demanded that the Seven Demoiselles answer him! Crackles of dying sentience polluted his mind and sickened his stomach. *Answer me!* he roared, and felt the returning wash of confusion and fear from the Happy Hogan clones who awaited his arrival near the RTI Lab perimeter fence. This cleared his head. He was Zola. He was a man of intellect and control. He soothed the Hogans, and searched again for signs of life in the wreckage of the copter.

Two of them lived. Two Demoiselles. He reached out and nurtured them back into consciousness, calling them out of the physical shock that dulled their minds. *To me*, he said. *To me. We will yet prevail.*

xxxii.

Happy Hogan, how did you come by your name? Is it because you have always been happy, or because people have taken advantage of your loyalty and bestowed upon you a nickname meant to patronize you and provide ammunition for cold jokes told when your back is turned? Ah, now I see. Because you would not smile, back in the days when you were a boxer. Such ironies are cheap. Harold is a kingly name, a heroic name; Happy is a simpleton's moniker, given by people who look down upon happiness and believe it to be synonymous with naivete and stupidity. What has your loyalty ever gained you, Harold? I have found your clones strong and worthy; but the people who employ you treat you as if you were a clone. The people you care about are trapped inside a building that burns, slowly. They are surrounded by superior forces. Why? Because they are surrounded by clones of you, Harold, and what normal man can outfight you? Not James Rhodes, not Nick Fury. No man. And Tony Stark has gone on his voyage to the disappearing reaches of his own mind. He will not return. He does not wish to return. He has abandoned you, and your beloved Pepper. Will you have them cloned, or will you strike to save them from the fate that has made you so despise yourself? You know, Harold. You know what you must do.

On his way up the steps, Tony allowed the prototype suit to grow around him and seal him in. He could be an avatar, too—an avatar of Iron Man, the Iron Man who had never yet existed in the Four-D but would as soon as he took care of his would-be usurping clone In Here.

He reached the last step and stood looking out over a

space so immense it seemed like his concept of space was revising itself to accommodate what his senses experienced. Nothing in the Four-D had ever seemed so vast . . . and there was nothing after the last step. There won't be nothing when you get there, the companion had said. Was it wrong? Lying? Slyly conniving against him with a slangy double negative?

None of the above, Tony thought. There was something. He couldn't see it yet. That was going to be part of Virtual Tony's bag of tricks. He'd gotten here first, and configured the space to his liking. Iron Man would have to deal with this problem before all others; he had allowed the enemy to choose the site of the battle. This was a fundamental error, but Tony didn't know how he could have avoided it. He did know how he could rectify it, though. That was simple. He had to be tougher and smarter and just a little meaner than Virtual Tony.

He thought of Pepper, and Serena, and Rhodey and Happy and all of the other people who meant something to him out in the Four-D. Bodiless and alone in the teeming emptiness of In Here, Tony had a bit of an epiphany about what he'd really been giving up by sealing himself off in the RTI Lab with his fantasies about instant control.

Virtual Tony was going to answer for that.

And then, so was Arnim Zola.

He stepped off the last step into nothing.

Five minutes into the PDM's countdown, one of the server rack's power cables blew out at the wall in a shower of sparks and smoke. The pickup wasn't burning as intensely as it had; Fury figured that as soon as it was approachable again, they could count on another HYDRA incursion from that direction. The last one had cost him three men. They could still hold the space—at least he thought they could—but if Zola showed up again, or

HYDRA came up with something unexpected, he was going to need Rhodey to fall back into the building. Nobody wanted that, except maybe Zola. If the SHIELD forces were stuck inside the building, he could stand outside and soften it up all he wanted before deciding to wander in. Already Fury had sent a man looking for a shutoff valve to cut off the sprinklers, but it was too close to a window. HYDRA had snipers covering all the windows. So they sat and got wet, and so did everything else. Sooner or later all that water was going to overwhelm even Tony's obsessive backup systems.

As the server rack's backup power kicked in, Fury looked over at Pepper. "Okay so far," she said nervously. Tony was the wild card in all of it, Fury thought. If he came back in one piece and fit to fight, things would change in a hurry. If he didn't, they were all going down the drain, quickly or slowly, didn't matter.

"Tony better hurry," Fury observed.

"Yeah," Pepper said. "Hope he knows that."

How much time had passed in the Four-D, Tony wondered? Maybe he needed to hurry. From the nothing came a floor. When he hit the floor, the sound echoed off walls newly created to receive the sound and reflect the echo. By the time the sound waves had created a space, it was fully realized: a cube of shining black with Tony standing in one corner. In the opposite corner, wearing Tony's favorite pajamas and smoking jacket, stood Virtual Tony. "So you got here," he said.

"Couldn't ignore the invitation," Tony said. "How did you know about the clothes?"

"Oh, these old things? In Here, not too many people have secrets. You sure don't, especially not from me." A martini glass appeared in Virtual Tony's hand. He sipped and let the glass fall. It vanished without a sound before it hit the floor, or maybe it fell through the floor and would fall endlessly through the vastness of In Here. "You know none of this is really like you're seeing it," said Virtual Tony.

"Far as I'm concerned, if this is how I'm seeing it, this is how it is," Tony said. "I thought that was one of the lessons of the place."

"Lessons? There are no lessons here." Virtual Tony took off the smoking jacket. It, too, disappeared after he dropped it. "Lose the suit," he said. "Let's do this like civilized men."

The last thing in the world Tony cared about was being fair. "No," he said.

Virtual Tony grinned. "No? Okay, then." He raised his hand and spread the fingers. Tony tensed. "You think I'm going to hit you?" Virtual Tony said. "Or shoot some kind of death ray? No. That's not how we do this. Raise your arm just like I did."

No, Tony thought. But his ~~arm~~ came up, palm facing forward and fingers spread.

"See?" Virtual Tony said. "Will. You think you have it. I'm made of it. I am walking willpower, and I can make you do whatever I want In Here."

Tony was conscious of time and fear but he couldn't think of why. Details, causes and effects, slid through his mind and were gone before he could get a fix on them. "You're soft because you've been you for so long that you've forgotten you have to keep trying to be you, to keep your you together," Virtual Tony said. "I was never supposed to have a real chance to be you, but as it turns out I'm going to get that chance, and lucky for me you're too weak to stop me. Raise your other hand, just the same."

Tony did, fighting it all the way. "Now I'm going to walk up and we're going to touch palms, and when that happens I'm going to be the only Tony Stark In Here or in the Four-D or anywhere else," Virtual Tony said. He took a step forward.

Something broke, like an invisible string that held the air

together. In the wake of the vibration, the room was a little less cubic, the black a little less black. Virtual Tony glanced around. "You have to be careful with Zola," Tony said. He'd had a brief moment when he remembered something about Zola, and knew that he wasn't to be trusted. He was dangerous. His danger had something to do with what had just happened.

"I'm not worried about Zola. He'll run out of bodies before I'll run out of will." Virtual Tony took another step forward, and another invisible string snapped. Tony could turn his head, couldn't hear anything different, but he felt like a large part of In Here had just disappeared.

"Is that happening to everyone In Here?" Tony said.

"What do you think?"

"Is what happening?" Virtual Tony sneered. "Nothing's happening to me. What's happening to you? Not strong enough to keep it together In Here? Stay right there. It'll all be over in a minute."

He came closer. Tony felt pixilated, in need of defragmentation, lacking vital robustness and redundancy. He could feel the tug of the limitless In Here, the tidal seduction of infinity. What did he want to go back for? Out There were people, Tony Stark among them, with their needs and their failures and their complicated and contradictory desires. In Here transformation was just a thought away . . .

No.

It came back to him, all at once. I know me, Tony thought. That wasn't the problem. "What I'm really having trouble with," Tony said, "is a little too much sense of self. What slack-jawed self-annihilating weakling would want to stay in here when all the girls are out in the Four-D?"

Nature versus nurture. Virtual Tony hated Tony for being first, and Virtual Tony loved In Here for not knowing that Tony had been first because they didn't know Virtual Tony was Virtual Tony. In Here you could be whatever you wanted. But that was all nurture, and somewhere inside

Virtual Tony there was the incorrigible kernel of Natural
Tony Starkness, and if there was one thing that defined Starkness, it was an appreciation of wine, women, and song. Virtual Tony wrestled for the briefest second with this eruption
of desire for the pleasures of life, real physical life—and Tony
seized on that moment of distracted weakness. His hands
were already up, palms out, and it was the easiest thing in the
world to blow Virtual Tony through the shining black wall
into the nothing.

Tony dove after him, force projectors still smoking because that's what your mind expected them to do even when
you knew how they worked. He accelerated faster than Virtual Tony could and caught him. Far below, Tony could see
the river of data, appearing exactly where he'd wanted it to.
Every terrain had its own rules. It had taken him too long
to learn these, but learn them he had. Now Virtual Tony
would suffer for it—and in all likelihood so would Tony
Stark himself. He and Virtual Tony tumbled. There was only
one way to survive, Tony thought. He'd learned enough
about isolation; it had failed. Now it was time to try union.
"Sorry, Junior," Tony said as they fell. "You haven't lived
long enough to know what will is." Virtual Tony fought to
get free of him, but he was Tony Stark. He was Iron Man.
He remade himself falling from nothing with an empty shell
of himself, and his grip did not break until they plunged together into the river of data that surged and roiled down-
stream, toward Out There.

"Thirty seconds," Pepper said. The server rack smoldered
and smoked, but according to the terminal, the PDM was
still functional. It was slow, though. God, it was slow. And
a mind was big, storage-wise. Would the system survive
long enough to get all of Tony out of . . . cyberspace? Was
that really the word?

What would happen if only part of him came back?

Fury was reading her mind, it seemed. "Don't think about it," he said. "Keep an eye on the system. Control what you can control. We need you on point, Pep."

She nodded, but she couldn't look at him. Couldn't look at anyone. All she could look at were the numbers counting down on the screen to the moment when the PDM would start recalling Tony Stark from the virtual wilderness of his exile.

Serena Borland hadn't flinched when the chocolate factory blew up behind her. A fierce joy rose in her when she turned to look and saw the mushrooming pillar of fire, blackening around its edges. *Die,* she thought. *All of you.* Pieces of masonry and glass and Zola's machines fell out of the sky, pinging and shattering on the broken asphalt of 49th Street. She assumed if she kept walking she'd hit a street she knew. It looked like the Bronx, maybe, but the street name was wrong. Wasn't there a 49th in Queens? Brooklyn, too. It didn't matter. She looked up at the sky she hadn't seen in three weeks and realized that she was alive again. All of those soldiers had died in there, but she was alive again. She could thank them for that.

Sirens started approaching. Serena didn't care. Part of her thought that she was probably suffering some kind of stress reaction. She should have been a little more freaked out, running down the street and shrieking at passersby, but she couldn't muster the energy. The one firm thought in her head was that she didn't want any part of Tony Stark's world anymore. He was a nice enough guy—also gorgeous, rich, and right at home in the social circles Serena liked to inhabit—but the truth was, if dating a guy got you kidnapped, cloned, nearly murdered, and almost blown up, you had to face the possibility that there were serious obstacles to pursuing the relationship.

She figured she should call him and tell him. But she

didn't have her phone, and he was probably busy with this Zola problem. He could call her. Right now what she wanted was to find a taxi, go home, call her mother, and do nothing but watch TV and look out the window. Just to see that it was all still out there, and she was still alive and part of it.

xxxiii.

PROVISIONAL APPLICATION FOR PATENT

TITLE
  Defensive energy shield projector

DESCRIPTION
  The Defensive Energy Shield Projector uses hyper-concentrations of electromagnetic energy to create a dual-purpose barrier, useful against both energy and projectile attacks. Supercooled electromagnets within an insulating shield release focused fields of energy whose power, duration, and distance from point of origin can be automatically controlled using existing suit-borne command-and-control systems (as in Stark Industries patent [redacted]).

CLAIM
  No existing energy-projection technology can reliably and repeatably create a shield of predictable strength at a predictable distance. Stark Industries has innovated in this area before, notably patent [redacted], and the Defensive Energy Shield Projector improves on this foundation by creating a more powerful shield that can absorb heat and electromagnetic energy as well as deflect the kinetic energy of physical projectiles. It has been tested on kinetic energies comparable to those delivered by the main turret gun of the M1A1 Abrams tank, heat energies comparable to the thrust delivered by the engines of the F-22 Raptor, and electromagnetic energies produced by a 1.4Mt nuclear explosion.

SECURITY STATUS
  Project undertaken under the auspices of Stark Industries agreements with the Department of Defense, SHIELD, and other

governmental agencies outlined in Senate Amdt. [redacted] to Senate Amdt. [redacted] to H.R. [redacted] (110th). Technology is proprietary to Stark Industries but will be shared fully with all eligible entities. Technology is classified and will not be licensed until such time as classification order is rescinded.

Zola picked through the constant electronic chatter among the SHIELD elements arrayed against him. The situation was more or less as he had anticipated. Forces were roughly equal until you entered his new body into the equation. The lab's security systems were much degraded by damage to the servers and by sabotage from HYDRA elements at the perimeter of the property. All was arranged for the final stage of his plan. Maheu, had he been present, would no doubt have offered acerbic commentary. As was so often the case, his pessimism would have been misdirected; if Tony Stark failed to extract himself from the infinite spaces of the virtual, Zola had already won. If Stark returned, Zola had every confidence that his new body—refined as it was by innovations adapted from Stark's own work—would prove to be the equal of Stark's vaunted prototype Iron Man suit. All was as it should be.

Fresh data intruded on Zola's assessment. "Oh," he said. This body had no external ESP Box because he had felt it would detract from the overall effect of the construction, but all of the ESP Box's functions were embedded in various parts of the cybernetic anatomy. He felt the jamming signals from within the RTI Lab, like electronically generated confusion. Out at the edge of the lab property, the signals were weak, and Zola could sense minds outside the signals' range. The one he was focusing on at the moment appeared to belong to the original Happy Hogan. What lovely symmetry, Zola thought.

He reached out and felt the contours of Hogan's mind, the texture of his fatigue and desperation, the simple fabric of his devotion, the spiky darkness of his fear. Some control had to be achieved by brute force; on other occasions, the subtlest of suggestions—the recalibration of one tiny assumption—could create a chain of thoughts that seemed perfectly sensible. A mind as frayed and exhausted as Happy Hogan's was the softest of targets for just such a gentle push.

Simultaneously he sent out the word to his soldiers using cruder physical means of communication. Hand signals relayed along the fence line, down into the creekbed where several squads of Hogan clones crouched in the brush near a hole they had cut into the fence. It was nearly time to settle the SHIELD problem, and the Tony Stark problem, once and for all.

The Two Demoiselles were with him again. They were damaged but functional, worth any ten SHIELD commandos even after the injuries they had suffered. "Soon, my Demoiselles," Zola said. "There's just one thing to arrange."

Happy approached the RTI Lab from nearly due west. He slowed down and called in to the SHIELD controller when he was about a mile away. "What can you tell me? What's it look like on the ground?"

"We're getting not very damn much at all," Control said. "Sounds like a stalemate, but something's happened to Tony and nobody knows where Zola is. We've got a bunch of clones on the outside, and our guys split between the parking lot and the lab space inside."

A realization dawned on Happy. SHIELD was praying for rain. They were stuck defending an asset that probably had no value at all. They were assuming that Tony was going to ride to the rescue like he always did, but they hadn't seen Tony this past month. He was gone, the old Tony didn't exist anymore, he'd been absorbed into his dream of instant control and disappeared into the cyber-ether. SHIELD was doing exactly what Zola wanted. They were concentrating themselves in a single spot under circumstances dictated by

HYDRA; every cadet two weeks into his first military history course knew that if you let the enemy choose the ground of the battle, you were well on your way to losing.

There were things worse than death.

"Control, I don't think Tony's coming back," he said.

"We have information that the PDM recall process is underway," Control said.

Happy shook his head, not caring that Control couldn't see the motion. "It won't work."

Being turned into raw material for a marching, mindless army of clones. That was worse than death. Down there, trapped in and around the RTI Lab, were all of the people Happy cared about in the world. He couldn't let that happen to them.

It's an awful choice, Happy, but in the end a clear one. You know what you need to do.

What he needed to do was take out the lab building. That much was clear.

Rhodey pinged the turbocopter as soon as he saw its electronic signature identified it as SHIELD materiel. "Thought all you guys were supposed to clear out," he said. "New orders?"

"Rhodey, it's Happy," came the reply.

"Happy? What are you doing out of bed?"

"Tony's not coming back," Happy said. "Zola's going to come in there and smear you guys around like mosquitoes. You haven't seen him, Rhodey. You don't know what you're in for."

"You sound like you need to land that copter and get some shut-eye," Rhodey said. "We're doing fine here." Which might or might not have been true, he thought. They had not in fact seen Zola—but how had Happy?

Silently he patched General Fury into the channel, muting Happy for long enough to say, "General, I think you need to hear this."

When he brought Happy back, he heard ". . . can't stand the idea of her being cloned, Rhodey. Can't stand it. Or Zola getting Tony's suit. Tony's not coming back. If Zola gets the suit it's all going to be clones, Rhodey. Do we want that?"

"Hell no, of course not," Rhodey said. "That's why we're here."

"Yeah, but it's no good. It's not going to work. I think we have to make sure."

Rhodey got a cold lump in his stomach. "Make sure of what, Hap?"

"Make sure Zola doesn't get what he wants. We've got to scuttle the ships, Rhodey. There's no getting out, but at least we can make sure that when Zola gets in, there's nothing for him to find."

Oh, no, Rhodey thought. *Zola already found him.* "Hap," he said. "That's Zola talking. Pull your copter back a couple of miles, or land it. Can you feel him?"

"He's right, Rhodey." The despair in Happy's voice was enough to germinate seeds of doubt that had been in Rhodey's mind all along. So that's how it works, he thought. Even doubt is like a virus. Zola starts it somewhere and watches it spread.

"You have to land that copter, Happy. Now," Rhodey said. "Whatever you've got, it can't hurt Tony's suit. You know that. Land, Happy, for the love of God, land."

"Soon as I take care of this one thing. You don't know how it feels, Rhodey. You want a million clones of you? Of Pepper? Not going to happen. No. I have to make sure."

"Happy, you can't—" Rhodey was talking into a dead channel.

"General," he said. "What do we do?"

"You are not authorized to arm missiles," an automated voice said. A moment later, Control came on the comm. "Happy, what's with the missiles?"

"Bad situation here, Control," Happy said. "But I think I can take care of it. Visual lock on Zola."

Outstanding, Happy. Improvisation under duress is one of the hallmarks of a fine soldier.

"Unconfirmed," Control said. "You will not, repeat will not, fire missiles in that area without direct authorization from General Fury or this location."

"Control, you're not seeing what I'm seeing," Happy said.

"Happy, I am deactivating your arms-control software," Control said. "I advise you to land that copter in the closest safe spot and watch the show. Tony Stark is due for PDM recall in less than a minute."

"It's too late," Happy said. "Too late."

He watched as the arms-control software froze up . . . and then, a few seconds later, rebooted. Yes, he thought. That's how it's done.

I will keep your channels free of interference, Happy. You know that there's something you have to do, something only you can do, something that must be done.

"Thank you," Happy said.

"Happy!" barked Control. "You will land that copter without discharging missiles or any other ordnance! Is that order understood?"

"Understood and refused," Happy said. He was calm and at peace. "There's something I have to do."

Pepper heard the exchange between SHIELD flight control and Happy. She wasn't one to cry at the drop of a hat, but tears stood in her eyes as she understood what might be unfolding.

"It's Zola, right?" she said. "Zola's got him."

"Looks like it," Fury said.

"General Fury, this is Control. Arms-control systems on that copter are no longer responding. Overrides executed by unknown agency."

"Understood, Control," Fury said. "I think we have an idea about the source of the overrides."

"Be advised that targeting simulations are being run on the RTI Lab," Control said.

Fury looked over at Pepper, and then around at the nearer SHIELD defenders. They'd all heard what Control was saying, and understood the implications.

"Control, please advise when and if a firing sequence is initiated," Fury said.

"Will do, General. Hope you have a plan."

"Me, too, Control. Out." Fury looked back to Pepper. "It's been more than thirty seconds."

She nodded.

"What's the PDM say?"

"It says it's finished with the extraction," Pepper said. "But . . ." She lifted both hands and let them drop again.

"Yeah," Fury said. Tony Stark's body lay where it had fallen in the matte-black prototype suit. Seemed like maybe they ought to move it, but what was the point?

"Pepper, I don't know what else to do," Fury said. "If the firing sequence starts in that copter, we're going to have to take him down."

xxxiv.

Do you see them huddled like rats in their holes, HYDRA? Do you see their machines and tactics, their laboratories and defensive perimeters? Soon you will sweep them away. SHIELD is broken! Gnawed and worried by the many heads of HYDRA! Stark returns, but only to die. Happy Hogan is ours, the template absorbed and made one with its superior iterations. We mass, we are one, we are HYDRA! Know that even if you cannot hear me, I am speaking, and you know what I say because I have built my words and my will into the magnificent architecture of your brains. You will follow me whether I am there to follow or not, because that is the nature of HYDRA. All heads move as one, all heads know that HYDRA is everywhere and invincible, all heads know that the loss of one head creates the space into which ten more will grow. The enemy, too, knows this—see how he does not come out to fight? See how he hides behind machines and walls, behind the illusion of shelter? Your signal will come, HYDRA. When the time is right, you will sweep down upon the SHIELD minions and destroy them. With their destruction will come the dawn of a new age, of the age of HYDRA! You are present at the creation, and the new world will sing of your courage! You are the first generation of supermen! You are HYDRA!

Instant control meant knowing and sensing and feeling everything in the world all at once—and being able to organize it. From In Here, Tony fell into the Four-D, into his body again, into awareness of instant control that once had been a dream and now was the organizing principle of how he experienced the world. It was like falling asleep deaf, dumb, and blind and waking up with senses you'd never known you could have. He heard, as instant control assessed and prioritized all of the information logged by the suit while Tony had been In Here, the important parts of the exchange among Happy, Rhodey, and Nick. This was his first priority.

"No, Nick, don't do that," Tony said calmly. He was aware of his surroundings, of himself lying on the testing floor, of the suit coming to life around him. He had a body again. The sensation was intense and strange, completely unlike the synthesized approximation of physicality he had experienced while In Here.

Out of the infostorm came Fury's answer. "Tony?"

"In the flesh. So to speak."

"Don't do what?"

"Just let me handle Happy." Tony reached out and plugged a hole. It felt as easy as that. There was a hole in Happy's mind that was letting Zola in. Tony plugged it. If he'd had to explain it to Fury—or to Happy himself—he could have said something about subtle alterations in the broadcast frequencies of a thousand different signals, setting up interference patterns that shunted Zola's ultra-low-frequency broadcast away from the cranium of Happy Hogan. And it would have been true. But using instant control, it felt like Tony had just plugged a hole.

But Happy's thumb was already on the firing stud.

To Happy, it felt like he awoke from a dream of betraying everything he had ever believed in only to find that it hadn't been a dream at all. The copter bucked ever so slightly as the two missiles launched. "Oh no," he said. "No no no, *get out! Get out of there! I didn't know what I was doing get out of there!*"

Zola stood and watched the initial flare of the missiles' launch. He felt the loss of his control over Hogan and briefly wondered at its cause—but it no longer mattered. The missiles were in flight. Their impact would annihilate the SHIELD defenders and leave the Stark suit intact. It would also destroy the computer routines that were Tony Stark's only way out of the virtual palace Zola had constructed for him. He would move in, take the suit, and retire to a location of his choice. There he would build out his own information superstructure, and turn Tony Stark into the central intelligence of HYDRA's newest and most fearsome head. The combination of Stark's enviable instant control routines, the intelligence and ego of the man himself, and Zola's own considerable scientific prowess meant that the boundless powers of the information universe were about to fall utterly under HYDRA's control. Which was to say, Zola's control. No packet of data would travel without his permission.

He would rule the world.

"We move, HYDRA!" he cried aloud to his soldiers. "Now is the time for the last decisive blow!"

HYDRA soldiers roared as the bright sparks of the missiles' exhaust fell through the night toward the RTI Lab and the doomed SHIELD defenders within.

Instant control meant that Tony felt the signal as it relayed from the firing stud on the copter's joystick through the switch inside the flight console. He felt the response of the onboard computer as it armed and triggered the missiles' engines and blew the cover bolts on the launch tubes. He felt the initial feelers of the missiles' guidance systems as they pinged SHIELD satellites and got their fix in the Four-D. If he had been paying attention, Tony could have directed any of these processes to go wrong; but he was not a machine, not yet, and his first thought had been to plug the hole that had been sinking Happy under an intolerable weight of despair.

The missiles talked in flight, checking to see if they were

going where they were supposed to be going. The satellites told them that yes, they were. Tony had eight seconds to do something about the missiles before they impacted, one at the inside corner of the RTI Lab's L shape and the other on the dead center of the testing floor, less than forty feet from where Tony was still organizing all of the stimuli from his newly reawakened body. He was born again, and at the same time feeling his consciousness expand through instant control to encompass a world he had briefly glimpsed at the moment of impact with the river of data In Here. He acted, and saw the consequences before he had articulated the command to act.

When the missiles hit, they would incinerate Pepper and Nick Fury. James Rhodes, out in the parking lot behind his picket line of bullet-riddled APCs, would suffer blast overpressures sufficient to kill him unless he was lucky enough to be shielded in exactly the right way by one of those APCs—and in that case, the vehicle might turn into a secondary weapon, crushing him as it tumbled over in the blast wave. All of the SHIELD defenders in the testing area would die without ever knowing what had happened to them.

Seven seconds. Tony ascended through the roof, feeling the impact like a gust of wind when he punched through the corrugated steel. Six seconds. He triangulated the missiles' location and trajectory using built-in instrumentation and an instant tap on the satellite guidance feed and the missiles' response. A menu of choices presented itself. He could trigger the missiles' warheads. He could deflect the missiles. He could anesthetize the missiles with EMP. He could destroy them with a simple, direct burst of kinetic energy that would shiver them into tumbling bits of shrapnel. Each of these choices brought consequences in the way of collateral damage. The missiles were twenty meters apart, the one targeted on the testing floor slightly ahead of the other due to ambient atmospheric factors. Five seconds. Tony accelerated toward them, leaving the crackle of a sonic boom behind him. He halved the distance between himself and the missiles. They were eight hundred yards from the RTI Lab. Four seconds.

He triggered a targeted EMP burst. The satellite guidance systems started talking to one another, asking where the missiles were. The missiles flew toward him, dumb and disarmed now but still lethal simply by virtue of their mass and speed. With his right hand, Tony discharged a pulse bolt. It shattered the missile that had been aimed at the corner into an expanding cloud of metal fragments, bits of high explosive, and sputtering chunks of solid fuel. With his left hand, Tony flicked out a force shield and angled it to deflect the other missile ever so slightly off course. Then with both hands, he created another shield that bounced the fragments of the destroyed missile downward, where they rained into a staging area for semi trailers, punching holes in the trailers and pattering on the ground.

Three seconds. Two, one . . .

The intact missile hit the ground fifteen feet from the group of HYDRA clones mustering around the immense figure of Arnim Zola. Disintegrating on impact, the missile turned into a five-hundred-pound cone of shrapnel aimed directly at the HYDRA position. The burst of earth obscured the immediate result from Tony's visuals, but he knew it wouldn't take Zola out. The immediate objective was to reduce HYDRA's fighting strength and thereby improve the survival odds of SHIELD personnel.

"Interesting trip you sent me on, Zola," Tony said as he pivoted in the air and waited for the cloud of dust and smoke to clear. "Ran into some complications getting a return ticket, but here I am."

Zola walked out of the cloud. From Rhodey's position, small-arms fire erupted. Tony saw each hit on Zola's body, and registered the fact that none of them seemed to have much effect. "Yes, Stark, there you are," Zola said. He spoke in a normal conversational tone, picked up by audio surveillance from within the RTI Lab and relayed through priority channels to Tony's desired frequency. All of it happened instantly and automatically. "And here I am," Zola said. He launched himself into the air, one more missile coming to meet Tony . . . but this one was stronger and smarter than the other two, and it had its own version of instant control.

"Hap, old buddy," Tony said. "I can only talk for a second, but I have to say you're in no shape to be flying. Put the bird down and take the day off, will you?"

Then he leaned forward and accelerated toward the showdown with this newly enhanced version of Arnim Zola.

Inside the lab, Fury nearly had a heart attack when Tony's voice came out of the control terminal speaker. Then he nearly had another one when the prototype suit abruptly shot up through the ceiling without having previously shown any sign of life whatsoever. He ducked away from a falling piece of sheet metal that spun down from the edge of the hole left by Tony's departure and clanged onto the concrete floor. "Well," he said after a pause. "I guess the PDM thing worked."

"I guess so," Pepper said.

From outside came the sounds of the missiles being destroyed. The comm picked up Tony's brief speech to Happy. "Second that, Happy," Fury said. Happy said something back, but he was nearly incoherent.

"He's going to crash if he tries to land that copter now," Pepper said. She leaned into the terminal mic at her station. "Happy, stay with it. You have to keep it together long enough to land. We'll be okay in here. Really. Tony's back."

No sooner had she said that than smoke grenades came skipping under the burned-out body of the pickup in the loading bay and a storm of automatic weapons fire broke over the rear wall of the RTI Lab. Not knowing what was going to follow the smoke grenades, Fury flipped down his helmet visor and went to infrared. The two nearest defensive positions laid down fire in and around the truck, just on general principles. As the smoke spread, sound seemed to take on strange qualities, too; Fury couldn't tell as reliably from what direction any particular shout or gunshot or impact was coming from. It was going to be a hell of a mess, these next few minutes.

From the control terminal, Pepper said, "Building infiltrated from one of the windows toward the front."

"Rhodey!" Fury shouted into the comm. "Where's your line of fire down the side of the building?"

"Intact, General," Rhodey said.

"Then why do we have enemy inside the building from that direction?"

A brief pause. Then Rhodey said, "We had no visual contact with enemy personnel on either side of the building."

"Well, I have a feeling we are about to have goddamn visual contact with them on the inside of the building," Fury said. "Keep your eyes open."

"Should we fall back into the building and support?"

"What's the situation there?"

"Well, we've got—" Static blew out the next few words. "Also, Tony and Zola are duking it out up in the air. HYDRA on the ground are coming our way, also headed around the fence perimeter. Assume they're looking to get into your spot."

Fury gave himself three seconds to think. Three, two, one, he counted. "Fall back into the building," he said. "Redeploy to cover the central corridor and all access to it including the front door. I think the rest of the dance is going to happen inside."

XXXV.

PROVISIONAL APPLICATION FOR PATENT

TITLE
Haloalkane accumulator and delivery coupling

DESCRIPTION
Using commercially available haloalkanes or proprietary Stark Industries refrigerants (see patents [redacted] and [redacted]), the haloalkane accumulator and delivery coupling creates a reservoir of concentrated refrigerant, kept at temperatures as near to 0K as is practically possible given the system's integration into the line of Stark Industries personal armor systems (see attached list of relevant existing and pending patents). From this reservoir, the delivery coupling feeds a high-pressure stream of haloalkanes that spread rapidly as ambient temperature warms them. The principle is akin to that of the fire extinguisher, but the HDC's nozzle is specifically designed to keep the haloalkane substance narrowly focused. This concentration of the delivered material creates new possibilities for military, industrial, and personal-defense uses.

CLAIM
Existing freeze spray technologies—such as those used to flash-freeze consumer goods or momentarily supercool industrial materials at a given stage of their manufacture—function only at extremely short ranges and in tightly controlled circumstances. The haloalkane delivery coupling (HDC) will deliver a highly organized, and therefore more effective and longer-ranged, stream of haloalkanes. This is possible only because of material advances in the structure of the delivery conduit and advances in the insulation of supercooled materials form surrounding systems that

operate at normal temperatures. Possible uses include civil policing and military engagement. The HDC is capable of freezing a human being solid at a distance of fifty yards, and of crippling damage to electronics and mechanical systems at ranges of up to twice that, depending on the nature and protection of the given target.

SECURITY STATUS

Project undertaken under the auspices of Stark Industries agreements with the Department of Defense, SHIELD, and other governmental agencies outlined in Senate Amdt. [redacted] to Senate Amdt. [redacted] to H.R. [redacted] (110th). Technology is proprietary to Stark Industries but will be shared fully with all eligible entities. Technology is classified and will not be licensed until such time as classification order is rescinded.

Before their initial impact, Tony knew a great deal about Arnim Zola's new body. From its spectrum of electromagnetic emissions, Tony inferred a set of sensors and instruments similar to his own. From the nature of its radar presence, Tony learned that the body was only 26 percent organic material by weight; the rest was a combination of complex polymers, high-tension alloys, and carbon-nanotube ligatures. Numerous apertures in the hands and feet hinted at weapons systems. It was, in short, a cybernetic version of the Iron Man armor. "You know, Zola," Tony said in the instant before their impact, "I tried the cyborg thing once. All it did was wreck my nerves. Literally. You'll find the same."

"Ah, but Mr. Stark," Zola said, "you're assuming that I do things the way you did, when the fact is that I do them much better."

The sound of their meeting rattled the remaining windows in the RTI Lab, five hundred feet below.

Happy landed the copter in the same truck yard where the remains of one of the missiles had fallen. He got out, ducked under the slowing blades, and looked around. Falling pieces of the missile had torn holes in at least half of the trailers. Some of the bits were still smoking. Probably there was highly classified technology lying around somewhere, and in a few weeks a worker at a warehouse in Denver, unloading one of the trailers, would kick a bit of highly advanced gyroscopic circuitry out of his way because it was hanging up the wheels of his pallet jack. Because already, SHIELD and DOD had decided that none of this had ever happened. The trucks would be bought and scrapped, or resold. The heroism and sacrifice of the SHIELD soldiers dying in the RTI Lab would remain secret.

As would the failures of Happy Hogan.

This was what it was like to have trouble living with yourself. Happy felt so awful about what he'd almost done that he didn't know how he would ever come to terms with it. Bad enough that he'd let himself get jumped by the clone of Serena Borland, but then to fly right into Zola's mind-control radius? To let Zola play on his reaction to being cloned, to the point that he was ready to kill Nick Fury and Pepper?

Never in his life had Happy thought of himself as weak, but the last ten minutes had proved to him that he had weaknesses he'd never imagined. The desolation of the truck yard fit his mood. He would quit Stark Industries, leave New York. He couldn't face any of the people he'd let down.

And then what? Become one of the guys who kicked bits of stuff away from the wheels of their pallet jacks?

"No," Happy said.

He'd never run from a fight in his life, and he was for goddamn sure not going to run from this one.

Leaning back into the cabin of the copter, he retrieved the light assault rifle from its rack behind the pilot's seat. He checked the load, tapped the holster of his automatic where it hung under his left armpit, and headed for the sound of gunfire. Redemption, he thought. Just like failure, it's always just one decision away.

Considering how many of them Fury's troops had already iced, there sure seemed to be a lot of Hogans left. They came in through the windows, around the crashed truck, through the fire door at the far end of the testing area. The only place they weren't coming from was the hallway that led up to the front of the building, and Fury couldn't figure that out. Hadn't the security routine detected an infiltration there? Where were they? If they hadn't come in to shoot SHIELD personnel, why bother using the window? He pinned down a pair of Hogans near the truck's rear wheels and periodically aimed bursts under the truck until one of his men would work around to get a better angle and finish them off. God. Fury winced. The HYDRA clones didn't make much noise, but when they did, they sounded just like Happy. This battle was like listening to a good friend die over and over and over again.

On the other hand, just about every battle was like that. The differences were one, usually it wasn't the same friend each time, and two, usually the friend wasn't fighting on the other side.

Tony, Tony, thought Nick Fury. *There must be some way to blame you for this.* He was half-serious, but only half. Truth was, he didn't know what to blame on Tony and what to thank him for. Could be awhile before he found out, too, because according to Pepper, Tony was tied up with Zola's latest body somewhere in the sky. "Rhodey!" he barked into the comm. "How goes the move?"

"Just a minute, sir," Rhodey said.

Fury glanced over at Pepper. "Long as he's not in a hurry," he said. She cracked a smile, but just barely. "Hey," Fury added. "You did a hell of a job wrangling the machines long enough for Tony to get back."

"Thanks," she said. "Now can I get a gun and kill some clones?"

Fury burst out laughing. "You want a gun? Look around you. Pick one up. Just don't kill anyone who doesn't look like Happy."

"Speaking of. Where is Happy?"

"Last I knew, he'd landed his bird. I don't know after that. Here," Fury said. "Take this." He scooted a rifle across the floor to her. "If it keeps up like this, we're going to need the extra firepower."

"Anything I should know about it?"

"You shot a gun before?"

She gave him a look. "Nick. Please."

"Okay," he said. "It's just like the other ones. Point it at the bad guy and pull the trigger until he falls down." Turning his attention back to the comm, Fury shouted, "Rhodey!" again.

"Sir. We're in position. HYDRA coming in through some of the ingresses we're no longer covering. It's going to be a long afternoon. Also there's—"

The transmission cut out. Simultaneously Fury heard the firing intensify down the hall toward the front of the building. Then he couldn't pay attention to that anymore because another wave of Hogans was banging down the doors.

Happy knew that he was running a serious risk of being shot on the assumption he was a clone. He was hoping that his civilian clothing and lack of HYDRA insignia would slow down anyone's trigger finger for long enough that he could convince them that he was the original and not one of the copies—which didn't have his finely rearranged nose, but there was no use expecting someone in the middle of a firefight to notice that. He got to the edge of the RTI Lab property and picked off two clones coming around the corner of the building from the parking lot to fire in through one of the office windows. Tony's office must be a wreck, he thought. The boss was kind of a crybaby about stuff like that sometimes. He didn't have a comm because he wasn't supposed to be part of any operation, and he wasn't sure where his phone had gone. The copter? Back at the hospital still? Happy was running on adrenaline and willpower. His body felt like it was made out of chicken wire.

How could he get in touch with Fury or Pepper so he could get in without being killed?

Lights flared in the sky. Happy looked up and saw massive discharges in every color between Tony and Zola. They looked to be rising; already they were high enough that he only knew what he was looking at because there wasn't really anything else it could be. What random pedestrians and motorists would be thinking, he had no idea. In New York City, the sky always seemed to be full of weird lights. Out here, not so much, although the proximity of the airport added some variety to the sky. Even so, it couldn't be an everyday occurrence to see that kind of light show. The sounds, too—crackles and thumps and booming thunderclaps—they must have had the neighbors convinced that there was a fireworks show for some occasion they hadn't heard about.

Down here at the edge of the RTI Lab grounds, Happy had his own problems. Tony could take care of himself, and if he couldn't, whatever Happy did wouldn't make much difference in the long run.

Except to me, he thought. *I owe it to myself, if nobody else.*

Keeping low, he made the run from the fence line to the edge of the building and risked a glance into the corner of a broken window. The room he saw was an office space, not yet furnished. Tony hadn't gotten around to the details before being swept away by dreams of instant control. Skirting the bodies of the two clones and not looking at their faces, Happy vaulted in and squatted under the window, letting his eyes adjust. The door was open, and in the corridor emergency light glowed, but he was in near-total darkness. There was a body in the room. He couldn't tell which side it had belonged to. From the corridor and deeper in the building came the sustained chatter of small-arms fire. A burst ripped pieces out of the door frame in front of him. He wanted to move, to get involved. The whole complex was a shooting gallery, though, and he had no way to prove he wasn't one of the bad guys.

Motion over his head made him flinch. He looked up and saw a long-limbed female form in a green bodysuit tumble in through the window, hit the floor in the controlled roll, and continue right out into the corridor before he'd even had a chance to raise his rifle. Just as she disappeared, another identical form came through in the same way. This time Happy did get his rifle up. He squeezed off a burst, but God they were fast; by the time he'd aimed and fired, she was gone. Two women in green bodysuits. With swords. Zola had some kind of wild card. Happy didn't know what it was, but he had a feeling it wasn't a positive development.

On his belly, he crawled to the door and peered in both directions up and down the corridor. Bodies sprawled along the length of it. As he watched, a spray of bullet holes appeared in one wall, two doors down; firing from inside the room continued, and then stopped. Happy heard men screaming, and not in his voice. He rolled out into the corridor and headed for that door. Just as he arrived, one of the women in green flickered through his field of vision. He saw a flash of steel and got his rifle up just in time to deflect a stroke that would have opened him up from collarbone to pelvis. The woman in green pivoted to strike again as Happy cracked his rifle butt into the side of her leg. Knocked off balance, she flipped away from his second swipe and came up with a throwing knife. Before he'd registered what it was, it was buried in his thigh.

Happy cried out and raised his rifle. His shots were wild

and the woman in green was gone. He bit down on the pain and scooted into the room to be out of the line of fire while he tried to pull out the knife without tipping himself over into shock.

The room was full of dead men. "Not me," Happy gritted. He worked at the knife, which was deep in the meat of his quadriceps but didn't seem to have caught bone or artery. He was lucky. As he worked the blade free, his vision dimmed and he nearly passed out. He breathed deep and evenly until the wave of nausea passed, then tested the leg. It would hold his weight, but neither of them was happy about it.

While he'd been working on his leg, that part of the building had gotten a lot quieter. Happy hated to think about why. He had to get moving. If he could get to Rhodey, or Fury, and nobody shot him along the way, maybe he could get another shot at the women in green.

xxxvi.

And now the body, the perfect construction, the final unification of techne and soma. I am man, I am machine. I am brute force and unconquerable will, incomparable intellect and indomitable strength. In the strength of my limbs I make the world the object of my will. I break what will not yield. Stark, in your clever eggshell you imagine yourself my equal—but you are a man encased in a machine and I am a new man who has cast aside the boundaries that limit your imagination. I am HYDRA, which is the legacy of visionaries and seekers. I am the emergent expression of a new world, the walking and thinking avatar of a humanity that does not yet know it exists. In me is the strength of the future, the latent power of the mind waiting to be tapped. I have seen what no one else has seen and created what no one else has created. I have made you, Stark, made you again, made a better version of you that waits patiently for the death of its predecessor to inch the world that much closer to its inevitable perfection. You do not hear me, but you would not listen even if you could hear, and that is your flaw. This pride! What have you done to earn it? I will break your limbs inside their eggshell, crush first your spirit and then your body so your death will be the final example to the idolaters of the machine that their idol has fallen.

For all that Tony could instantly tap everything from Saharan weather reports to bandwidth deviations in Stark Industries servers to climatological data piped from satellites to usage peaks at New England electric utilities, he still got caught looking the other way the first time Zola landed a solid punch. Without the suit on, the impact would have caved Tony's skull in and sent his eyes shooting out of their sockets like paddleballs. As it was, he saw double and lost his airborne equilibrium.

It always came down to this. You could fight your infowar, your psyops war, your high-level strategic war . . . in the end, it came down to mano a mano. Even when both parties were tricked out in the best human technology had to offer. Tony should have known this, should have planned for it, but he'd been dreaming of something different, forgetting that war always ends up down in the muck and the mire with one guy's hands wrapped around the other guy's throat.

Zola had not forgotten this. He wasn't as fast as Tony, or equipped with as much in the way of electronic enhancement, but he was immensely strong. Stronger than Tony. *I can block his mind-control powers,* Tony thought. *And I can deflect the energy weapons he uses, because they're the last generation of stuff I designed.*

But I can't do a damn thing about the fact that whenever he gets in close, he pounds the hell out of me.

Tony hit him back, no doubt about it. And he did damage. Zola's body seemed designed to absorb an endless amount of punishment. Freed from the dictates of biology, he put all of the vital organs way down deep where Tony couldn't get to them. Normally, when you hit a man in the head, you rattled his brain around; do that enough times, he's going to go down. But Zola's brain wasn't in his head. Tony wasn't sure what was, but hitting him there sure didn't seem to have any effect. "You can't beat me by fighting me like a human being, Stark," Zola crowed, and delivered another eye-crossing haymaker. "I'm the next stage. I am everything I have learned, every clone I ever designed, every experiment I ever ran just to know whether it would work. You're like Australopithecus fighting Homo sapiens; you're giving up not just physical strength and size, but brainpower as well. And I say that as someone who respects your talents in the area of engineering."

Next tactic, Tony thought, and delivered a blast of liquid haloalkanes, close up, into Zola's eyes. He followed up with a punch to the bridge of Zola's nose, shattering both the nose and the flash-frozen eyeballs on either side. Zola made a gratifyingly agonized noise as pieces of his face fell away into the turbulent wind of their passage. "That's where Australopithecus comes after Homo sapiens with a sharp stick," Tony said. His head was still spinning a little from Zola's shots, but he was starting to get his equilibrium back. "And don't forget; even Australopithecus gets pissed when you kidnap his girlfriend."

Is she my girlfriend? Tony thought. Didn't matter. He couldn't have passed that line up. He hammered away at Zola with pulse bolts, thinking that sooner or later, it had to make a difference.

The Two Demoiselles danced a double line of blood and steel through Rhodey's unit. They were fast, way faster than they should have been, and when they struck they never seemed to miss. Smoke from the grenades in the testing area had drifted throughout the building along with mist from the sprinklers, deepening the near-darkness in the hall. The SHIELD commandos who would have fired on them never seemed to have a clear line; always one of their comrades was in the way, usually at the moment of dying, and every one of the men who didn't take that shot would wonder for the rest of his life whether he should have. But they wouldn't wonder long, because the Two Demoiselles struck and were gone.

Rhodey and six men had taken up a position behind the reception counter in the RTI Lab's front lobby. The Two Demoiselles were in among the seven men before they'd heard a sound. Rhodey shoved one of them toward the hall. "Go tell Fury!" he shouted. The man ran.

Rhodey was a skilled martial artist, and a handy man with gun or knife, but he couldn't shoot because the Demoiselles were in among his men and he couldn't close because in close combat, you had a better chance against an opponent with a gun than you did against a knife. He held his rifle on the two women, glad he'd saved one of his men but already feeling the edges of his field of vision turn red with atavistic fury at losing the others. He fired, and missed. Fired again, and missed. The Demoiselles went in different directions, and Rhodey knew they had him. All he could do was pick one and try to get her before the other one got him. He swiveled left, had her in his sights—and then saw the soldier he'd sent to Fury, gun pointed over Rhodey's right shoulder. He ducked at the same moment the soldier fired, and a split second later the back of Rhodey's head lit up and the red in his vision faded to black.

"General? General?"

The voice was plaintive and ragged. Fury didn't recognize it. "Fury," he said.

"General, Rhodey's down. Rhodey's down, there's these two women with swords—"

The transmission cut out. Fury flicked over to Rhodey's direct channel. "Rhodey. Report," he said.

No answer. Women with swords? Fury wondered. What next? He had his hands full with clones. They'd blown a fresh entrance to the testing area, between a simple drill press and a sealed-in miniature clean room where Tony designed circuitry and something he called a kinesis reservoir. Four Hogan clones were behind the stainless steel walls of the clean room, creating a hell of a cross fire with the other clones shooting down the length of the testing floor from behind the burned-out pickup.

That was about all HYDRA had left, though. Fury thought that SHIELD had won. The Hogan clones would fight until they were dead because that was what they did, but they didn't have the numbers to root Fury's people out of the lab. Getting to be time for a push to take care of them once and for all, Fury thought. He had twenty-one able-bodied soldiers left, plus Pepper, plus however many of Rhodey's men survived . . .

Thinking of Rhodey distracted him. Women with swords?

He fired off a burst at the Hogans behind the clean room and glanced toward the corridor entry, thinking he'd better see if he could link up with Rhodey's unit since communications seemed to be compromised. Then he saw one of the women with swords.

It was Madame Hydra. He'd seen her before, tangled with her before, lost men to her before—and a month ago, he'd seen autopsy photos of her taken after the midair collision that had killed her and ninety-four other people. Looked like Zola had one more card to play.

Then the second Madame Hydra appeared and both of them went into action. The first slipped down the wall of the testing area, weaving in and out of the machinery so fast that Fury couldn't get a bead on her. She was on two of his men before they knew she was there, and had killed them before Fury's answering fire pinged off the machines she used as cover. From the corner of his eye he saw the second leap onto the railing that separated the control terminal area from the main part of the floor, and spring into a leap that would land her right on him. He swung his rifle around but knew he was going to be too late.

A burst from across the room tore into her, and her leap became a graceless fall. She hit the deck near Fury and stayed there. He looked back toward the other Madame. With a collective yell, the remaining Hogans charged into the room, energized by the arrival of the clones of HYDRA's former leader.

Fury knocked one of them down with a textbook three-round burst, then closed to take on a pair of Hogans who were already on the control terminal platform. From behind them a SHIELD commando rose up and fired, killing one. Fury shot the second one through the head, suppressing a shudder at the sight of the wound on Happy Hogan's face . . . and then the Madame on the floor jerked his feet out from under him and twisted around to straddle him. He'd lost his grip on his rifle, and he barely managed to get his head out of the way of her first thrust. Instead of driving into his good eye, it cut off a piece of his ear and laid the side of his scalp open. He caught her wrist, but she shook his grip off like he was a child and drove the stiff fingers of her other hand into his throat.

His vision went dim. He swung blindly and felt his fist connect, but he didn't have the leverage to knock her off him and he couldn't see the knife. He turned his head and shoulders away from the direction he guessed the blow would come from, but instead of a knife in the throat Fury felt the Madame's body convulse at the same time as he heard a burst of rifle fire from somewhere down by his feet. She fell away from him and he reached for his rifle as he registered that the saving bullets had come from none other than Pepper Potts. "Finally I get to do something other than wrangle computers," she said.

The SHIELD commando who had killed the first of the two Hogans lay dead, a throwing knife in the hollow under his jaw. Fury had never even seen the Madame throw it.

"Good shooting, Pepper," he said. "Appreciate it."

She shrugged. "I could hardly miss from here. Sorry about the mess."

Fury was covered in the Madame's blood, and a fair amount of his was leaking from the side of his head. "Part of the job," he said, and turned to join the last of the battle.

There wasn't much to do. The Hogans' charge had been desperate, and once they'd broken the organized siege, the well-trained SHIELD forces had cut them apart with little ceremony. Commandos were moving from Hogan to Hogan, checking to make sure they were dead or to wave over a medic. Fury was a little sorry to see that some of the Hogans were alive, not because he begrudged anyone life but because he couldn't imagine what kind of life they would have after HYDRA. Some things were worse than death. Happy had been right about that.

Speaking of Happy, where had he gotten to? Soon as he found and got rid of the other Madame, that was the first order of business. Or second, if Tony hadn't gotten back in touch by then. "SHIELD," he called out. "There is one more Madame Hydra clone somewhere on these premises. We need her found and eliminated. Get on it."

The commandos formed into four-man search teams and started marking out territories in the darkened spaces of the testing floor. As they searched, more shooting echoed down the corridor from the front of the building. "Stay sharp, people," Fury said. He wondered whether that was Rhodey's people confronting holdout Hogans. Seemed like the only possibility. He popped Rhodey's comm channel again. "Report, soldier," he said. "You're missing the last bit of the fun."

No answer.

"Keep it tight in here," Fury said. He pointed at one of the search teams. "You, with me. We're going to do a sweep for Rhodes' unit. One of you a medic?" One of the team raised his hand. "Good. Let's go."

xxxvii.

PROVISIONAL APPLICATION FOR PATENT

TITLE
  G-Force dispersal and conversion system

DESCRIPTION
  Much like the nanoscale force converter (NFC) system (cf. Provisional Patent Application [redacted], attached for reference), the G-Force Dispersal and Conversion System (GDCS) is designed to trap and repurpose ambient and incoming energy as a power source. NFCs operate within a medium such as the kinetic attenuation gel (cf. Provisional Patent Application [redacted], attached for reference); GDCS operates by means of a lining inside a Stark Industries personal body armor product. When the suit operator changes directions or accelerates, creating lateral or linear G-forces, the lining absorbs and transmits that energy to the armor product's existing energy reservoir.

CLAIM
  The attenuation of gravitational forces is a critical concern of any engineer working in the areas of manned flight. Advances in pilot gear and cockpit features have made possible significant increases in the performance threshold of aircraft. GDCS takes the next step in this process by building on existing G-force attenuation technologies to capture and store both lateral and linear acceleration energies for later use by the operator of a Stark Industries personal body armor product. Current harvesting efficiencies run approximately fifteen to twenty percent, depending on the fit of the armor and the nature of the acceleration-creating maneuver. Experimental models predict future harvesting efficiencies could

approach 50 percent, making gravitational energy a valuable potential resource in energy-intensive operational environments.

SECURITY STATUS

Project undertaken under the auspices of Stark Industries agreements with the Department of Defense, SHIELD, and other governmental agencies outlined in Senate Amdt. [redacted] to Senate Amdt. [redacted] to H.R. [redacted] (110th). Technology is proprietary to Stark Industries but will be shared fully with all eligible entities. Technology is classified and will not be licensed until such time as classification order is rescinded.

Even without eyeballs, and with parts of his face gone so deep that Tony could confirm that Zola didn't keep his brain inside his head anymore, Zola kept coming. He tried to drag Tony out of the air and Tony, knowing that whatever advantage he had would be gone as soon as their feet were on the ground, fought just as hard to keep out of Zola's grip. "You are dancing," Zola said. "Dancers tire. And the fighter only dances when he knows he cannot beat his opponent."

"You think I can't kill you?" Tony said. "I blew off your ESP Box before, right? I didn't see you moving after that."

"That did not kill me, Mr. Stark. It was General Fury's bullets that killed my previous body. I had a clone standing ready to receive the transfer of my mind."

Ah, Tony thought. He hadn't noticed that because he'd been too busy being sucked out of his body via PDM to In Here.

"That clone, too, was killed shortly thereafter, but not before I was close enough to the facility that I could take up residence in this specimen you see before you. Feel its strength." Zola caught Tony's forearm. His hands were large enough to close completely around Tony's wrists. He squeezed and even through the armor, Tony felt his bones creak with the pressure.

He had an idea. *I've been going about this all wrong,* he thought, *thinking about protecting myself from my disadvantages instead of taking advantage of his.* Twisting into Zola's grip, Tony pirouetted around until his imprisoned forearm was locked across Zola's chest. He hooked his other arm under Zola's, creating a midair piggyback. "Sure, I can still kill you," Tony said. "You know how?"

Zola twisted his hands in opposite directions. A bone in Tony's wrist cracked. "Do tell," Zola said.

"I can kill you because you still need to breathe air," Tony said.

There was no way to make the tested maximum 37-g acceleration, not with the additional load of Arnim Zola. But when the suit's booster jets kicked in, Tony felt it in his eyeballs and the pit of his stomach. He rocketed straight up, Zola screaming the entire way, locked in a mortal embrace.

Fury had advanced down half the length of the corridor, stopping to check on obviously dead SHIELD personnel seemingly every five or six feet, when he heard a voice from a doorway to his right. "Nick." He spun, leveling his rifle, and if he hadn't been between the doorway and the search team, Happy Hogan would have eaten four rifles' worth of bullets.

"Happy, Jesus Christ, I've heard of death wishes . . ." Fury didn't know what else to say. "What are you doing in here?"

"I had to do something, Nick. After the, you know. The thing in the copter. I had to make it good. I took down some of the clones, but there were these women in green. I couldn't get a clear shot at them. Man, you should see them move."

"General?" said one of the search team. "General, I strongly suggest we disarm and immobilize this subject until we determine that he is not another clone." The commando looked Happy in the eye. "If you're the real Happy

Hogan, I apologize. If not, I hope they hang you for a spy, you underhanded son of a bitch."

"Whoa there, soldier," Fury said. "Look at him. See that nose? See the gray hairs? Look along the line of the jaw. A wrinkle here and there, right? This here is a real human being. You can tell the difference being on Earth for a few years makes as opposed to being grown in a tank."

"Plastic surgery, sir," the soldier said stubbornly. "I don't mean to be disrespectful."

"You're not being disrespectful. You're being careful. That's a good quality in a soldier." Fury chucked the soldier on the arm. "But you're also wrong this time. Now let's get on with the mission."

They found Rhodey behind the reception desk with a big gouge taken out of the back of his head. Bone gleamed in the beam of the flashlight one of the search team kept on him while the medic went to work. "He's alive, sir," the medic reported. "But out cold, and I don't think he's coming around any time soon. It's a survivable wound. Get some blood into him and wait for him to wake up, and other than a hell of a headache and forty or fifty stitches, he'll be okay."

Fury felt an enormous weight lift away that he hadn't known he'd been carrying, or hadn't allowed himself to consider carrying. How long had he and Rhodey been friends? How did you lose someone like that . . . but how did you not know that it was always possible that they would be lost?

Not today, he thought. *Not today.*

They found a few other survivors of the twin Madames' rampage through Rhodey's unit, and got them stabilized in the front lobby. Fury left the team to guard the casualties, and he went with Happy back toward the testing floor. They kept a sharp eye out for the color green, but there was no sign of the remaining Madame Hydra.

Back in the testing area, Fury tried to raise Tony, but there was no answer. "Pepper," he said. "With that instant control, Tony should get a signal right away anywhere in the world, right?"

"Anywhere there's satellite coverage," she said. "Which, yes, is everywhere."

"So he's just not answering."

"Say it, Nick. Or he's dead, and we're all just waiting for Zola to show up and turn us all into clones." Pepper turned away from him to Happy. "And you. What the hell are you doing here? You should be in the hospital."

"Pep, hey, I had to do something," Happy said. "I never ran from a fight in my life."

"I thought you were dead, Happy," she said. "I thought you were dead, I thought if you didn't get shot down in the helicopter that someone would mistake you for one of the clones or that you'd just disappear because who knows what Zola was going to do . . ." She caught herself exactly at the moment when to continue would have meant starting to actually cry. After taking a deep breath to compose herself, Pepper finished up by saying, "You better never steal another helicopter."

"I promise," Happy said. The shadow of a smile appeared on his face, for the first time Fury could remember. Everything was almost over. As soon as they heard from Tony, they'd know for sure.

He raised SHIELD Control and asked what they knew. "We had a bogey moving real fast straight up a couple of minutes ago," Control said. "Signature was a mess, all different kinds of materials, and the shape was not something that should have been able to move that fast against gravity. So that was probably him. Current altitude is, let's see . . . I got one hundred twenty-one kilometers. Well into the thermosphere. Cold as hell there; hope he's wearing his winter woolies."

"Active signals?" Fury asked. "His suit's on line and working?"

"General, I hate to tell you this, but Tony's been doing

everything he can to make the signals from his suits confusing for the last couple of years. I'm getting signals, yes, but I don't know what they mean. There's also a second body up there. I'm not sure what it is."

Zola, Fury thought.

"Keep me posted. To the second," he said. "The next time Tony moves or does anything that tells you he's alive, you let me know."

"Yes, sir," Control said.

"And while you're waiting, do you suppose you might send in some medevac for wounded SHIELD personnel, seeing as how you work for SHIELD and all?" Fury felt his temperature rising all over again at the incredible cowardice of the elements within the government who, once the extent of Zola's power had been demonstrated, had sealed off the whole battle and pretended it wasn't happening. How many lives had that cost?

"What's your combat situation there, General?" Control asked. "I've got a specific set of guidelines from You-Know-Where."

"I do know where. Our combat situation is one enemy unaccounted for. The rest KIA except for maybe half a dozen wounded. And Zola, whose current state is unknown to anyone in the world except him and Tony Stark. What you need to know is that we have thirty-one SHIELD wounded and we can't save them all with goddamn first aid. Now are you or are you not dispatching medevac?"

"The guidelines are specific, General," Contol said. "I'm sorry. You know I would."

Fury was nodding despite the audio-only connection. "Sure. I know you *would.* I know what lots of people *would* do."

The SHIELD commando who wanted Happy Hogan disarmed and immobilized was named Kirk MacFarland. He had been recruited to SHIELD from the Navy SEALs at the age of twenty-four, five years ago, and was as loyal to Nick Fury as he was to his own father. Now that the HYDRA clones had all been taken care of, he was helping move the wounded back toward the testing floor, where the large bay doors would mean easier movement out to the medevac helicopters . . . when and if they ever came. Four SHIELD soldiers were bouncing the burned-out truck on its springs, building toward a final heave when they would flip it over out of the doorway. The truck squealed and stank something awful. Kirk's stomach hurt. He carried a stretcher over to the open part of the floor near the loading bay, and was turning around to head back up front and get the last survivor of Captain Rhodes' unit when he saw Happy Hogan—the one who looked older, the one who said he was real—raise a rifle and level it at the back of Nick Fury's head.

Happy was looking out over the ruins of the testing floor and thinking that Tony had some serious work ahead of him when he got back. There was beginning to be light in the sky. Birds were chirping. Happy realized he was as tired as he'd ever been in his life. The search teams had reported in, one by one, each saying they'd found a ton of HYDRA clones and SHIELD personnel but that the second Madame Hydra was nowhere to be found. "You think she just got away?" Pepper was saying. "Where would she go?"

Happy shrugged. "Don't know. Maybe Zola had some kind of programmed rendezvous. But if Zola's not around anymore, I don't know what she would do."

It was as the last words were leaving his mouth that he saw the flash of green under the blue tarp covering the server stack, and the inhumanly fast motion of Madame Hydra springing toward Nick Fury, who was consulting with one of his team leaders to make sure he had an accurate count of what had happened to all of his men. One final surge of adrenaline ripped through Happy's nervous system. He swept the barrel of his rifle up and over toward Fury, leading the green blur that was Madame Hydra, and fired.

At the same time, Kirk MacFarland got his rifle as far as his hip before snapping off a shot. He was an expert marksman, and even in the conditions—smoke, fatigue, poor shooting position, and moving target—he would normally have expected one hit out of three at this range. He got Happy twice.

Pepper screamed and Fury jumped up and over the control area railing, blocking Kirk's firing line. "Cease fire! Cease fire now, soldier!"

The truth of the situation was dawning on MacFarland even as he pulled the trigger. Realizing too late what he had done, the commando looked shocked. "Oh God. General, I didn't know. He looked—"

Someone was shouting for a medic. On the control terminal platform, MacFarland could see Happy's legs kicking and scrabbling as he tried to get up. "Get your muzzle down!" Fury screamed. MacFarland went further, dropping his rifle and taking a step back.

"He looked—" MacFarland started to say again.

Fury cut him off by holding up a hand. "I know he did," Fury said. "I know. It's not your fault. We've all had a long night. But now the show's over, and nobody has to get shot anymore."

He turned away from MacFarland, wrestling with the impulse to cashier the soldier on the spot. It was a dangerous time, the aftermath of a firefight. Everyone always thinks there's one more target . . . and in this case there had been, just not the target MacFarland had assumed. It was a bad mistake, but an understandable one. Fury called to the medic. "Got one in the meat of the arm, one just above the hip," the medic said casually. "He can probably walk to the dustoff."

"How about I shoot you a couple of times and we'll see

how far you want to walk," Happy said through gritted teeth.

Fury got on the comm to Control. "All enemies accounted for," he said. "You feel like it might be possible to evacuate and treat all these wounded soldiers I got here?"

"Confirm elimination of HYDRA personnel," Control said.

"Yeah," Fury said, not bothering to hide the bitterness he felt. "I confirm. It's safe for you to come in now." He broke the connection and looked around. "Now where the hell is Tony?"

xxxviii.

Stark, I find you worthy. You are no match for my intellect, and your scientific prowess is the rude, forceful advance of the gifted amateur, but your determination I admire. So much, in fact, that I will not try to sway you to join forces with me—although the world would truly be our oyster were that to come to pass. Now we fight, but if we stood shoulder to shoulder, you in your prototype suit and instant control and I in my cybernetic apotheoses, who could stand against us? And isn't that what you have always wanted, to stand above others and know that they understood your superiority. You have no secrets from me, Stark. I have known other men like you, and I know the recesses of your mind. I have plumbed its architecture while watching a copy of you grow in my departed Bushwick fastness. The shapes of it are clear to me. Men's minds are as different as fingerprints or retinas, not because of any metaphysical transformation of matter to soul but because variations in the individual structures of an individual brain demand that it should be so. I have seen your mind accrete, molecule by axon by neuron by lobe. I have a picture of it in my mind now. Do you know it as well as I do?

It took forty-five seconds for Tony to burn high enough that his repulsor-designed thrusters no longer had anything to repel, and another three minutes for Zola to break Tony's grip and twist away. Already it was too late for him. Zola's mouth was moving, but of course Tony couldn't hear him. He monitored every frequency from alpha all the way up to UHF, and didn't see any high-volume data transmission leaving Zola. When Zola was dead, Tony watched his body drift away and then down, gradually heeding the call of gravity. Tony tracked it visually and through the entire spectrum of instruments available to him, dispassionately noting the decreasing temperature, the lack of electromagnetic activity. Dead. Tony fired pulse bolts at the body to accelerate it downward; even though there was no kinetic energy for them to harvest along the way because they weren't passing through an atmosphere, they still packed their initial punch. He wanted to know Zola was destroyed before he himself assented to the grip of gravity again. When Zola's body was far enough away that Tony could no longer maintain visual contact, he followed via satellite and military radar, which registered an object decaying out of low-Earth orbit. Five minutes after Tony had let him go, Zola's body began to burn. The last of it broke up over the North Atlantic, falling anonymously into the ocean out of sight of any land or human observer.

"Pepper," he said. "How's everything down there?"

"Oh, peachy," came her answer. "Rhodey's got his head split open, it looks like. Fury nearly lost his other eye. Happy's been stabbed in the leg and shot. The lab's on fire, there are bodies everywhere . . . and where are you?"

"Low-Earth orbit. About to head back down."

"Care to enlighten us on the status of Arnim Zola?"

"Arnim Zola has been rendered back into the raw materials from which he was created," Tony said. He turned belly-up and unleashed haloalkanes. The pressure of their expansion drove him downward. He let himself fall, thinking that he should get back as soon as he could, but maybe he could squeeze in a thermal test along the way. Reentry would, if nothing else, burn away the little bits of Zola that probably still clung to the outside of the suit.

"I'm on my way," he said before atmospheric reentry effects could block his communications.

* * *

He arrived twenty minutes later, dodging a SHIELD mede-vac copter on his final approach. A line of ambulances and meat wagons clogged the access road in front of the RTI Lab, and news helicopters were circling trying to get footage despite the coordinated blackout SHIELD and the Defense Department continued to impose. "God," Tony said when he walked into the lab and got a look around. He took off his helmet. "What a mess."

Fury heard his voice and stalked over. A fresh bandage taped to the side of his head was spotting with blood. "You mind updating us on the Zola situation?"

"The Zola situation is that I flew him up to space, where he died—I imagine of pulmonary edema or something related—and then his body burned to nothing on reentry. Whatever's left of him is probably just now coming to rest on the bottom of the Atlantic Ocean." Tony looked at the suit. Reentry had left faint streaks of it as intense heat and pressures broke the atmosphere apart. Inside the suit, he'd felt the heat the way you felt sunshine on the back of your neck. A gentle warmth, gone as soon as he'd decelerated in the upper reaches of the troposphere. "What's the situation here?" he asked. "You look even more piratical. How are Happy and Rhodey?"

"Happy's back in the hospital," Fury said. "And he's go-ing to stay there for a little while this time. Pepper went with him. Rhodey had the back of his head unzipped by some kind of samurai sword, but he's got a thick skull so all he's going to need are a lot of stitches and a lot of aspirin. We ran into two clones of Madame Hydra. All these highly trained SHIELD personnel around, and it was Pepper and Happy who got them."

"Pepper killed someone?" Tony said. "She hates guns."

"She hates being dead worse," Fury said.

"News from the chocolate factory?"

"I would have thought you'd already know," Fury said. "What with your instant control and all."

"Yeah, I turned it off on the way down," Tony said. Fury arched an eyebrow, but Tony didn't elaborate.

The truth was that after all his seeking and after his sojourn In Here, the actual experience of instant control made Tony uncomfortable. It fully integrated him with the suit in a way he never had been before, not even when he'd built the interface into his nervous system. When instant control was on line, Tony was faster, stronger, more aware . . . and maybe a little less human. He lusted after the feeling and feared it at the same time. Maybe it was the trip In Here that had done it, but Tony wasn't quite the same person he'd been before Zola's virtual mousetrap had sucked him up through the PDM. It might have been transcription error as his personality was up- or downloaded, or it might have been some subtle psychological consequence of the experience. In the end, the reason mattered less than the effect, and the effect was that Tony had a deeper appreciation for the flaws and foibles inherent in humanity. Or he thought he did. Probably that feeling would evaporate the first time he ran into someone being criminally stupid again.

"Hey, Nick," he said. "My head's been in a weird place this last month or so."

Fury's eyebrow crept higher. "Is that an apology?"

"Yeah, it is." Tony triggered the suit release and it unsealed itself from around his body. He stretched and reveled in the feeling of air on his skin. "Yeah," he said again. "I'm sorry. It's been a strange couple of days."

"You can say that again."

"So," Tony said. "Chocolate factory?"

"The extraction team didn't come out. They did manage to get Serena out, and they did manage to blow the building to hell with all of Zola's toys in it," Fury said. "Including something like forty extra bodies he had stashed away."

"No kidding. Forty?"

"Forty. NYPD picked Serena up at a White Castle on

Metropolitan Avenue when she asked to use the phone and then started screaming about women running around with severed heads." Fury inclined his head toward the control terminal platform, where the last Madame Hydra lay dead. "Apparently there were eight of those initially. I sure am glad only two of them got here."

"Is she okay? Serena, I mean, obviously," Tony said.

"Last word we had was that they were giving her a ride home, and she was going to spend some time with family. The cop I talked to also said that I should mention to you that Serena thinks you two shouldn't go out anymore," Fury said.

"Some people aren't cut out to live exciting lives," Tony said. He looked around the lab. "You know I'm going to bill SHIELD for fixing this place up."

"Why don't you go to the hospital?" Fury said. "I bet Happy and Pepper would be glad to see you. God knows why."

After taking a shower—the bathroom seemed to be the only place in the RTI lab not riddled with bullet holes and carpeted with dead bodies—Tony hopped a SHIELD copter and got a ride to Governors Island. On the way, despite the third-hand advice he'd gotten about the status of his relationship with Serena Borland, he gave her a call. She didn't answer. He left a voice mail suggesting that when everything had gotten back to normal, or mostly, maybe they could catch some jazz again sometime. When he hung up, he knew he'd never hear from her again, but it wouldn't have felt right not to make the offer.

Happy looked like ten miles of bad road, and Pepper—although she had been neither shot nor stabbed—didn't look much better. "How long has it been since you've slept?" Tony asked her.

"Probably not as long as it's been since you have," she said.

Drifty and slow from the painkillers, Happy sketched a wave. "Hey," he said.

"Hap, you don't have to let every clone in New York take a piece out of you," Tony said. "For future reference."

"The SHIELD guys got me, too," Happy said. "I'm an equal-opportunity target."

"While I've got you both here, I'm going to tell you I'm sorry whether you want to hear it or not," Tony said. "Both of you are better friends than I deserve."

"Agreed," Pepper said.

The moment was in danger of becoming overly sentimental. Tony was looking for a way to forestall this unwelcome possibility when Pepper's phone made a strange sound, a cross between a guitar riff and the quacking of a duck. "What is that?" Tony asked.

"That," she said, "is the specific sound my phone makes when it receives a communication intended for you but that you have decided I should get first so I can screen it."

"Don't look at it," he said, but she already was. After he'd watched her stare at the screen for maybe half a minute, Tony couldn't stand it anymore. "What?" he said.

She held the phone out so he could see the screen.

"It's from Zola," she said. "Time-stamped about twenty minutes ago."

I speak to the world that has never listened, this world that lies below, blue wreathed in white against the marvelous black of space. This time, perhaps, I am bested. This time, perhaps, my commands go unheard, my visions unrealized, my advances unheeded. Arnim Zola dies knowing that his life has been dedicated to the pursuit of knowledge and the betterment of those elements of the human race which are worth bettering. And he dies knowing that nothing ever really dies, and that even if this Heraclitean truism fails a test of gravity or seriousness, it speaks to the situation. Cut off the

*head of a HYDRA, Mr. Stark, and it grows ten more.
Cut off the body of a Zola . . . you get the picture.
Every innovation in your suits, those marvelous
exoskeletal extravagances, brings you closer to a
juncture at which your goals and mine will be
indistinguishable. You improve humanity by means
of mechanical contrivance, I by means of root-level
transformation. Both of us remain dissatisfied with the
limitations of the human animal, and both of us strive
for something better. Our disagreements, and the fatal
result of this most recent encounter, do not change
that incorrigible truth. This has not been our final
engagement, and the timing of our next rendezvous is
not for either of us to know at this time. But know
that you have been a worthy adversary, and that I
have learned much from you. Enough, I trust, that
next time our contest will conclude on terms more
favorable to me. You have that rude energy of the
American. This time it was enough. Next time might
be a different matter.*